Praise for *Vampire T...*

2014 RT ... ...ee,
Bes...

"Humphreys is ... ...enre... The sparks th... ...le are totally irresistib... ...the tension that unfolds between the vampires and the werewolves will have readers on the edge of their seats!"

—*RT Book Reviews* July Top Pick
for Paranormal Romance

"A wonderfully engrossing read... Sara Humphreys's storytelling talent shattered the pages of my e-reader into vibrant colors and hypnotized me with blazing action."
—*Night Owl Reviews*

"A powerful love story that proves that while our past is inescapable, it is the core of our strength."
—*The Washington Post*

"This series is wildly addictive, and this book is totally awesome. It's a five-star book that you do not want to miss. I can't wait for more."
...*eviews*

"Full ... ...e, and suspen... ...*Mamas*

Also by Sara Humphreys

The Amoveo Legend

Unleashed
Untouched
Undenied (novella)
Untamed
Undone
Unclaimed
Unbound (novella)

Dead in the City

Tall, Dark, and Vampire
Vampire Trouble

SARA HUMPHREYS

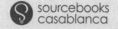
sourcebooks
casablanca

Published by Sourcebooks Casablanca, an imprint of Sourcebooks, Inc.
P.O. Box 4410, Naperville, Illinois 60567-4410
(630) 961-3900
Fax: (630) 961-2168
www.sourcebooks.com

Printed and bound in Canada
MBP 10 9 8 7 6 5 4 3 2 1

*"Love one another and you will be happy.
It's as simple and as difficult as that."*

—Michael Leunig

For my children...

Chapter 1

BEING A RESPONSIBLE ADULT SUCKED ASS.

Sadie let out a beleaguered sigh and folded her arms over her breasts while surveying the crowd with her heightened senses. The lights of the club pulsed and throbbed in time with the music. Beneath it all, she could feel the thrumming heartbeats of the humans, like a swarm of butterfly wings constantly rushing around her.

As a two-century-old vampire, Sadie had done a damn fine job of avoiding major responsibility. Until a year ago, her toughest choice had been what playlist to use at the nightclub on Friday and Saturday nights. However, with all of the recent changes to their little NYC-based coven, everyone's roles had undergone serious adjustments.

Life had been simple and predictable.

That was then and this is now.

When Olivia, her maker and dearest friend, had offered to sell Sadie the nightclub, she'd thought it was a joke. Olivia loved this place and had busted her butt for twenty years to make The Coven one of the hottest dance clubs in Manhattan. Housed in an old church in Greenwich Village, The Coven had become *the* place to party for humans who liked to dress up like vampires—or what they thought vampires looked like. Little did they know the place was owned and operated by actual vampires.

Sadie had officially taken over the club about six months ago and was finally finding her groove. Olivia even admitted that Sadie was doing a hell of a job running the place. For a year, Olivia had tried to do it all—czar, nightclub owner, mother—but in the end she just couldn't. Something had to go. Olivia had said she'd have to sell the club to strangers if Sadie didn't buy it from her.

That was when shit got real.

Sadie scoffed audibly as she moved along the edge of the leather-clad crowd. No way in hell would she have let some stranger buy The Coven. Not only did the other girls in the family work here, but they all lived in apartments beneath the club. Nope. At that moment, Sadie had known it was time to nut up or shut up. She'd avoided being a real grown-up for more than two hundred years, but as with all creatures, time eventually caught up with her.

She was now an official grown-up, and as she'd suspected, it wasn't all it was cracked up to be. Making her way past the two VIP booths, one of which was empty for the first time in a long while, Sadie cast a look of longing at the DJ platform. At first she'd tried to manage the club and DJ, but it had simply been too much. Like Olivia, Sadie knew something had to give. Much to her chagrin, it had been the duties up on the platform.

The young vamp she'd hired from Los Angeles was one hell of a good spinner, bringing years of experience to the table. Not only that, but Justine was absolutely fucking gorgeous in a pierced-and-tattooed sort of way. The male portion of their human clientele had doubled since she took over and that, in turn, had pumped up the human female attendance. There was no denying that having a hot girl on the DJ platform helped the bottom line.

Sadie walked the floor of the busy nightclub and surveyed the writhing crowd of humans before giving Justine a nod of acknowledgment. Headphones around her neck, the DJ winked and pumped her fist in the air at the same moment the tune changed. A deep, pulsing beat rippled seductively through the club, which triggered some serious dirty dancing by the patrons. Sadie laughed and shook her head, knowing Justine loved watching the humans practically fuck each other on the dance floor.

That girl sure can spin her sexy little ass off. Trixie's voice touched Sadie's mind with wonderful familiarity. *I haven't seen a vampire girl with that many awesome tattoos in a long time. Please tell me we can keep her. She's a badass.*

You're supposed to be worrying about the customers and serving wicked drinks. Not inspecting the new DJ. Sadie captured her sibling's gaze and pointed toward the end of the bar. *Meet me down there.*

Now, you know me better than that. I can do both, sister. Trixie didn't miss a beat and continued pouring shots for the three patrons seated in front of her. She'd been turned at the height of the NYC punk movement, and her spiky pink hair and leather getup made her look just like one of the club-goers. Sadie had been jealous when Olivia first brought Trixie into the fold. She'd never had to share her maker with anyone before, but she didn't need long to see how awesome Trixie was. She was spunky, feisty, and swore like a sailor. Then again, so did Sadie, which was probably why they got along so well. *She's bringin' 'em in alright. We've been jammin' from open to close ever since she started.*

Standing by the end of the mahogany bar, Sadie kept her sights on the two bartenders. A sense of pride filled her. Maya's blond, innocent look was the perfect complement to Trixie's punk-rock chic, and they were really good at keeping the drinks flowing. Sadie's smile faltered when Maya caught her staring and then immediately made a beeline for her. Another sign of the times. Maya could no longer telepath with the rest of the coven.

Like Olivia, Maya had found her bloodmate and become a daywalker. Sadie didn't begrudge her sibling the joy of feeling the sun on her skin or finding true love with Shane. But all of the bloodmate stuff would have been easier on the rest of the coven if they hadn't lost the ability to telepath with each other.

All vampires could telepath with their siblings, maker, and progeny—unless they found a bloodmate. Then they could only telepath with their mate. There were pros and cons to everything, and the lack of telepathy was one of the cons.

Big time.

Sadie's non-beating heart clenched in her chest and she looked away, worried her emotions were written all over her face. She desperately missed the intimate mental connections with Maya and Olivia—but especially Olivia. Not hearing Olivia's voice in her mind crushed her soul a little bit every day. The deafening silence made Sadie feel alone for the first time in two hundred years.

She could still telepath with Trixie, Damien, and

Suzie, the other members of the coven, but for how long? How long until the rest of them found bloodmates and Sadie was left alone?

"Hey." Maya leaned both elbows on the bar and kept her voice low, pulling Sadie from her thoughts. Maya tucked one long strand of platinum-blond hair behind her ear. "Since it's kind of quiet tonight, would it be okay if I split a little early? I'll come back later and clean up so Trixie doesn't have to do it all."

"Let me guess," Sadie said with a knowing look. "Shane wants you to go out on the end of his patrol with him tonight."

Shane Quesada was Maya's bloodmate and a sentry for the Presidium, the vampire government. He and two other sentries kept watch over the NYC area and reported directly to the czars. It was a sentry's job to ensure the safety and good behavior of all supernatural citizens. Which, until about a year ago, had pretty much only meant vampires.

"Maybe." Maya's eyes twinkled. She gave a noncommittal shrug before glancing over her shoulder to the door, likely keeping an eye out for her man. She locked her blue eyes onto Sadie's and put her hands together as if in prayer. "Pleeeeeeazzzee?"

"Oh, fine." Sadie rolled her eyes and suppressed the laugh that threatened to bubble up. Since hooking up with Shane, Maya had gone from spoiled brat to thoughtful professional in the blink of an eye. She was settled and at peace in a way that Sadie both admired and envied. Sadie smoothed the lapels of her jacket and adjusted the lacy cuffs of her long white shirt, trying to look like a hard-ass. Wearing a suit was awful, but it was important to at least try to look like a grown-up. The lace shirt was her way of rebelling. How pathetic.

"But you better get back here after closing and help Trixie clean up the bar. I have a new cleaning crew coming at six in the morning to take care of the club and the bathrooms, but you know that the bar area is all you and Trixie."

"Thank you so much." Maya squealed with delight and clapped her hands. "You're the best, Sadie."

"Yeah, yeah." Sadie shook her head and jutted both thumbs at her chest. "That's me."

You're a sucker, that's what you are. Trixie's voice shot into her mind with a curt laugh. Cleaning glasses in the sink, Trixie looked at Sadie through the mirror above the bar. *You're the boss now, and you gotta learn to say no sometimes.*

Really? I'll remember that when you ask me for something. Sadie winked at her sibling, but when she looked back at Maya, her smile was gone. If the look on Maya's face hadn't been enough of a clue, the tingling from the scar on Sadie's shoulder would have been. Oh fuck.

Aside from finding her bloodmate last year, Maya had discovered her gypsy heritage and a rather unique power. In addition to detecting the presence of wolves in the area, Maya had the innate ability to turn a werewolf into a human.

King Heinrich, the werewolf king, and pretty much everyone else had believed that Maya's power to render a werewolf mortal lay in the emerald necklace that King Heinrich destroyed. They had all assumed that once the necklace was gone, so was the power to take the wolf.

Not so much.

As fate would have it, the power was inside Maya. Necklace or no necklace, the girl could turn the most ferocious of werewolves into mortal men if she so desired. The only reason the wolves hadn't hunted Maya down and destroyed her was because one man—one wolf—kept her secret.

And at the moment, *that* wolf stood in the doorway of *her* club.

"It's them." Maya's voice shook. Based on the tense vibe she was sending out, Sadie knew it could only be one thing. Maya's violet-blue eyes were wide and fixed on the massive double doors of the club. "The wolves are—"

"Here," Sadie said in a barely audible tone. "Damn it all. One of the things I used to love about New York City was its lack of werewolves. Truce or no truce, they make me nervous."

"Well, our kind and theirs never have gotten along," Maya said quietly. "You're not the only vampire in the city who's upset they're setting up house here."

Sadie rolled her left shoulder in an attempt to ease the weird tingling sensation she got every time Killian and his pack came around. The dark, circular scar on her left shoulder blade was left over from the night Olivia turned her, a memento from the attack that left her an orphan and a vivid reminder of all she had lost. She figured the tingling in the scar was her body's way of telling her something—or someone—dangerous was in the area.

Someone like Killian Bane.

Killian, the werewolf prince and heir apparent, was the newest supernatural resident on the island of

Manhattan. He was also the thorn in Sadie's side, now standing in the vestibule like he owned the place. The guy had been making a habit of bringing his little pack to The Coven, and it was starting to grate on Sadie's nerves. She'd never been a fan of wolves, due to an encounter right after she was turned, but this guy irked her more than most.

Vamps and werewolves had maintained a delicate peace for about two hundred years, and Sadie felt uncomfortable as hell that this guy—this *wolf*—knew Maya's secret. With one word, he could bring a world of shit down on Maya and the entire coven—not to mention blow up the treaty. It almost felt like Killian was blackmailing them or something when he showed up every night at the club. Passive-aggressively reminding them, *You'd better play nicely, or I'm telling my daddy what your little friend can do.*

"But seriously? They're here again?" Sadie gritted her teeth and glanced at the empty VIP booths. "You know, ever since these guys started coming to the club, the few vamp clients we had have stopped coming around. Darius and his crew haven't been here for weeks."

"Ah, those assholes hardly spent any money anyway," Trixie said with a snort of derision. "I mean, they'd get maybe three bottles of blood between them. Not only that, but they don't tip worth a shit, and if I had to get Darius's hand off my ass one more time, I was gonna bite his ugly face off." Trixie wiggled her eyebrows. "At least the wolf boy is hot."

"Yeah, well, he still bugs me." Sadie fought the urge to bare her fangs and instead plastered on the biggest, fakest smile she could muster. Killian's sharp, brown-eyed gaze captured hers from across the club. He tilted his head in deference but made no move to come farther into the club. To her dismay, the instant those eyes met hers, her stomach flip-flopped as though a fucking nest of butterflies resided there. "I definitely need to go for a swim. It's been too long and I need to blow off some steam."

"Oh man." Trixie shook her head and laughed while wiping a glass dry. "Are you still squatting at that rooftop pool on the west side? You better watch your ass, girl, or you're gonna get busted and give some poor human a fucking heart attack. Finding a naked woman skinny-dipping is enough to send most folks over the edge."

"Yeah," Sadie said absently. "Swimming is the only thing that seems to calm my nerves lately. Besides, if anyone sees me, I'll just glamour them and they won't remember a thing." She latched eyes with Killian again. "Jeez. After hanging around all these freaking were-wolves, I'll need to do about a hundred laps to relax."

Killian's grin widened and he leveled a challenging stare in her direction. *Damn it.* It was like the big jerk *knew* the effect he had on her. Sadie narrowed her eyes and clenched her teeth against the sensation. Holding his gaze, she barely noticed that Maya had moved next to her at the end of the bar.

"The arrogant SOB is waiting to be escorted to the table, even though he damn well knows where it is. What's his deal anyway? They've taken over one or both of the VIP booths weekly for the past six months. He does know there are other clubs in the city, doesn't he? Besides, the hotel he's been *living* in has two bars.

He has hundreds of other places to choose from," Sadie groused.

"He does," Maya said quietly. She waved to Killian quickly before grabbing two bottles of Cristal from the fridge and whipping up their usual order. "I guess they like coming to a club owned by supernaturals. The Coven is the only one in the city now, Sadie."

"Yeah, maybe." Sadie snagged a few drink menus off the bar. She knew what they would order; she gave them drink menus anyway just to pretend she didn't. She glanced at David and Ivan. Killian's two friends were nice enough, at least as far as wolves were concerned, but they still made her uncomfortable. It wasn't just them, though. All werewolves set Sadie on edge. Maya and Trixie were different; they had been turned after the treaty was in place. They hadn't seen what it was like when rogue wolves were around every corner and the bastards only had one thought on their furry minds—killing every vampire they could find. "I still don't like him."

Steeling her resolve, Sadie held the menus in front of her and strode over to Killian and his pack with the most confident air she could muster. This was her place, and she'd be damned if she was going to let an arrogant alpha werewolf and his cronies throw her off her game.

Ah-ah-ah. Trixie's teasing tone slipped easily into her mind. *Don't start trouble with our resident werewolf royal. Besides, if you ask me, he's coming here for more than the music or the constantly flowing Cristal.*

I know exactly why he's coming here. Sadie glanced at Maya and then to Trixie before moving past them.

He's keeping an eye on Maya. The son of a bitch probably reports back to his father and tells good old King Heinrich her every move.

Yeah, right. Trixie laughed. *Keep telling yourself that. You and I both know that our furry friend clocks your every move when he's in here. He can get overpriced champagne anywhere in this city, but he comes here to annoy you. I think he gets off on bugging the shit out of you, and if I didn't know better, I'd say you're starting to enjoy it.*

Trying to ignore Trixie's commentary, Sadie stopped directly in front of Killian and tilted her head back to look him in the eye. He was just over six feet tall, broad shouldered and impeccably dressed as always. Unlike the club patrons, he was dressed more like a Wall Street tycoon than a club rat. The man exuded wealth and class. She had to admit that the devilishly handsome Killian Bane cut a striking figure.

The sidelong smile, the one that almost always curved up those firm-looking lips, made him look like he was up to something. His wavy brown hair brushed the edge of his jacket collar, and the crisply pressed white button-down was undone just enough to give her a glimpse of dark chest hair. Her gaze skittered over his perfectly chiseled jawline with the ever-present five-o'clock shadow until finally settling on those brilliant caramel-colored eyes.

Damn it. Sadie put on a tight smile. Butterflies. It felt like a damn swarm of them swirling in her belly, and she gripped the menus to keep her fangs from unsheathing. *Why on earth am I attracted to him when I don't even like him?*

I knew it! Trixie's victorious claim sliced into Sadie's mind.

Sadie cursed and shut her mind off from Trixie's laughter. Being around this wolf was making her crazy and sloppy. She couldn't remember the last time she'd accidentally let her thoughts be exposed.

"I was beginning to wonder if you'd forgotten about me," Killian said through a widening smile. Hands clasped in front of him, he bowed his head while holding her stare. He dropped his voice low, to a level that only another supernatural would hear above the noise of the club. "You don't mind if my pack and I settle into one of the VIP booths again, do you?"

Sadie held her ground and glanced at David and Ivan. The two men stood about a foot behind Killian. Flanking him the way bodyguards would, they scanned the crowd with the same intensity she'd seen on the faces of Shane or the other sentries. She wasn't stupid. These two wolves weren't Killian's pack members, not really. They were more like secret service for the heir to the Werewolf Society throne.

It made sense, didn't it? The prince would surely have extra protection in a city that was run by vampires. But that's what didn't make any damn sense at all. Why would the werewolf prince be living here in a vampire-dominated city? Why not stay in Alaska or go to Canada where the wolves owned most of the territory?

The question that nagged at her the most? Why was Killian Bane frequenting her club week after week? They drank while they were here but not enough to get a werewolf hammered—a wolf's tolerance for alcohol being notoriously high. They never danced. In fact, come to think of it, all they ever did was watch what was happening in the club. Once in a while, Killian would chat up a pretty girl or two, but only in passing.

The wolf was definitely up to something, and she'd bet her left fang it had to do with Maya. She flicked her gaze back to Killian, and a slow smile spread over her face. Come hell or high water, Sadie would figure out Killian's game plan.

"Why would I mind?" Sadie said sweetly. She swept her left arm wide. "Follow me, gentlemen."

Without glancing back, she led them around the dance floor full of heaving, grinding bodies and directly to the empty VIP booth. Above the odor of sweat and sex that flowed among the humans, Sadie could smell Killian's earthy, woodsy scent and it was remarkably unsettling.

Unhooking the red velvet rope, she stood at the end of the curved red leather booth and waited for the three of them to settle in. Ivan and David slipped into the booth easily, and as usual, neither of them gave her more than a cursory "hello" and head nod. Well, weren't *they* a couple of chatty Cathies?

As focused as the two men were, Sadie didn't miss the fact that David had his sights set on Justine. She cast a glance over her shoulder just in time to catch the sexy wink her DJ shot back to the wolf. Sadie's eyebrows flew up. She shifted her attention to David, who immediately looked away and cleared his throat.

Interesting.

When Sadie turned around, she found Killian Bane standing right in front of her. Instead of sitting with his friends, he'd sidled up to her at the end of the booth. His massive frame loomed over her, and he invaded her personal space with calculated precision. The son of a bitch was trying to get her to submit to his big, bad alpha wolf.

Not likely.

Meeting his challenge, she held her ground. The heat from his tall body wafted over her in thick waves, and to her surprise, the onslaught made her a bit dizzy. A werewolf's body temperature was significantly higher than a human's and they had a distinct scent, like wood burning on a cold winter night. Killian's surrounded her like a thick cloud of smoke and had her head spinning.

Killian's heartbeat thrummed strong and steady in his chest, and even with the thundering music pulsing around them through the club, Sadie could practically hear the pulsing flow of blood as it rushed through his veins. His blood called to her like a seductive siren song, willing her closer, tempting her with its forbidden power. Drinking from wolves was a big, fat no-no, and doing so could effectively break the delicate treaty between the two races.

Logically she knew that. Sure. What vampire didn't? But bloodlust was anything except logical. It was carnal, primal, all consuming, and savage. It could turn even the most sedate vampire into a horrid, vicious creature—and that was something Sadie *never* allowed herself to forget.

Unfortunately for Sadie, she had tasted werewolf blood once before, and the two-hundred-year-old memory was still gut-wrenchingly fresh. Her fangs hummed as she recalled, with haunting clarity, the rush of energy she'd felt when that wolf's blood had seared through her body.

Sharp. Intense. Powerful. Intoxicating.

Just like Killian.

Damn it all.

Before she could stop herself, Sadie took an involuntary step back. Killian countered, taking one step closer, and his lips tilted into a lopsided grin. Shit on a stick. How annoying. She blinked first in their little game of chicken, and the worst part was that Killian knew it. He folded his arms over his broad chest and cocked his head while studying her more closely than she cared for.

"You don't like me much, do you?" Killian asked with mild amusement.

"You're a customer, Mr. Bane." Sadie kept her voice even. She placed the drink menus on the table and slid them toward the other two without looking away from Killian. "Your money is as green as anyone else's."

"True." His eyes glittered with mischief, and she could tell he was trying to get her riled up. "But you didn't answer my question."

"Fine." Sadie folded her arms, matching his stance and meeting his challenge. "Let's just say I don't trust you. Liking you has little to do with it."

"I disagree."

"Shocking." Sadie rolled her eyes.

"Why?"

"Why, what?"

"Why don't you trust me?"

"Are you kidding?" Sadie scoffed and placed her hands on her hips as she leaned closer. "Let's see. Where do I start? You're a werewolf, a royal one at that, *and* you know—" She stopped herself before mentioning Maya's secret and cast a sidelong glance at

Frick and Frack, who were staring at her with predatory gazes. "*And*, of all the clubs in this city, you come to the *only one* that's owned and operated by vampires. You never dance and you barely drink, at least by werewolf standards. So, yes, I think it's a little suspect that you keep coming here night after night. To be quite honest, I would like to know why."

Silence hung between them for three beats of his heart, with only the surge of the music surrounding them. If he didn't respond soon, she was gonna scream.

"Fine, you want to know why I drag Ivan and David here? Because they're about as happy about it as you are." Killian's grin widened as he leaned closer. Sadie's jaw clenched when his crisp scent wafted around her enticingly. Looking her square in the eyes, he whispered, "It's you."

Sadie blinked, like he'd just proposed marriage or something equally ridiculous.

"Me?" Her body hummed with anticipation, shock, and much to her dismay, a pure shot of lust. Of all the things this guy could have said, that response was nowhere in the litany of items she expected. Trixie's teasing words drifted through her mind. "Y-you come here because of me?"

"Yup," he murmured. Those glittering eyes skittered over her face. Sadie swallowed hard against the sudden surge of desire that had her fangs vibrating and clenched her thighs together at the unexpected rush of heat between her legs. For a second, just a second, he leaned even closer and she thought he was going to kiss her— which was both terrifying and intriguing. "Who else can teach me about running a nightclub in this city?"

Sadie's mouth fell open, and Killian smiled broadly before stepping back and casually slipping into the VIP booth.

"What?" Sadie sputtered. She gaped at Killian, who was now leaning back in the booth with both arms stretched out over the back of the seat. "What are you talking about? I thought your family had some kind of handmade furniture business."

"That's my father's business," he responded abruptly. The cocky exterior wavered briefly, and if she didn't know better, Sadie would swear she saw the eyes of a wounded little boy. It only lasted a split second, and then the wolf was back. "I've been looking to branch out on my own and try something new. In about a month, I'm going to be opening my own place. I thought Olivia would've told you." He lifted one shoulder and flicked his gaze to the DJ stand before giving Justine a friendly wave.

"I knew that coming here and checking out the way you handle business with the humans would benefit me. And it has." The smug smile on his face widened, and she wanted to give him a good punch in the nose. "My place will be different, but the customers are the same. I'll cater to both humans and any supernaturals who might be interested in what we're offering. I knew your expertise would be helpful…and it has been. I have to admit, it would be a hell of a win if I could get your DJ as well. Once we open, of course."

Anger shimmied up Sadie's back and now she really wanted to smack the smug, satisfied look off Killian's face. A million different responses ran through her head, but she was so angry she could barely see straight…

angry and embarrassed. Why hadn't Olivia told her about this? And why, oh for the love of all that was holy, *why* had she assumed that he wanted *her*?

What. A. Dummy.

"Why?" He cocked his head to the side and his lips tilted. "What did you think I was talking about?"

"Nothing." Sadie wrestled to compose herself and plastered a smile on her face. Before leaving, she said, "Trixie will be over with the bottle of Cristal shortly."

"So you do know what I want?" Killian asked with more than a little innuendo. Sadie's face heated with embarrassment. He saw right through her, which was more than a little annoying. "You just might be the woman of my dreams. Well, except for the vampire part." He sighed and looked her up and down. "Unfortunately, that's a deal breaker."

"Yeah," Sadie snorted. "A real bummer. And for the record, *Your Highness*, vampires don't dream."

"Really?" Killian's brow flew up in surprise before his gaze slid over her in one slow, lazy stroke. "Now, that's a damn shame."

"Yes," Sadie said sarcastically. "It's a real tragedy. Right up there with world hunger."

"Nah. It's just that I've had some lovely dreams." His eyes twinkled at her mischievously. "You give me a drink menu every time I show up just to make me think you don't know what I want. Don't you?"

"I just want to be sure you have plenty of options." She scooped up the drink menus, and keeping her voice even, she murmured, "And I assure you I'm well aware of what you're after, Mr. Bane."

Without another word, and with Killian Bane's stare

drilling a hole in her back, Sadie strode to the bar. As she cut through the crowd, one voice stood out amid the cavalcade of sounds. "I'm counting on it."

Chapter 2

THE CLUB WAS FINALLY EMPTY AND QUIET, EXCEPT FOR the familiar sounds of cleanup—bottles clanking, chairs scraping across the wooden floor, and the playful banter of her friends while they closed the place. Sitting at the end of the bar and tallying the night's receipts, Sadie tried to keep her cool. Everything was going to be fine.

She swore and slammed the pen onto the bar.

Like hell it was. She'd been fuming all night after what Killian told her.

The son of a bitch was opening a competing club here in Manhattan, and when he said it, he acted like he'd just given her a diamond ring or something. Not only that, but he had the audacity to all but come right out and tell her that he was going to steal her crowd-attracting DJ. She'd even caught him up there talking to Justine right before he and his pack left for the night. Why on earth would he think she'd find that even remotely amusing?

Because he's an arrogant alpha werewolf, that's why.

Annoyed and lost in her thoughts, it took a minute for Sadie to realize that Justine was calling her from the DJ platform.

"Boss!" she shouted for what was probably the fifth time. "Yo, Sadie."

"What?" Sadie whipped her head over her shoulder and forced herself to smile. The look on Justine's face instantly made her feel shitty. She'd barked at the poor girl. "Sorry." Sadie laughed and shook her head. Placing the calculator on the bar with the receipts, she shifted her position on the bar stool. "I guess I was concentrating too hard on these numbers."

"Yeah, right," Trixie said with a snort of laughter. Drying glasses behind the bar, she shot a knowing look at Sadie. "You were concentrating, but it sure as hell wasn't on those receipts. I'd bet my money on a six-foot hunky wolf."

"What's up, Justine?" Sadie cast a narrow-eyed look at Trixie.

"There's somethin' I should tell ya 'bout," she said with her thick cockney accent. Justine flew down from the DJ platform and landed quietly on the center of the empty dance floor. Smoothing the spikes of her colorful, long hair in a nervous gesture, she strolled over to the bar before pulling up a stool and sitting next to Sadie. "It's 'bout our furry friends."

"Okay," Sadie said slowly, a nagging sense of dread creeping up her back. "What about them?"

"Let me guess." Trixie tossed the dishrag over her shoulder and leaned on the bar. "That big blond one has the hots for you."

"Trixie," Sadie said warningly as Justine shifted nervously on the stool. "Why don't you go get Damien? Have him help you replenish the stock behind the bar."

Sadie had barely finished her sentence when Damien, the club's bouncer and one of the newest coven members, came in through the front doors of the club. He threw the bolts on the inside of the massive wooden doors and cast his big pearly white grin in their direction.

"Did someone mention my name?" he called in his typically playful baritone and strolled into the club. He placed the velvet rope and brass stand by the wall and waved to them. Dressed in a black T-shirt and jeans that covered his tall, sturdy frame, the guy reminded Sadie of a big teddy bear.

"Justine, man, you rocked the freaking house tonight. I tell you, sister, I can't remember the club ever being this packed. Seriously. We've had a waiting list almost every night for the past two weeks. You are a lucky charm, my friend."

"I second that emotion," Sadie said. Giving Damien a weary smile, she pointed at Trixie. "And yes, you did hear your name. Would you give Trixie a hand restocking the booze? You can pull whatever we need from the storage room. Trixie has a list of what we're low on. Maya will be back later but I'd just like to get it done."

"Aw, man," Trixie whined. She pushed herself away from the bar and tugged the dish towel off her shoulder. "Just when the conversation was getting good."

"Sure, boss." Damien put the clipboard on the bar's smooth mahogany surface and slid it down to Sadie. "Everyone on the list showed up tonight except for Darius and his crew. It's been a while since they've been in." Damien's brow knit together and made his olive-toned complexion seem even darker. "I know it's because the wolves have been hanging out here a lot, but I thought Darius was cooler than that, you know? Killian and his crew aren't so bad."

"Darius? Cool?" Trixie scoffed and hoisted herself onto the bar before swinging her feet over and hopping off on the other side. She landed silently next to Damien and punched him in his massive arm. "I think all that time standing outside with the line full of whiny humans is giving you mental problems. Darius is kinda letchy. Vampire or not, I don't like him. Shit, man. I'd rather hang out with the wolves than have him and those two old stooges of his here. Shane told me those guys are almost as old as he is, which would be fine if they were cool." She made a face of disapproval and glanced at Sadie. "I can't believe you slept with Darius. I mean, of all the vamps to choose from, you banged old man Darius?"

"Yeah, well." Sadie rolled her eyes and pushed her long hair off her forehead. "It was a long time ago and he's not that old. Well, he doesn't *look* old. Anyway, that's ancient history."

"You never told me that," Damien said.

"Would you brag about it?" Trixie asked with a snort of laughter.

"Very funny." Sadie smirked.

"You and stuffy old Darius?" A laugh bubbled up and shook Damien's broad shoulders. "I'm sorry to laugh, but talk about an odd couple."

"Whatever," Sadie said through a giggle of her own. "We weren't a couple. It was just sex. And like I said, it was a long time ago. At any rate, I don't think Killian and his friends will be hanging out here much longer, and that means Darius will probably be back. So, letch or not, he's a customer. Play nice when he's here, Trixie. No one is saying you have to bang the old vamp, just placate him. Like Olivia always says—his money is as green as anyone else's." She flicked her gaze to Justine. Based on the DJ's expression, she already knew about Killian's club. "You know about Killian's plans, don't you?"

"What plans?" Trixie asked.

"Yeah." Justine nodded and rested her tattooed arms on the bar. "That's what I wanted to talk to you 'bout."

"What's going on?" Damien asked with his typical big-brother concern.

"It seems our werewolf friend is opening a club right here in the city. He and his pack have been spending all their time at The Coven to learn more about the business." Sadie gave Trixie a pointed look. "See? Killian's hanging out here had nothing to do with me."

"Right." Trixie elbowed Damien. "She won't admit that the hot wolf man has the hots for her."

"Don't start." Sadie sighed. "And Killian's not that hot." Trixie and Justine gave her doubtful looks. Even Damien arched an eyebrow at her denial. "Fine." Sadie lifted one shoulder and gathered the receipts in a semi-neat stack while avoiding their inspecting stares. "He's kind of hot, if you're into the arrogant alpha-male type. Anyway, he and his pack are opening a club next month here in Manhattan." She made a scoffing noise. "Whatever. It'll be out of business before the next full moon. I'm not worried."

"Does Olivia know about it?" Damien asked.

"Apparently, yes, she does." Sadie tried not to show her irritation but it was no use. "I guess she didn't think it was important to mention."

"Let me get this straight." Trixie put up both hands and looked at Sadie like she had a screw loose. "You'd diddle with Darius and his old balls, but you turn your nose up at a hot, sexy badass like Killian?"

"We aren't talking about my sex history. We are talking about business."

"Yeah, but the sex stuff is more interesting."

"You're too much." Sadie shook her head and answered Trixie's question. "Darius may be old, but he's a vampire. And in case you've forgotten, Killian is a werewolf."

"So?" Trixie shrugged. "There's no rule against having sex with their kind. Not really."

"No, but it's certainly not encouraged," Sadie said slowly with a glance at Justine who seemed increasingly uncomfortable with the topic. "We all know that lust and bloodlust go hand in hand. Sleeping with a wolf isn't illegal, but feeding on one is." Sadie shook her head quickly and rested her arms on the bar. "Wait a minute. We aren't here to talk about the ill-advised idea of vampires and werewolves hooking up. I've got a business to run. Speaking of which, aren't you two going to get that stuff from the storage room?"

"Whatever you say, boss." Damien started toward the back hallway. "Come on, Trixie."

"No way." She sat on the stool next to Justine. "I want to hear more about the wolves."

Sadie was about to protest when Damien grabbed the defiant pink-haired bartender and tossed her over his hulking shoulders. He turned around and winked at Sadie before disappearing into the dark hallway, Trixie protesting through a loud laugh.

"You were saying?" Sadie turned all of her attention to Justine who was fiddling with the skull-and-crossbones ring on her forefinger. "You know about Killian's club?"

"Yeah." Justine cracked her knuckles and tapped the bar with her fingers. "Ya see, gov, the thing is that the bloke wants me to DJ for him on their opening night. I wanted to—"

"Fine." Sadie shrugged and smiled as though the request wasn't totally annoying.

"What?" Justine's jaw dropped. "I wasn't gonna ask ya to do that, Sadie. Honest. I just wanted to tell ya about it. Y'know, open lines of communication and all that." A wide grin bloomed slowly across her face, showing off the gap between her two front teeth. "But I gotta be honest. It would be a freakin' thrill to open a big, new club like that. I ain't never been a headliner b'fore."

"You're always a headliner *here*, but I get it and I think it's a cool opportunity for you." Sadie nodded and patted Justine's arm reassuringly. Personally, she hated the idea of her star attraction working at a competing club, especially Killian's, but she figured she'd get more flies with honey. Protesting might push Justine away, but giving her leeway would keep her loyal. At least that's what Sadie was hoping. "You and I have been talking about hiring a DJ to fill in for you once in a while anyway. Why don't you test out a couple of the new guys over the next few weeks and then we can hire a part-timer."

"That's bloomin' brilliant." Justine grabbed both of Sadie's hands and lavished them with kisses. "And it'll just be one night. I promise."

"Yeah, yeah." Sadie winked at her before gathering up the receipts. "I'd prefer a vamp DJ, for obvious reasons, but if you want to audition a human, just give me a heads-up."

"Done." Justine was about to say more, but the phone in her back pocket interrupted their conversation. She grabbed it, and a sheepish grin cracked her face when she read the text. "Thanks again, gov."

Justine hopped off the stool and flew up to the DJ platform. Sadie was about to go to her office when a knock on the door of the club brought her to a halt. She let out a whimper of frustration. The last thing she wanted to deal with right now was some half-drunk human girl looking for her phone or something. With Damien and Trixie still downstairs, the responsibility clearly fell at her feet.

Ready to give whoever was outside a hundred different reasons why they couldn't come in the club after closing, Sadie slid the bolts aside. Pushing open the enormous wooden door, with the "We're closed" mantra lingering on her lips, she found herself face-to-face with the last person she would have expected to see.

Darius Lockwood.

"Do you have a few minutes for an old friend?" Darius asked with a regal bow. Dressed in his usual all-black ensemble, he reminded her of Johnny Cash. Tall and slim with slicked-back salt-and-pepper hair, he stood patiently on the cracked sidewalk. The grin faded and his pale blue eyes glinted in the lights of the streetlamps. "It's important."

"Sure." Sadie stepped back and held the door open for him before checking to see if his sidekicks were around. To her surprise, neither of his usual companions was in tow. Closing the door, she gestured toward the bar. "Have a seat. Where are Thomas and Lawrence? I can't remember the last time I saw you out alone."

"They had other *engagements*," he said in his typically evasive way. Darius perched himself on a bar stool and rested one elbow on the bar. Looking elegant and stiff, he did resemble the stodgy old vampire Trixie pegged him for. The guy had been turned in his early thirties but acted like the old world soul he was. "My apologies for bothering you after hours, but something has been nagging at me."

"Let me guess. This something wouldn't have anything to do with our newest supernatural residents, would it?" Sadie nodded and sat on the stool next to him. "You're upset that Killian and his pack have been coming to The Coven, which is why I haven't seen you guys here in a while."

"Perceptive, as always." Darius tilted his head and delivered a tight smile. Gathering his hands in his lap, he paused as though carefully choosing his words. "We are not the only ones who are…concerned. I was asked to speak with you about this issue. Some of our friends are quite uncomfortable with the wolves settling into this city."

"Okay." Sadie's defenses immediately went on high alert. "Who are 'our friends' exactly?"

"Others like myself, Lawrence, and Thomas." Darius waved his hand dismissively. "It was bad enough when the prince and his little pack lingered here in the city, but my sources tell me he's moved out of his hotel. From what I hear, Bane signed a lease agreement on a penthouse apartment. Can you believe it? I realize the new czars want to modernize our community, but just how much change do they expect our kind to handle? You're close with Olivia. You're her oldest progeny."

"I am." Sadie kept her voice calm and crossed her legs while leaning one elbow casually on the bar. "What's your point?"

"We were hoping you could talk to the czars." Darius leaned closer and covered her hands with his in a suggestive gesture. His blue eyes crinkled at the corners as they drifted down, lingering on her breasts. "I, better than anyone, know how persuasive you can be when you want something. Perhaps you can explain to the czars how distasteful this latest development is to the vampires who live here. The city is crowded enough with humans, and the last complication our community needs is an influx of these werewolves. We thought she would take the complaint better if it came from you."

"I see." Sadie kept her eyes locked on Darius while removing her hand from beneath his. Irritation flickered up her back. She wasn't thrilled about Killian's plans either, but the last thing she wanted to do was go whining to Olivia. The woman had plenty of other fish to fry. "I am Olivia's friend, which is exactly why I will not go speak to her about this. Aside from the fact that it would be an abuse of our relationship, I'm not going to be a mouthpiece for the restless vampires of Manhattan. If you have a problem, then I suggest you and the rest of the whiners go to the Presidium's offices and file a formal grievance."

However, even as the words escaped her lips, she knew what she was saying was a lie. She would be speaking to Olivia—but not for Darius's sake. Sadie would be giving Olivia a heads-up about the rumblings as a courtesy to her maker. If any trouble broke out with the wolves, then Darius and his crew would probably be involved.

"That is disappointing." Darius's jaw set and the muscle flickered beneath his fair skin, belying his annoyance with her refusal. "Perhaps I misjudged our relationship."

"We don't have a relationship," Sadie said flatly. "We fucked twice back in the sixties, and to be really honest, I chalk it up to the fact that I'd fed on two hippies who'd smoked everything but the sofa. Two rolls in the hay do not make a relationship. It was fun, but still, it was just sex, Darius."

"But it was good sex," he said with a widening grin.

"Most sex is," Sadie said through a curt laugh. The wounded expression on his face instantly made her feel guilty. "Sorry…I think I'm just cranky. It's been a long night."

"You always have been direct," Darius said, rising to his feet. "It is one of your finest qualities." His eyes flicked down to her cleavage again as he tugged the cuffs of his shirt from beneath his jacket sleeves. "So there's no way I can convince you to speak with Olivia?"

"Sorry." Sadie hopped off the stool and started toward the door of the club to let him out. "If you and your friends have a problem, then make an appointment with Suzie and speak with Olivia and Doug yourselves. I'm not a politician, Darius. I just want to run the club with as little drama as possible. Okay?"

"I suppose," he said with a sigh. Darius stopped by the door and moved closer to Sadie, intentionally invading her space as his eyes flickered over her in clear invitation. "Perhaps you and I should take another tumble.

It seems I didn't leave you with a very good impression, and I just don't think my ego can take that."

"Good night, Darius."

Sadie pushed the door open and waited for Darius to leave, but he didn't. Instead, he drifted closer and ran one finger down the length of her arm, which did not have the desired effect. It was meant to turn her on, but all it did was make her want to roll her eyes. She was about to tell him to piss off when a familiar intriguing scent filled her head and sent a pang of desire through her body. Her gut clenched with a sudden and ferocious need as a deep, seductive voice sliced through the night.

"Am I interrupting something?"

Sadie let out a yelp of surprise that was rivaled only by the curse that Darius uttered when Killian Bane appeared on the sidewalk outside the club. The stretch limo he always rode in was idling at the curb behind him, and Ivan, the fiercer of his two pack members, stood a few feet away looking less than amused.

"Like I said," Darius said without taking his fierce stare off Killian. "It's already a crowded city." He stepped back and flicked his gaze to Sadie before making a wide path around Killian. "And think about what I offered, Sadie. The door is always open."

"Right." Sadie ran a hand over her hair in a pathetic attempt to get herself under control, or at least look like she was. That expression "fake it 'til you make it" flew through her head. Her belly swirled with need and her legs felt unsteady. Sadie gripped the handle of the door tighter and leaned against the large wooden surface, praying she wouldn't fall on her ass.

She could feel Killian's eyes on her as Darius disappeared around the corner. Steeling her courage, she turned to face the inescapable presence that was Killian Bane. "What are you doing here?"

"Did I interrupt something?" Killian asked quietly. He slipped his hands into the pockets of his slacks and glanced over his shoulder at Ivan, who nodded and got back in the car. "You two looked like you were in a deep conversation."

"Conversations with Darius are never deep." Sadie forced a smile and tried not to notice the way her body was reacting to Killian on a primal, carnal level. That scent of his was going to drive her wild. The cozy, comforting aroma of wood burning on a cold winter night oozed off him like fucking pheromones or something. Sadie cleared her throat and met his stare as he moved closer. "It's late. What can I do for you, Mr. Bane? Did you leave your phone here or something?"

"No." An amused expression covered his face and he shook his head slowly, stopping about a foot away. Heat fired off his tall, broad-shouldered body in seductive flickering waves. "Actually, I—"

"Or did you come to try and steal my DJ again?" She tilted her chin in defiance and glared up at him triumphantly.

"Justine told you already?" Killian rose to his full height, his mouth set in a grim line. "Shit."

"You arrogant son of a bitch." Irritation crawled up Sadie's back, swiftly cooling her attraction to him. Standing in the open doorway of the club, it took every ounce of restraint she had not to haul off and deck him. "What? Do you think werewolves are the only ones who show loyalty to the people they care about?" A homeless man was picking bottles out of a garbage can down the street and Sadie lowered her voice. He probably wouldn't hear her, but that didn't mean she should be careless. "Well, I have news for you. Justine may not be in my coven, but she's loyal to me. She told me all about your conversation."

"Right," Killian said with a surprisingly apologetic look. "Listen, maybe I overstepped my bounds. I didn't plan on asking Justine to DJ at our opening night. It was a spontaneous decision. David and I were talking about how good Justine is at what she does and how big the crowds have been at The Coven and, well, I guess I let my passion take over." He shrugged, a cocky grin playing at his lips. "Sorry. My father would tell you that I don't always think before I act. Sometimes my enthusiasm gets me in trouble." He extended his hand in a peace offering. "Can we call a truce?"

Sadie gaped at him in pure shock. The big, bad wolf was apologizing to her? At least it sounded like an apology. Part of her wanted to tell him to stick it in his hat, but that wouldn't help her or vampire-wolf relations.

Time to suck it up. Shit, she hated politics.

Flicking her gaze to his hand, she reached out slowly and placed her palm in his. The instant the searing heat of his flesh settled against hers, white-hot streaks of pleasure zipped up her arm and went right to her core. A slow smile cracked his face as he curled his strong fingers around hers and moved closer. His massive frame loomed large in front of her, blocking out the streetlamps and pretty much everything else. His warm brown eyes drifted over her face as he gently shook her hand, running his thumb over the curve of her wrist and sending tiny electric shocks beneath her skin.

She was in big, fat trouble.

"A-apology accepted," Sadie said, quickly taking her hand from his. She tucked her hair behind her ear and looked away. A yellow cab zipped by, hit a puddle, and splashed the poor homeless guy. "I told Justine that she's welcome to work at your club—that night or any other night. She can split her time between both if she wants. But first she has to find me a part-timer to fill in when she's not here." Sadie tried to act nonchalant about the whole encounter, not wanting him to know how much he unnerved her. "It's a big city and there's plenty of business for all of us."

"I'm glad you feel that way. Thanks." Killian turned to leave but stopped and gave her a curious look. "I've got one more favor to ask you."

"Could I stop you?" Sadie asked all too sweetly.

"No," he said flatly.

"Right." Sadie rolled her eyes. "Okay, tough guy. What is it?"

"Come by my club and give me your honest opinion about it." Killian's grin widened when Sadie couldn't hide her shocked expression. "From what I gather, your honesty is one of your best attributes."

"Yeah." Sadie sighed. "I've been hearing that a lot lately."

"From your friend?" Killian asked, referring to Darius. He lowered his voice to just above a whisper and a dark cloud flickered across his face. "Or is he more than a friend?"

"You ask a lot of questions, Mr. Bane."

"And you aren't answering them, Ms. Pemberton."
Killian took two steps closer and lowered his voice
further still. "Are you *involved* with that vampire? He
seems too old for you, but I get the feeling you two
have…tangled."

Sadie held his stare and fought the rising surge of lust
that swamped her, right along with his enticing scent.
His physical attributes weren't all that turned her on.
Oh, no. His forthright tone and alpha-male confidence
had her fangs begging to be freed. Killian possessed a
powerful, commanding presence. It flipped every switch
inside Sadie and made her want to throw him against the
wall and see what he was hiding underneath all those
clothes. He definitely wore too many.

Damn it all to hell.

"That's none of your business," she said hastily. Too
hastily. Shit. She'd tipped her hand.

"Maybe not. But I'm asking anyway."

"Fine. No," she said quickly. Holding her ground,
Sadie gripped the door handle so tightly she was afraid
it might snap off. "I mean, yes, but it's ancient history."

"Yeah, he seems ancient." Killian smirked. "Like I
said, way too old for you."

"Is that so?" Sadie said through a laugh. In spite of
the fact that he should be her natural enemy, she found
herself charmed by his flirting. "Exactly how old do you
think I am?"

"Twenty-five." Killian narrowed his eyes and quickly
said, "No. I take that back. Younger than that. Twenty-
two, maybe, but you're definitely in your twenties."

"Really?" She arched one dark brow and her
grin widened. She was thoroughly amused by this

conversation. "And how long do you think I've been in my twenties?"

"Longer than most." Killian glanced over his shoulder at the idling limo and lowered his voice. "Tell me."

"A couple hundred years." She shrugged. "Give or take. Honestly, after fifty, who's counting? I mean, I don't age. So it doesn't really matter, does it? I stopped aging as soon as I was turned. At least my body did."

"How did it happen?" Genuine curiosity laced his voice, and his brow furrowed as he folded his arms over his chest. "Your turn? I know that Olivia is your maker, but what exactly happened? I'd really like to know."

"You don't know much about vampires, do you, Mr. Bane?" Sadie swallowed the lump in her throat and the sudden tightening in her gut. What was it about this guy that made her body go haywire? Lots of people had asked about her turn story over the years without ever making her feel this uneasy. "Or vampire etiquette."

"I know some. Why?"

"Asking a vampire to tell you the story of when they were turned is really personal." Sadie bit back a moan as his scent grew stronger with each passing second and the tension in her belly loosened. Tension was replaced with simmering desire. "It's not something you tell just anyone."

"Okay," he said abruptly. He wagged a finger at her and winked. "You don't have to tell me now, but you'll tell me eventually."

"Oh really?" Sadie cleared her throat. "That's a hell of an assumption, *Your Highness*."

"Yup." Killian nodded and silence hung between them as a sidelong grin cracked that handsome face.

"Now, back to that favor. Will you come to my club and give your honest opinion? How about tomorrow?"

Sadie held his challenging stare as she weighed her options. Saying no would only make her look like a jerk, and it certainly wouldn't do anything to help race relations. Saying yes would give her a chance to check out the competition and it would be politically correct. It was a win-win.

"I can't tomorrow. I have plans." That wasn't really true. She didn't have anything going on outside of the usual business of the club, but he didn't need to know that. He opened his mouth, probably to ask her what her plans were, but she held up one hand. "Before you ask me what my plans are, I'll just tell you they're none of your concern. The day after tomorrow should work." She nodded toward the club. "Pick me up here at sundown. I can give you an hour, but then I have to be back here to get my place ready for the night."

"Great." Killian tilted his head and smiled before turning around and heading for the limo. Anticipating his arrival, Ivan got out and opened the back door for the prince. Killian lingered in the open door for a moment before he winked and said, "It's a date."

He slipped into the car and the door shut before Sadie could tell him it was most certainly *not* a date. As the shiny stretch limo pulled down the New York City street, however, part of her wished that it was.

Chapter 3

SADIE KNOCKED ON THE DOOR TO OLIVIA AND DOUG'S apartment and prayed she wouldn't wake up the baby. She had desperately wanted to go for that swim tonight, but her two unexpected visitors ended up changing her plans. Tomorrow night she was going to get a swim if it freaking killed her. Letting out a sigh, she tipped her head back and stared at the stone ceilings of the Presidium's hallways. Buried deep beneath The Cloisters and Fort Tryon Park, the vampire government operated freely with humans none the wiser. Sadie envied their blissful ignorance of the supernatural world.

Olivia and her bloodmate, Doug, were the Czars of New York City, and after they bonded, both became daywalkers—vampires who could walk in the sun. Then, as if that wasn't enough change, they also had an adorable baby girl, Emily. Sadie's mouth curved into a smile when she thought of the redheaded cherub. All of them loved Emily like a daughter, and given the oddity of her birth, she was probably the only child any of them would have. Doug's angel bloodline, combined with the two of them being bloodmates, had resulted in Olivia's highly unusual pregnancy.

Well, that was what everyone thought, but who the hell knew what to expect anymore?

The changes they'd been going through as a coven reminded Sadie of how she'd felt when Olivia first turned her. The world had shifted, making her feel unsettled, like the ground beneath her feet could rumble at any moment and swallow her whole. The winds of change always seemed to be lurking around the corner lately. Sadie hated change. She'd loathed it when she was human, which was probably why she liked being a vampire so much. Life for the undead was steady and predictable—at least it had been until recently.

"What's up?" Doug asked with a loud whisper as he swung the door open. His short blond hair was in a state of disarray and the pajama pants he wore were horribly wrinkled. The poor guy looked like a disheveled mess. Pressing his finger to his lips, he stepped back and gestured for Sadie to come in. "Emily is finally asleep, and if she wakes up, I might actually cry. Have you ever seen a grown man cry? It's not pretty."

Doug shut the door silently before plopping onto the brown leather sofa. A moment later, their German shepherd, Van Helsing, trotted silently into the room and went directly to Sadie.

"Sorry to bother you guys." Sadie kept her voice to barely above a whisper and stood in the open living room of their spacious apartment while trying not to laugh at the new father's predicament. The dog sat at her feet waiting for the scratches she always gave him, and two seconds later, Oreo appeared next to him. "Are you sure Oreo knows she's a cat? I swear she thinks she's a dog."

"I have no idea, but you should be honored." Doug opened his eyes briefly. "Those two rarely leave Olivia's side. What's going on, Sadie?"

"I really need to speak to Olivia." Sadie squatted down and stroked the two furry creatures lovingly. The black and white cat purred like a freight train as she rubbed up against Sadie's leg. "It's important."

"It must be if you're here and not getting some shut-eye after sunrise. She'll be out in a minute." Doug let his head fall back on the couch and closed his eyes. "Emily must have had a nightmare or something. The poor kid cried for an hour. Let me tell you something. I thought seeing Olivia get upset was the worst thing in the world, but I was wrong. Hearing my baby girl cry is like getting shot with silver. It hurts like a bitch and I can't do a fucking thing to stop it."

"It's worth it, though, isn't it?" Sadie slipped her hands in the pockets of her slacks and strolled over to the far wall with the animals at her heels. It was filled with black and white photos of their unusual little family. Sadie's chest ached as she stared at the three of them smiling into the camera.

Memories of her own human family, now long dead, drifted through her mind, and a swell of loss and sadness tugged at her. She hated to admit it, even to herself, but she hadn't thought of them in years. However, ever since Killian asked her about the night she was turned, their faces hadn't left her mind. "Having the love of your family makes all the crappy stuff okay."

"Are you alright?" Doug asked with obvious concern. "Maya and Trixie can be kind of hotheaded, but you're usually the even-keeled one. What's up with you? Early morning visits aren't usually your style."

"I'm fine." Sadie faked a smile and waved him off. "I just had a question for Olivia about the club."

"Right." Doug made a snort of derision and flopped his head back on the sofa. He closed his eyes and a smile played at his lips. "When a woman says 'I'm fine,' she is anything but fine."

Sadie squirmed at his typically perceptive nature, the quality that had made him such a good cop when he was a human. As a vampire, it made him a really good czar. The guy could smell bullshit from a mile away, and right now he had a whiff of hers.

"She's out like a light."

Olivia's voice cut through the room and saved Sadie from Doug's impending inquisition. Sensing her uneasiness, Olivia immediately came over and swept Sadie up in a hug. Wearing a green silk bathrobe, the same shade of emerald as her eyes, and with a cascade of red curls over her shoulders, Sadie's maker looked as beautiful as ever. In most cases, she would make it a quick hug, but this time Olivia hung on and the tenderness of the embrace tugged at Sadie's heart. They may not be able to telepath with each other anymore, but their connection ran deeper than that. Words weren't necessary.

"I'll leave you two girls to talk about the club or whatever." Doug waved before flying out of the room, presumably to the bedroom.

"Come on." Olivia linked her arm through Sadie's and led her to the front door of the apartment. "Let's take a walk."

Arm in arm they strolled through the Presidium's stone hallways with Oreo and Van trailing close behind as Sadie relayed the evening's events to her maker. The iron lamps' flickering light illuminated the ancient halls with an ethereal glow and, as always, made Sadie feel as though she had stepped back in time.

"Okay," Olivia said slowly. "I'm sorry I didn't tell

you about Killian's club, but Doug and I thought it would be a good idea to keep it under wraps for a while. We knew that once the word was out, the inevitable bitching would begin."

"I'm not just anyone." Sadie stopped walking and captured Olivia's serious green gaze. "I'm your progeny and your friend." Her lip trembled. "We're family, Olivia. You and the rest of the coven are the only family I have left."

"I know that," Olivia said gently. She gathered Sadie's hands in hers and looked at her earnestly. "I'm not perfect, okay? I'm still new at the whole czar thing. I was just trying to keep things calm for as long as possible, you know? Let the vamps in the city get used to having the wolves around before we announced the opening of the club. It looks like Darius and his crew aren't going to make this easy for anyone."

"What are you gonna do?" Sadie smiled when Oreo kept trying to capture Van's tail and the enormous dog dutifully ignored the cat, keeping his intelligent brown eyes on Olivia. "Will you formally announce it to the community soon?"

"Probably." Olivia sighed. "That shithead Darius is obviously starting to make noise, so we'll have to get ahead of it." She squeezed Sadie's fingers gently. "But something tells me that Darius's visit isn't what's really bothering you."

"No, it's not." Sadie held her maker's intent stare, and images of her human family flickered through her mind. "Killian asked me about the night I was turned."

"Really?" Olivia said slowly. Van whined at their feet, sensing a spike of tension in the air that wasn't lost on Sadie either. "Did you tell him how personal that question is?" She linked her arm back through Sadie's and started walking with her again, irritation edging her voice. "You would think that a member of the royal family would be more informed about proper etiquette when dealing with vampires." She stared straight ahead, her body tensing. "Did you tell him the story?"

"No." Sadie shook her head. "But I might at some point."

"Really?" Olivia shot a sidelong glance at her. "How much do you remember about that night? We haven't talked about it in a long time."

"Most of it." Sadie let out a shuddering breath. "I try not to think about it, and until Killian asked me, I'd done a bang-up job of keeping it off my mind. It's weird, you know?"

"How so?" Olivia's tone grew serious and she stopped walking. "In what way?"

"Well, lots of other vamps and a few humans have asked me about my turn story, and I've told them without hesitation." She let out curt laugh. "I mean, I know it's personal and everything, but for some reason, when Killian asked me… I can't explain it… It was like a kick in the gut and now I can't stop thinking about it." She made a sound of frustration and ran her hands through her hair. "Jeez, I sound like such a girl. This guy is making me crazy."

"I see," Olivia said quietly. "Are you going to help him and go check out his new club?"

"Yes." Sadie quickly added, "I mean, I thought I should. You know, it will be good for race relations and politics. Right?"

"Sure." A knowing smile spread across Olivia's face. Sadie's face heated with embarrassment because her maker saw right through her. "It will be great for...relations."

—⁓—

The beat of the music in the nightclub thrummed through Killian insistently but he barely felt it anymore. All he could think about was the sexy vampire with the long, dark hair, and when he closed his eyes, he could still feel her hand when it had settled so perfectly inside his. Beautiful, soft, and cool, she reminded him of a crisp December morning in Alaska. That was weird, wasn't it? A werewolf prince should not be so insanely attracted to a vampire—and yet he was.

What was it about Sadie that had him twisted up in knots? It was ridiculous to come to this nightclub night after night and drool over a woman who could never be his. And yet here he was, in a perpetually horny state, fantasizing about a vampire who, by all accounts, thought he was a dick.

He was so screwed. Royally fucking screwed.

"Can we get out of here?" Ivan asked abruptly. Leaning back against the red leather booth, his bodyguard made a face that expressed his displeasure. "The place is closing anyway. Most of the humans have already left."

Killian was about to respond when the sweet familiar scent of mint captured his attention.

"Time to settle up, gentlemen." Sadie's dark eyes drifted over the three of them but she artfully avoided his gaze. Sliding the leather billfold on the table, she pushed it toward Killian. "You get the good news, if I'm not mistaken?"

"Absolutely." Killian went to grab the billfold and his fingers brushed hers in one brief electric pass. Her dark eyes widened when her fingers clashed with his, confirming his suspicion that she'd felt it too. "Thank you."

"Of course." Dragging her gaze from his, Sadie straightened her back and smoothed the lapel of her blazer in a soothing gesture. Perhaps he wasn't the only one who felt a dangerous attraction. "If you'll excuse me, I have business to tend to. Trixie will close out your tab."

Sadie glanced at him briefly before making a hasty exit toward the hallway that led to the restrooms. As she disappeared around the corner, Killian took his credit card out of his wallet and handed it to Ivan with the bill.

"Take care of this at the bar with Trixie." He slipped out of the booth and sent a glance at David. "I'll meet you two at the car."

"Your Highness." Ivan got out of the booth and stepped in front of Killian, blocking his path. The man was a wall of muscle. "You shouldn't go anywhere unattended."

"Really?" Killian kept his voice low and arched one brow at his overprotective bodyguard. "I've been taking a piss by myself for a while now. I'm pretty sure I can handle it."

Before Ivan could say another word, Killian stepped around him and followed Sadie's scent. He knew that Ivan was less than thrilled about spending time at The Coven, and his distrust of vampires was common among their kind. But none of that mattered. All Killian could think about was finding out if his suspicions about Sadie were correct. Propriety, rules, and political correctness could be damned.

Moving down the dark corridor, he paused outside the ladies' room and a growl rumbled in his chest as her distinctly sexy scent filled his head. Eyes closed, he tilted his nose and sucked in a deep breath. At that same moment, the door swung open and with the subtle shift of air came a pulse-pounding surge of Sadie's perfume. He flicked his eyes open and found himself face-to-face with the source of his obsession.

"Wrong door, Your Highness." The door shut silently behind her and she stood only a foot away from Killian, who was blocking her exit. Music from the now almost-empty club drifted over them but he barely noticed it. "The little boys' room is behind you," she said, pointing over his shoulder. "See? It's got the nifty outline figure of a dude on the door."

"I know," Killian bit out. Curling his hands at his side, he remained stone-still with his eyes pinned to hers. "That's not what I'm looking for."

"Oh really?" Settling her hands on her hips, Sadie tilted her chin, and her lips curved as her dark gaze flicked over him from head to toe. "Then what are you looking for? A restraining order? Because that's what you're gonna get if you start staking out the women's bathroom."

"No." Killian inched closer, intentionally invading her personal space. He studied her closely, wanting to see if he affected her even a fraction of the way she affected him. Sadie held her ground, but the slight widening of her eyes and subtle flare of her nostrils as he closed in spoke volumes. He sucked in a deep breath and picked up the unmistakable scent of desire. Oh yeah. He was definitely not alone. "I was looking for you."

"Me?" Sadie blinked. "Why? I gave you the bill. Was it wrong or something?"

"No." A smile played at his lips and he let his eyes drift over her slowly from head to toe. "I realize that I forgot to give you something," he murmured.

Killian leaned in, so that his face was just inches from hers. Sadie wavered slightly but still didn't back away. He breathed deeply, inhaling her scent, which was mixed with the clear aroma of her arousal, and his entire body tightened in response. Sadie's mouth parted and her tongue flicked over her lower lip temptingly.

"My business card." Killian smirked as he snagged his business card out of his pocket and held it up between two fingers. "I realized that I forgot to give this to you last night."

"Right." Sadie held his challenging stare as she grasped the edge of the card and tried to take it. Killian didn't let go. Her grin widened and her voice, low and husky, swirled around him like smoke. "Well, are you going to give it to me or not?"

"Absolutely," he whispered. Holding the edge of the card, his fingertips brushed hers again, sending that delicious electric shock through his body and straight to his dick. "And I'm not just talking about the card."

His suspicions confirmed, Killian turned on his heels and strode away. With her scent lingering in his head and the effects still impacting his body, Killian made his way out of the club. He knew, without a doubt, that merely flirting with Sadie wouldn't be enough.

Not by a long shot.

Chapter 4

THERE WAS NOTHING KILLIAN ENJOYED MORE THAN a challenge.

His father used to say that Killian would build a mountain just so he'd have something to climb or conquer. Whether he was building forts on their property in Alaska as a human or chasing rabbits in his wolf form, Killian was always seeking something to test himself. That was the true sign of a future king, according to his father. And if all went as planned, Killian would assume the throne on his thirty-fifth birthday.

All he needed was a mate.

Ugh.

He stretched his legs out and leaned back against the leather seat of the town car before casting a glance at Ivan and David in the front. The two men were his assigned security detail and had become something akin to friends. As the heir to the throne, he'd always found friendships difficult to maintain, and having any kind of relationship with a woman was even more difficult. Sex wasn't a problem. He'd had plenty of that with more human women than he could count. A ready and willing woman wasn't the issue. But finding the right one seemed downright impossible. Killian was beginning to believe she didn't really exist.

His parents' marriage had been arranged, like so many royals before them, but the difference was that they actually loved each other. And that was what Killian wanted. He didn't want to marry just for the sake of the throne. If he was going to bind his life to a woman, it would damn well be with the right woman.

His father had been after him for the past two years to settle down and take a mate. For shit's sake, the old man had ensured that every available she-wolf from all of the *acceptable* families had been paraded in front of Killian since he reached adulthood. They were lovely, really, beautiful women who would undoubtedly make fine mates—but none of them were *the one*.

Aside from the fact that not one of the females captured his interest beyond a passing fancy, none bore the mark. Since childhood, Killian had been dreaming of the same woman, with the mark of the full moon on her left shoulder blade. Each time it was the same. Naked, she emerged from the water like some kind of ghostly vision. Her alabaster skin glistened in the light of the full moon, and only one thing marred that perfect flesh: a dark circle on her left shoulder—the mark of the moon.

Killian would chase after her, call to her, and beg the nude beauty to turn and face him, take pity on him, and put an end to his loneliness. It wasn't just her beauty that drew him to her. He sensed a strength in her that could rival his own, along with a glimmer of loneliness that he recognized all too well.

Yet each morning he would awaken just as she was turning around...and find himself alone again. The vision was always the same, and as he got older, the recurring dream became more frequent, frenzied, and desperate.

He'd made the mistake of telling his father about the

dream, and the old man had simply brushed it off as childish fantasy. The only person who didn't give him shit about it was his baby sister, Naomi. She was about ten years younger than he was and, when she was a little girl, would beg Killian to tell her about the dreams. Each time she'd sigh and tell him that it was just like a story in one of her books.

Too bad life wasn't a fairy tale. Not even for a prince.

Time was running out and his father was losing patience with him. Maybe he should just pack in this ridiculous idea of opening a club in the city and go back to Alaska, pick a mate, and raise a litter of children.

That's what he should do—but not what he was going to do.

Killian had five years until his father retired and he would have to take his position as king. If these were going to be his last years as a free man, a man beholden to no one but himself, then he was damn well going to make the most of them. He sure as hell couldn't do that back in Alaska with everyone watching his every damn move and playing matchmaker every other day.

When Killian told his mother and father that he wanted to open a nightclub, there had been the inevitable pushback. The only way the old man would agree was if Killian allowed the king and one of his friends to invest in the club. Killian owned controlling interest and having his father as a silent partner wasn't the worst thing in the world, but he would buy his father out as soon as possible. The king said his "friend" wanted to remain anonymous, and even though that set Killian on edge, he was so eager to get his club going that he agreed.

Living in a city run by vampires might seem like an odd choice, but only to those not looking to keep a pack of werewolves out of their business. So far it had been going well. The czars and their coven had been surprisingly welcoming. Most of them, anyway. He had received a couple of anonymous threatening letters about the club, warning him that his kind wasn't welcome in the city, but Killian paid them little mind. He had the approval of the czars, and their opinions were the only ones that mattered.

Maybe not the *only* ones.

A smile played at his lips as he recalled the look on Sadie's face when he'd revealed he was opening his own club in the city. She was quite possibly the most interesting woman he'd met in his life—and he'd met a lot of women. Sadie Pemberton was a challenge for many reasons, not the least of which was because she was a vampire. Aside from that, she was also one of the czar's progeny. If he and Sadie got involved and things went south, it would create a messy situation politically. Then, of course, there was the fact that Sadie seemed to have a clear dislike and distrust of werewolves.

As Killian stared out the window of the limo at the city streets flashing by, Sadie's beautiful face and her fiery dark eyes drifted into his mind.

Vampire or not, that woman would be a challenge. Her dislike and distrust of his kind had been evident from the second he met her last year. She was defiant and outspoken, making her feelings about him perfectly clear, and that outspokenness lit a fire in his gut. For his entire life, people had done whatever he wanted and the word "no" was scarcely heard, unless it came from his father.

He was heir to the throne and constantly surrounded by yes-men.

Not Sadie, though. She seemed to delight in defying him, and he found that spirit remarkably refreshing. It was as though, from day one, she had dared him to seduce her, and damn if he wasn't attracted to her.

There was something about Sadie, something he couldn't put his finger on, and that *something* kept him coming back to her club night after night. Telling her that he was observing the club operations wasn't a total lie. It wasn't the total truth either. At first, he'd gone to the club to study the business, and it had been helpful. But the sexy dark-haired vampire had him returning time and again. It was stupid to get hot and bothered over a vampire, especially when a relationship between them had no future.

Aside from the fact that his father would blow a gasket, his own people would freak the fuck out if they heard the heir to the throne was messing around with a vamp. Yet, here he was, night after night, at The Coven because of Sadie. Fixating on her had to make Killian either the biggest idiot ever born or a gigantic commitment-phobe. After all, if he got involved with Sadie on any level, their relationship would eventually have to end. Killian was going to be king of the Werewolf Society and that meant mating with another wolf. Not a vampire. Hooking up with Sadie would be a waste of time.

Maybe that was why he was chasing her.

God. Was he that big of an asshole? Was he only fixating on her because he knew it would go nowhere? No. He needed her help. Sadie was a smart, intuitive businesswoman and her input on the new club would be valuable. There was nothing wrong with developing a working relationship with her, even if a personal one was outside the realm of possibility.

Yeah, keep telling yourself that.

Lost in his thoughts, Killian made a scoffing sound, leaned his elbow on the bottom of the window, and pressed his mouth against his fist. He was so absorbed in images of Sadie that he didn't hear Ivan.

"Yo!" Ivan shouted. "Killian, you okay back there?"

"What?" Killian snapped his head forward and adjusted his position, feeling embarrassed for spacing out like he had. "I'm fine. Just been burning the candle at both ends."

That wasn't a total lie. He had been pulling double duty with days at the new club site and nights at The Coven. He sure as shit wasn't going to admit he was fantasizing about a vampire vixen. Talk about breaking protocol or tradition. Killian was the heir to the throne, and his mate had to be a she-wolf from one of the proper bloodlines.

Period.

End of story.

Fuck.

He pressed his fingers against his eyes and let out a long, slow breath.

"Killian, are you sure you're okay?" David gripped the wheel tighter and flicked his dark eyes at Killian in the rearview mirror. "For a second I thought you fell asleep with your eyes open."

"Sorry." Killian dropped his hands and rolled his shoulders, rigid with tension. "I was just thinking about something."

"You mean Sadie?" David asked. "That's why we go back there every night, right?"

"I don't know what you're talking about." Killian's eyes narrowed and he looked back out the window. They were driving up the West Side Highway and would be at their new building in a few minutes. "As I said to Ms. Pemberton, I've been watching how they run their club and how they handle the humans."

"Hey." David raised one large hand off the wheel. "Don't get me wrong, man. I'm not complaining about going." He cleared his throat and glanced in the rear-view mirror. Killian wasn't stupid. He knew David had developed a fascination with the DJ, Justine. He also knew that David slipped out from time to time for trysts with the vampire, and out of respect for his friend's privacy, Killian opted never to bring it up unless David did. "That Sadie broad is gorgeous, but she's also a vampire."

"I get it," Ivan interjected. "The attraction to someone different and forbidden is hot, and I know lots of wolves that have dallied with a vamp or two. Let's be honest, hookups like that happen. People just don't talk about it. You, however, aren't just anyone."

"It's true," David replied without looking back. "Your Highness, I—"

"Cut that shit out." Killian gave him a bored look. "I told you not to call me that."

"Right." David held up one hand in surrender and shifted his hulking frame in the seat. "Sorry."

"I've heard stories from my grandfather," Ivan said firmly. "Shit that went down before the treaty was signed. I have to be honest. I'm hoping you're about done there. It makes me highly uncomfortable to be around them."

"Ah, they're not so bad." David turned the wheel and pulled the car into the garage of their building. "Even that Damien guy, the bouncer, is cool. In fact, he cut me in to the pool for the big game next week. I've got fifty riding on it. Vamp knows his sports; I'll give him that. Justine and the girls are cool too, although that Maya chick gives me the creeps more than the others."

Killian stilled. He knew exactly why Maya made them uncomfortable, even if they didn't.

"Maya or that mate of hers, Shane?" Ivan scoffed as the car came to a halt in their parking spot. "Shane is one dangerous sentry. I wouldn't want to have to fight him, and I get the feeling that if we even look at his woman sideways, he'll kill someone. Dude knows this city too. I'm sure he could hide a body with no problems."

"What's the matter?" David teased, shutting off the ignition. "Afraid of a couple vampires? I thought you were a tough guy."

"I am." Ivan punched David on the arm in a not-so-playful manner. "Fuck you."

"I dunno, you kind of sound like a pussy," David said through a gritty laugh.

"Shane isn't a problem." Killian got out of the car and slammed the door. He took off his jacket and breathed in the scent of the garage, instinctively searching for anyone or anything that might be lurking. Finding nothing other than the distinct scent of wet cement, he headed for the elevator, Ivan and David right behind him. "Neither is Maya."

Ivan and David didn't respond and their silence spoke

volumes. They weren't convinced that Maya was harmless, and he couldn't really blame them. Killian knew exactly why Maya made them uncomfortable, but as promised, he'd kept her deadly secret.

Killian swiped his key card and pushed the button for the penthouse before they rode in the elevator in silence. He sensed his friends' uneasiness, and even though he wanted to tell them more to put their worries to rest, he knew he couldn't. He'd promised Olivia and her coven that he would keep Maya's secret, and Killian always kept his word.

No matter what.

If a man didn't have his honor, he had nothing. His late brother, Horace, had failed to grasp that particular concept and it cost him his life. Killian's mouth set in a tight line as a cavalcade of unpleasant memories roared to the surface. Horace had been a traitor, and when his plans to overthrow their father were revealed, he'd challenged Killian—and lost.

When an alpha is challenged, it's a fight to the death.

The soft ding of the elevator signaled their arrival. Killian shoved the unpleasant memories aside as the doors opened. He strode into the entry hall of the lavish penthouse duplex, intent on not feeding nightmares that couldn't be undone.

He liked this new place so much better than the hotel where they'd been staying. With the open floor plan and floor-to-ceiling windows, it felt more like home than living in that damn hotel suite ever did. His father had even given his blessing on the long-term living arrangement. For years, the king had wanted to improve the relationship between their people and the vampires.

Having his only surviving son and heir to the throne living in New York City was a good place to start.

"Good night," Ivan said. He slapped David on the shoulder and waved to Killian before heading toward his bedroom. "What time do you want to head out tomorrow, Your—Killian?" He corrected himself before Killian could.

"About noon. I have some emails I need to catch up on before we go to the site." Killian smiled and gave his friend a nod. "And not to worry, our visits to The Coven will be fewer and farther between. After all, I have my own club to worry about now. First thing tomorrow, I'd like to head over and check on the construction. They should be almost finished, and if all goes well, I can let the interior designers have at it before the end of the week."

"Yes, sir."

"One more thing," Killian said, stopping Ivan in his tracks. "At sundown the day after tomorrow, we will be picking up Ms. Pemberton and bringing her to the club."

"You're the boss." Ivan gave him a tight smile and tilted his head in deference before striding through the large living room and disappearing into the hallway that led to his bedroom.

"Good night, Ivan." Killian let out a sigh and stuck his hands in the pockets of his slacks. Ivan was a wall of muscle and looked like an escapee from a military unit. Most people would expect a brute, and while the guy may have been hell of a fighter, he could be surprisingly formal.

"Are you pissed?" David asked.

Killian blinked and turned toward him in surprise.

Standing in the sprawling kitchen, with its gleaming stainless-steel appliances and shiny granite counters, the fighter looked remarkably out of place. A pang of guilt hit Killian like a ton of bricks. David and Ivan wanted to be in this loud, crowded city about as much as Killian wanted to bond with a mate just for the sake of the throne.

"Why would I be pissed?" Killian tossed his jacket on the mahogany dining table and went to the fridge in search of a midnight snack. He glanced at the digital clock. Actually it was more like a really, really early breakfast. Pulling out a container of leftover sesame chicken, he grabbed a fork from the drawer and dug in. Chinese food tasted even better when it was a day old.

"I don't know." David shrugged and leaned back against the counter. Killian offered some chicken to David, who politely refused. "Maybe 'pissed' isn't the right word. But something is up with you, Killian."

"What are you getting at?" Killian swallowed the food in his mouth and leveled a serious gaze at David, who looked like he had something important he wanted to spit out. "You can be honest with me."

"How honest?" David narrowed his eyes and sucked in a deep breath. "Like friends honest or the king hired me to have your back honest?"

"Friends." Killian looked at him earnestly because he meant it. Ivan and David had both become more like friends, but especially David. "What's up?"

"Why are we here?" David asked quietly.

"You know why." Killian kept his voice even. "I'm opening the club—"

"Right." David held up one hand. "You could open

one in Anchorage on our territory. Why have you decided to work and now *live* in a city run by vampires?" He ran one hand over his cropped blond hair and let out a slow breath, a wry smile playing at his lips. "I don't get it, man. You could be back in Alaska and up to your ass in willing she-wolves who would do just about anything to be the next queen. Hell, Christina's made no secret that she wants you for herself," David said, referring to the she-wolf who was at the top of the king's potential daughter-in-law list and also happened to be the daughter of the general of their military. "The entire society knows she's the most suitable choice for queen."

"It's a moot point." Killian shrugged. "Christina doesn't bear the mark."

"Oh man." David ran his hand over his head and rolled his eyes. "So you're telling me that you're only gonna mate with some dream-woman who has the mark of the moon on her shoulder? With all due respect, she may not even exist."

"I believe she does," Killian said firmly. "Don't make me sorry I told you about that."

"Yeah." David laughed. "If it hadn't been for too much champagne the other night, you probably wouldn't have."

"True." Killian pointed at him with his fork before dropping it in the sink with the empty Chinese food container. "But it doesn't change the fact that I have no intention of ever mating with Christina."

"Fine. Don't hook up with her," David said quickly. "You could be looking for your dream girl with the moon mark in wolf packs in the other territories, and instead you're hanging around a coven of vampires. This city is crowded and dirty, and it stinks. I can only imagine what the stench will be like in the heat of summer." He let out a sigh and shrugged, his voice edged with sadness. "Don't you miss the fresh air? The mountains? I mean, I don't know about you, but if I don't get to run as a wolf soon, I think I'm gonna lose my fuckin' mind. I know your father wants to improve relations with the vampires…but…"

"We've run in Central Park."

"It's not the same, man, and you know it." David looked at him earnestly. "It still feels like we're caged in. That's what this city is, Killian. It's one enormous cage."

Silence hung heavily between them and regret flickered over David's face, showing he undoubtedly believed he'd been a bit too honest with the prince. Killian nodded slowly and stood to his full height, about a half a foot taller than David. The guard squared his shoulders and his jaw clenched, as though bracing for the how-dare-you flogging he obviously expected.

"Well, I did ask for honesty, didn't I?" Killian narrowed his eyes as a smile cracked his face. "I know my choices don't make sense to you—or anyone else, for that matter—but I have my reasons."

"That reason wouldn't be named Sadie would it?"

"Maybe." Killian kept his voice calm. Snagging a paper towel, he wiped his hands and leveled a serious stare at David. "And maybe the reason you don't mind going to the club is because of a certain DJ."

"I—I don't—" David paled.

"It's fine, David." Killian's expression softened and he tossed the paper towel in the trash can. "My point is that all of us have secrets. Your private life is your own…just like mine is."

"Understood." David stilled and paused before adding, "But with all due respect, I'm not the heir to the throne."

"Good night, David." Killian patted his friend on the shoulder and gave him a sad smile. "I'll see you in the morning."

David's voice stopped Killian as he reached the top of the open staircase to the second floor.

"I see the way you look at her." Killian stilled at the top of the stairs but didn't turn around. "You're playing with fire, Your Highness."

The truth of that statement plowed into Killian with all the force David intended as his friend hit the lights and sank the apartment into darkness. The sound of David's bedroom door clicking shut downstairs echoed through the dark, cavernous space.

"Shit," Killian said, letting out a long sigh.

He knew David was right, and based on Ivan's comments earlier, Killian figured that Ivan suspected the same thing. The only difference was that Ivan was too worried about protocol to call the prince out on his dangerous fascination. Unbuttoning his shirt, Killian strode across the loft hallway to his bedroom. The entire second floor was essentially his bedroom and he loved it. The space was private and the bird's-eye view from the building's top floor almost made it feel like he wasn't in the city at all.

Not even bothering to turn on the lights, Killian shed his clothing and tossed them into the corner, missing the laundry basket entirely. Standing naked in front of the

massive bank of windows, he looked out at the spectacular view of the Hudson River. The lights sparkled on the
surface of the choppy winter water, and with the light of
the almost full moon, the world outside was surprisingly
light. Although with the heightened eyesight of his wolf,
Killian didn't need the moonlight. Werewolves could
see clearly on even the darkest of nights.

He should sleep, but he was too wound up. And
Killian had developed a nasty habit of doing anything
except what he should do. He should go back to Alaska,
mate with Christina like his father wanted him to, and
forget about the stupid fantasy of some perfect woman
with the mark.

And Sadie. He should forget about her too.

He *should* and yet he couldn't get her out of his mind.
Those dark eyes, full red lips, and long, silky hair came
together to create an exotic and dangerous-looking
woman. David was absolutely right; Killian couldn't
deny that part of the allure was that she was a vampire.

Forbidden.

The sound of splashing water brought him out of his
thoughts and immediately set his senses on high alert.
Someone was in the pool on the private rooftop terrace.

The sound grew louder, and based on the level of dis-
ruption in the water, it couldn't be something small like
a bird. There was definitely *someone* in the pool. Who
the hell could it be? Who would be swimming out there
in the middle of May other than another wolf? David
and Ivan were downstairs, and the only way to get out
there was through Killian's office down the hall.

Moving swiftly and silently, with his wolf clamoring
to get out, he crept along the dark hallway. The door to

his office was open a crack, allowing him to slip into the room without alerting the intruder to his presence. The sound of water sloshing grew louder as Killian moved closer to the sliding glass door, and a low growl rumbled in his throat as he spotted a body moving in the water. A pile of discarded clothing was draped over the bench.

Stark naked, with his body wound tight, Killian curled his hands into fists as he prepared to rip the door open. The growl in his throat fell silent and heat flashed in his gut when he got an eyeful of the intruder and a wave of recognition flooded him.

The crystal blue water of the pool was lit up from beneath, giving him a clear view of the most perfectly shaped female body he'd ever seen. Ripples of dark hair skimmed behind her as she stretched her long, lithe body through the water, pull after pull. She moved with absolute grace, and every curve on her nude form was exquisitely shaped.

It was like watching an underwater dancer—one who didn't need to come up for air.

If the lacy cuffs on the shirt amid the pile of discarded clothing hadn't given her away, the lack of a need for oxygen would have. With all that long, dark hair and the curve of those hips, he knew exactly who it was— Sadie. His lips tilted. She couldn't possibly be aware that this was his place, and even though the temptation to go out there and bust her for trespassing was strong, he refrained.

Killian didn't know how long he stood there staring at the beautiful water nymph that had invaded his pool. Seconds? Hours? He didn't care. All he could see was *her*. The trance was finally broken when she ascended the stairs at the far end of the pool and sat on the edge with her back to him. His heart thundered in his chest as her alabaster skin glistened in the light of the moon. Every single inch of him hardened as his gaze skimmed over the dip of her waist and along the curve of her round ass.

Vampire or not, he didn't give a shit. Killian knew, in that moment, he had to have her. It wasn't a matter of should or shouldn't—it was a matter of need.

Part of him, for just a second, felt guilty for being a peeping Tom, but to be fair, *she* was the one skinny-dipping in *his* pool. Any guilt he might have felt was instantly squashed by a surge of desire when she arched her back and stretched her arms over her head. She reminded him of a cat stretching out in a patch of sunshine. She was loose and languid, and he swore he could practically hear her purr with contentment as she basked in the light of the moon. Still with her back to him, she gathered her long, wet hair in both hands and pulled it over her right shoulder to squeeze out the water—and that was when he saw it.

On her left shoulder blade was a perfect dark circle—the mark of the moon. As the steam rippled off the water's surface, blurring her from his vision, everything finally made sense. This moment and this woman were his vision come to life.

Sadie Pemberton, a two-hundred-year-old vampire, bore the mark of the moon.

Before he could stop it, Killian's eyes shifted to the glowing amber eyes of his wolf. His muscles rippled, straining against the desire to shift, and every animal instinct went into overdrive. The primal need to claim her and mark her as his was beyond any other sensation he'd ever experienced. Without thinking about the consequences, Killian slid the glass door open and stepped out into the crisp early-morning air, the inky darkness just beginning to give way to glimmers of the impending dawn.

The moment his foot hit the cement, Sadie leaped to her feet, spun around, and bared her fangs.

Standing on the steps of the pool, gorgeous and naked as the day she was born, Sadie looked ready to pounce and rip his throat out. The look on her face went from fury to shock within a split second and the change was almost comical—almost. There was nothing funny about the way Killian's body was responding to hers.

Nude and fully aroused, he stood at the edge of the pool and let his burning gaze drift over her gorgeous form. Nudity wasn't a big deal among the wolves, and based on the way Sadie wasn't running for her clothes, it wasn't for her either.

Thank God she didn't cover herself.

The woman looked like she was carved from marble, a statue of the goddess Aphrodite come to life. Her round, full breasts were tight and high, and rivulets of water trickled over her erect nipples as though begging him to lap at them. A narrow waist and flat belly gave way to full hips, and his gaze lingered briefly at the juncture of her lean, toned legs. A dark patch of hair hid the treasures he so desperately wanted to discover.

He expected her to fly off in a furious huff, but to his delight, she met his burning stare with her own as Killian stalked slowly around the edge of the pool toward her.

"What the fuck are you doing here? Spying on me?"

Sadie seethed. Her dark, almost black eyes clocked his every move and her lips peeled back, effectively showing her razor-sharp fangs. "How did you know I'd be here?" Her eyes flicked over him quickly. "And why are you naked?"

"Actually, I was going to ask you the same thing," Killian murmured. He was just a few feet away from her now and he lifted his nose, inhaling her rich, feminine scent. It was a combination of mint and violets. Feminine and fresh. His gaze drifted to her breasts that swayed enticingly. Sweet Mary, this woman was sexy. She was totally and completely comfortable in her own skin and seemingly unaware of her beauty. And that made her even more desirable. "This is my pool and I was going to go for a swim. So, tell me, what are you doing here? Vampire."

"Your pool? I've been here before and never picked up the scent of your kind."

"I haven't used my pool yet."

"When did this become your pool?" Sadie's voice wavered ever so slightly and her brow furrowed. "I thought you lived at that hotel." She smirked. "*Wolf*."

Killian knew she meant the word "wolf" as an insult, but damn if it didn't sound sexy coming out of her mouth. It was a challenge. Like she was daring him to come at her one way or another.

"As of last week." Killian stopped just a foot away from Sadie and kept his voice low. "Ivan, David, and I just moved in. In fact, I signed a five-year lease."

"Really?" Sadie arched one dark eyebrow and scoffed. "That's a hell of a commitment. It must be love. I heard your kind was into the ménage à trois. Congratulations. They're both very handsome."

"Hardly." Killian held her fiery stare. "I have nothing against a threesome. In fact, I've enjoyed a few over the years and I can assure you—I'm the only male."

"I knew it." Sadie rolled her eyes. "Homophobe?"

"Alpha," Killian growled and shook his head slowly. Sadie's expression faltered briefly. The tough exterior gave way momentarily to a heated look of lust, and that was all the encouragement Killian needed. "Looks like there are lots of things you don't know about me, Ms. Pemberton."

"I know enough." Sadie straightened her back and tilted her chin defiantly, steeling her stance and making no move to retreat. Her sharp gaze flicked down to the evidence of his desire, which he was doing nothing to hide. Killian didn't miss the slight widening of her eyes before she met his stare once again. "For example, it's time for me to leave."

"Chicken?"

"Don't flatter yourself." Sadie jutted a thumb to the brightening horizon. "Sunrise. But since I have you here, I want to tell you something. I should have said this to you when you first started coming to the club."

"Be my guest." He took one step closer.

"If you sell Maya out or reveal her secret to your father or any of the others…" she said in a firm, steady voice. "Make no mistake about it. Treaty or no treaty, I *will* kill you."

"I swore that I would keep Maya's secret, and I always keep my word."

"The word of a werewolf doesn't hold much water with me."

"Do you know many wolves?" he asked playfully.

"I've known enough." Sadie's voice wavered briefly. "They seemed more interested in savagery than promises."

"If a man doesn't have his honor, then he has nothing."

"Really?" Her voice dipped to a low, challenging tone. "Like your brother?"

"Yes." Killian stilled for moment. Bringing up his brother was a low blow and she knew it. "Just like him."

"Sorry." Sadie's voice softened and a look of regret flickered across her face. "That wasn't fair."

"If you don't believe me, then why not taste my blood and read my blood memories?" Killian's voice dipped lower to a challenging tone, daring her to break the rules. Which of them would crack first? "Your kind can do that, can't they? Read the memories of those they feed on?"

"Not wolves. Only humans." Sadie's voice was tight with restraint. "Besides, I don't get blood memories from anyone. Not anymore. I taught myself how to block that shit out. I have too much of my own history to carry around. I don't want or need anyone else's problems."

"Interesting. You can shield yourself from blood memories?" He inched closer. "Is that a common ability?"

"That's none of your business."

"You brought it up," he murmured playfully.

"Whatever." Sadie didn't give an inch. "I will do anything to protect my family." Her eyes seemed haunted by something, a memory perhaps, and she whispered, "Family is precious and too easily lost."

Silence hung between them with only the sounds of the city filling the air—car horns, wind whistling between the buildings, a siren wailing in the distance, and the savage pounding of his heart.

"I thought you were leaving," he murmured. Killian leaned closer, ever so slightly, and breathed her in. When her fresh, crisp scent filled his head, a deep growl rumbled in his chest. Sadie held her ground and didn't retreat, although he sensed her body quivering, almost humming. He closed his eyes and reveled in the unique vibrations and musical hum her beautiful body emanated. The erotic pulses thrummed through him, called to him. Damn it all to hell, he itched to touch her. To taste her. "You *could* leave…and yet, here you stand."

Eyes still closed, Killian inched his large frame nearer so that her nipples scraped lightly against his chest and the heat of his erection brushed against the cool skin of her belly. His body twitched as flesh met flesh, and still Sadie did not retreat. The vibrations rippling off her damp, quivering body skittered over him like music and, combined with the whisper of her touch, his last ounce of resolve evaporated.

His fists clenched and unclenched at his side until he finally gave in to the driving desire and trailed one finger up her arm. Sadie flinched almost imperceptibly as he traced the curve of her shoulder and then along the line of her collarbone. A moan escaped her lips when he brushed the back of his knuckles up her neck before gently cupping her face.

"I never run from a challenge," Sadie murmured. She pressed her breasts against him, the soft mounds of flesh searing against him.

Killian felt like he was in the middle of a game of

double dog dare—and it was a surefire bet he was going to lose. Sadie sighed, a seductive sound that made his cock twitch.

Oh yeah. Dead wolf walking.

"Me neither." Killian lifted his head and clapped his hungry gaze onto hers. Her eyes were wild, her mouth parted slightly, revealing the tips of her fangs so there was no mistaking her desire for him. Her body molded against his in all the right places, and the beast inside him fought for control. "This goes against the laws of nature."

"Yeah? So does a werewolf who wants to live in the middle of Manhattan." Sadie's lips curled back, flashing more of her fangs. Killian's gut clenched when she popped up on her toes and flicked his lower lip with her tongue. A wicked look twinkled in her eye. "I'd say it's time to nut up or shut up. All this talking is gonna make me think you're all bark and no *bite*."

"Wouldn't want to let you down." On a curse, he covered her eager mouth with his, and the world he knew ripped wide open. She tasted cool, sweet, and rich, like ice cream in the summertime, and in that instant Killian knew he would never, ever get enough of her. Laws of nature could be damned. This woman's taste was all he would ever crave. Were there other women? Who the hell cared?

Sadie's soft, pliant lips opened to him as he ran his tongue along the seam of her mouth and she welcomed him in. Grasping her head with both hands, he groaned and took full control of the plundering kiss. He tangled his hands in her long, wet hair, which felt like ribbons of satin as it rushed through his fingers. Killian groaned when her tongue swept along his, seeking him out with the same desperation and urgency.

This was what he needed. This woman. Her touch. Her taste. How on earth could this be wrong?

"Killian?" The sound of Ivan's voice shattered the moment and yanked him from the haze of lust. The fear of discovery was enough to have them both put on the brakes with gut-wrenching speed.

Sadie shoved him away with far more force than he would ever have thought she possessed, and easily extricated herself from his grasp. Breathing heavily and feeling completely stoned from that kiss, Killian stumbled back but caught himself before he fell into the pool. *Could Ivan's timing suck any worse?*

In a blur of motion, Sadie grabbed her pile of clothes. She looked at him, stunned.

"Sadie, wait."

"No way," Sadie whispered shakily. Her quivering hand went to her mouth and she stared at him with wide, frightened eyes. The tough-as-nails vampire had been replaced by a terrified young woman. She looked almost…fragile. "That's never happening again."

Before Killian could respond and assure her that was definitely not the last kiss they'd be sharing, Sadie shot into the night like a ghost.

"Damn it!" Killian shouted.

Killian heard Ivan coming and realized he was standing outside, naked, with a raging hard-on and a growing case of blue balls. Thankfully, he had enough of his wits about him to jump into the water in an attempt to hide his condition. Ivan came out just as Killian surfaced and swam to the edge of the pool.

"Everything okay up here?" Ivan, gun in hand and wearing only a pair of sweatpants, looked around the rooftop with more than a little curiosity. "I could swear I heard you talking to someone and I got…I don't know…a weird vibe." He tilted his nose to the air and Killian stilled. "I smell a vampire…and something else."

"Nope." Killian swiped his wet hair off his face and perched both arms on the edge. "Just me. I was feeling a little wound up and decided to take a swim before I hit the sack. You didn't shower tonight, did you?"

"No." Ivan looked around the area suspiciously. "Why?"

"I can smell the club all over you, man." Killian laughed and swiped water from his eyes, hoping this would satisfy Ivan's curiosity. "Vampire. Humans. Sex. Shit, Ivan. I hate to break it to you, but you stink."

"Yeah, you're probably right." Ivan nodded and looked around one last time. He was about to go inside when he snapped his nose to the air and stilled. "I smell blood, and I know that wasn't at the club tonight." Turning back to Killian, he squatted down and pointed at Killian's face. "What the hell happened to your lip? You're bleeding."

"I am?" Killian licked his lip and swiped at his mouth. Sure enough, the unmistakable coppery taste of blood bathed his tongue and his fingers came away with a streak of red. "Huh. I bumped the bottom when I dove in," he lied. "I guess I scraped my lip." Killian shrugged and waved Ivan off. "No big deal. I'll see you in the morning."

"No wonder the king wants you to have a two-man security team." Ivan gave him a doubtful look and rose to his feet. "We leave you alone for a little while and you hurt yourself."

"Very funny." Killian laughed as Ivan disappeared into the penthouse. "See you in a few hours."

Licking his lower lip, Killian looked to the purple and indigo predawn sky in search of Sadie. As he suspected, she was nowhere in sight. Hoisting himself out of the pool, he went inside and dried off, replaying that kiss over and over again in his mind. Kiss? Hell, that didn't cover it. He had never kissed a woman—human, wolf, or whatever—and experienced anything like that.

After a cold shower, Killian settled into the massive king-size bed and stared at the ceiling as golden light from the rising sun streamed into his bedroom. With sleep flirting at the edge of consciousness, one image haunted his mind—the fearful look on Sadie's face just before she flew away. Maybe she was afraid of getting caught by Ivan or breaking the no-fraternizing rule? But deep in his gut he knew that wasn't true. There was something more to it. Because up until that second, Sadie had been just as into it as Killian was. The question was, what had scared her so badly?

Killian made a silent vow to find out so he could put her fears to rest and claim her as his own.

Chapter 5

THIS CAN'T BE HAPPENING.

Sadie's body hummed with power, making her feel like she was hooked up to some kind of generator. Aside from flying to the underground tunnel entrance in record time, she ran through the old subway channels in the blink of an eye. Sadie had always been fast—but not that fast.

Her fang had scraped his lip. The moment his blood touched her tongue, Sadie's entire world exploded in a cavalcade of light and sound.

Killian's blood memories stormed into her mind like a hurricane, a flash of whirring images. In that split second Sadie glimpsed the werewolf prince's idyllic childhood and his tempestuous adolescence in the wilds of Alaska. She felt the heartbreaking betrayal he had endured from his brother and practically whimpered under the weight of the looming, oppressive future he couldn't escape.

Sadie was left confused and scared by the surprising experience of absorbing Killian's blood memories but her feelings weren't limited to herself. The man was trapped by his birthright and dreaded the notion of taking a mate. The boy had serious commitment issues.

Aside from the unexpected event of absorbing his memories, Sadie's body had been energized by Killian's blood although she'd barely tasted it. If only a few drops of his blood affected her like this, what the hell would happen if she had more than that?

The answer was simple. Nothing good.

No. Sadie shook her head as if she could shake away the crazy thoughts. What on earth was wrong with her? Lust. That's what. Good old-fashioned, fuck-me-blind lust. When she'd heard someone come out of the penthouse, she fully expected a human. But when the scent of a werewolf filled her head, panic had swamped her.

Until, that is, she set eyes on the preternaturally sexy, naked body that belonged to Killian Bane. His tall, well-muscled form was a gorgeous sight to behold, and she'd been right about what he was hiding under all those clothes. She didn't know what to stop staring at first: his perfectly sculpted legs, the broad chest covered by a dusting of dark hair, or that thick beautiful cock.

She should have flown out of there that instant. Should have grabbed her clothes and hightailed it to anywhere other than that roof with him in all his hot, sexy nakedness. But she couldn't. She quite literally couldn't make herself leave. He was like a magnet, drawing her closer, pulling her into his orbit.

A swirl of need gathered in her belly as she recalled the feel of his lips on hers. Letting out a groan, Sadie fought the unreasonable attraction she had for the arrogant wolf and focused on getting to the Presidium's offices. The feral, predatory look in his eye as he stalked toward her around the pool had made her wet. His long, toned, well-muscled body was taut with desire, and she had been more than a little impressed by the erection the guy was sporting.

An ache throbbed between her legs at the memory of

the hard feel of his body pressing against hers. In that moment it hadn't mattered that he was a werewolf. All that mattered was getting closer, and as strange as it was, being naked in his arms felt remarkably *right*.

Strong. Powerful. Irresistible.

Every single bit of him drew her in, and she had fooled herself into thinking she had control, that she could handle the situation. Yeah, right. That veil of bullshit had evaporated when she let him kiss her. Because from that moment forward, Sadie knew she'd never get enough. He tasted hot, feral, dangerous, and forbidden, and the effects of that kiss continued to hum through every cell of her body.

Then, of course, there was the blood.

She didn't mean to cut him, and normally she was great at maneuvering kisses when her fangs were out. Hell, she'd kissed plenty of men—and women, for that matter—and never once had she been so sloppy. But when she'd heard Ivan coming and picked up his scent, her instincts for self-preservation had kicked into high gear. She must have scraped Killian with her fangs when she pushed him away. Then when his blood hit her tongue, every one of her senses exploded and went into hyperdrive.

It wasn't the taste of his blood that frightened her, or even the fact that it was forbidden. Hell, not even getting his blood memories was as scary as what had happened next. Nope. What she had felt when his blood rushed through her veins paled in comparison to the shock of what she *heard*.

Could Ivan's timing suck any worse?

The deep baritone growl of Killian's voice had ripped

into her mind with shocking intensity, and Sadie's entire world had started to spin out of control. Killian had telepathed to her, and since vamps and werewolves could not speak to each other telepathically, that it had happened at all was plain old crazy. Other than mental illness, there was only one reason why she'd be able to hear Killian's voice in her mind. It simply *couldn't* be possible.

Bloodmate.

"This can't be happening." Talking to herself was a sure sign she was losing it, taking a ride on the crazy train. "It was just a fluke—a one-time thing because I tasted his blood. That's all."

She pressed her hand to the smooth, black panel next to the iron-hinged wooden door and waited not-so-patiently for the entrance to the Presidium's New York office to open. The vampires' central offices provided shelter and a safe haven for all vamps. Just being within these walls made Sadie feel safe. And a little less crazy. After what seemed like an eternity, the antique door swung wide and allowed her access. Letting out a huff of impatience, Sadie made her way quickly through the stone hallway, the sound of her boot heels echoing around her with obnoxious clarity.

Olivia and Doug lived in an apartment at the other end of the Presidium's underground chambers, and with any luck they were preoccupied with baby Emily. While both of them were daywalkers, they still kept vampire hours for the most part, and by now they should be going to bed. The last complication she needed was to involve the czars in this latest development, and she'd already intruded on them last night. She wanted to handle this

situation on her own and only involve Olivia if she absolutely had to.

When she came to the intersection of the two grand
hallways, Sadie took a left turn beneath the ornate
stone arches and made a beeline for Xavier's laboratory. Xavier was their resident genius and inventor.
Aside from making the latest and greatest weaponry, he
dabbled in chemistry and potions. If anyone could help
her find a way out of this mess, it would be him.

Sadie nibbled her thumbnail nervously before banging
on the massive steel door. The sun was just coming up
and she prayed their resident weapons master and Mr.
Fix-It hadn't gone to sleep yet. She was about to pound
on the door again when she heard a muffled clicking
sound and the double doors opened. Stepping back so
she didn't get bowled over, Sadie quickly slipped inside.

The cavernous room looked like a mad scientist's lab.
Ancient weapons dangled from the ceiling like some
kind of macabre mobile. Assorted experiments were in
progress on several tables, but Xavier was nowhere to be
seen. She was about to call out to him when a familiar
fluttering sound, almost like the wings of a giant butterfly, filled the air.

"Hello, Bella." Sadie looked toward the ceiling for
the Presidium's resident ghost, but so far the Romanian
specter wasn't showing herself. She barely revealed
herself or spoke to anyone other than Xavier. "I'm here
to see Xavier."

A clicking noise echoed through the room, making
Sadie jump. She spun to the right just as a panel along
the far wall slid open. A moment later, Xavier flew
out in a blur. Sadie let out a sigh of relief as her friend

landed on the stool in front of her and threw out his arms in welcome.

"Sadie girl!" Xavier exclaimed. "Get on over here and gimme a hug. I've barely seen you since you started running that dang club."

Standing on the stool and wearing his usual ensemble of a lab coat, shirt, and slacks, he looked like a miniature Albert Einstein. A shock of white hair stuck up in a thousand different directions, and his wire-rim glasses were perched precariously on the tip of his nose. The vampire's signature hundred-watt smile was gleaming brightly, instantly making her feel better.

Sadie ran over and wrapped him up in a big hug. He may have been small in stature, but Xavier had one of the biggest hearts of anyone she'd ever known. The brilliant man was the closest thing Sadie had to a father, since she'd lost her own so many years ago. She squeezed her eyes shut and fought the flood of tears that threatened to come.

"Hey, now." Xavier pulled back and patted her arms, looking at her with genuine concern. His pale blue-gray eyes studied her intently, and he pursed his lips together as he gave her the once-over. "What's going on with you, Sadie girl? You seem wired or hopped up or something. I mean you're almost…buzzing. Seriously."

He gripped her hands tightly in his far smaller ones. "I've never seen you so rattled. What happened?"

"I'm in deep shit." Sadie swiped at her eyes and released Xavier before pulling up a neighboring stool and sitting down. "And I know that if anyone can help me, it will be you, but I'm going to need you to keep this between us for now."

"You got it." Xavier nodded and crossed his heart with one pudgy hand before sitting down. "Your secret is safe with me." The fluttering noise above them grew louder, and he jutted a thumb toward it. "And with Bella too." He winked. "She won't say a word. Only speaks Romanian anyway."

"Thank you, Bella." Sadie gave a cursory wave toward the ceiling and smiled before turning her attention back to Xavier. "You make a lot of potions and elixirs and stuff, right?"

"Right…" he said slowly. He pushed his glasses up onto his head and clasped his hands in front of him. "I take it you're looking for something specific."

"Well, I know you've been working on a cure for a werewolf bite."

"Yes." Xavier nodded, his expression pensive. "Their saliva is fatal to vampires when delivered through a bite, and with a few more of them now residing in the city, Olivia asked me to work on something just in case. No luck so far, though." He gestured toward two large tables at the back of the room with bubbling liquids and tubes twining in and out of a scaffold-like structure.

"That's what I've been spending most of my time on lately. The virus that turns a human into a werewolf is a fatal virus for us. It attacks our cells with frightening speed. I haven't even been able to slow it down, let alone stop it." His expression darkened. "Watching it happen, even under the microscope, is one of the most terrifying things I've witnessed."

"It's so bizarre." Sadie shuddered and wrapped her arms around herself once before rising and walking over to the lab tables. As she stared at the equipment, her mind went to the kiss she'd shared with Killian and the euphoric sensations she'd experienced. "How can their saliva from a bite kill us but their blood energize us? I just don't get it."

"I think it has something to do with the way the virus is introduced into our bodies. The saliva is introduced through a bite, but the blood is ingested. I think that's the difference, but the truth is I just don't know." Xavier flew over and landed on a stool on the opposite side of the table. He put his glasses back on and pointed at one of the beakers. "I've been looking at both microscopically."

"Wait a minute." Sadie pointed at the beaker. "Where are you getting the werewolf blood and saliva for your tests?"

"The prince." Xavier shrugged.

"Killian donated his blood and saliva to help vampires figure out how to cure a werewolf bite?"

"Yes." Xavier grinned and pushed his glasses back on his head. "He made one donation about six months ago as a sign of good faith and to assure us that the wolves aren't a threat. In fact, King Heinrich insisted on it. I like him very much," Xavier said with a smile. "He's progressive and willing to make changes, like Olivia and Doug. Anyway, I'm sure that's the reason the czars didn't put up a fight when Killian decided to stay here in the city." Xavier's eyes narrowed and he lowered his voice. "Now, why don't you tell me why you're here? Since you obviously haven't suffered a werewolf bite."

"I did something really stupid." Sadie puffed a stray hair from her face and stared at Xavier for what felt like forever before finally spitting it out. "I kissed Killian."

"Ah, I see. I guess it's a good thing that their saliva is only fatal when introduced through a bite." Xavier's white eyebrows flew up and a look of understanding covered his face. "So, how exactly can I help you with that?"

"You don't seem surprised."

"I'm not." Xavier chuckled. "From what the girls tell me, our royal friend has been spending a lot of time buzzing around you at the club. They all figured that it was only a matter of time."

"Great." Sadie cringed inwardly, realizing she'd been fooling no one but herself regarding her attraction to Killian. "Kissing him? That's not the I-fucked-up part."

"I'm listening."

"I tasted his blood."

"I see." Xavier's playful expression evaporated as the weight of her words settled over him. "I'm still not sure why you're here. I'm not a priest, my dear, and this isn't a confessional," he said, a glimmer of humor returning after a second.

"I think it did something to me—his blood, I mean," Sadie added quickly. She started pacing around the room, hoping that if she said it all out loud she wouldn't sound as crazy as she felt. "I tasted werewolf blood once before. It was just before the treaty was signed and right after Olivia turned me. We got ambushed by a pack of three wolves, and in those days, it was kill or be killed. Olivia took down two and I got one of them—barely. Anyway, when I tasted *his* blood, it was definitely supercharged, you know? Made me stronger and I felt kind of invincible for a little while. It's probably what humans feel like when they're on cocaine or something."

"That's what I've heard. But that's not what happened with Killian?" Xavier asked in his typically calm, fatherly tone.

"No," Sadie whispered. She hugged herself tighter and rubbed her arms, wishing she could rub away her fears and uncertainty. "It wasn't just what I felt, Xavier." Her voice quivered as she finally forced herself to say it out loud. "I saw his blood memories…and…I heard him."

"What?" Xavier's voice was barely audible. He flew around the table and, hovering in midair, grabbed Sadie by both arms and looked her dead in the eyes. "How exactly did you hear him?"

"In my head." Sadie swallowed hard and whispered, "Telepathically."

"Do you mean to tell me that Killian—a werewolf—spoke to you telepathically *and* you saw his blood memories?"

Sadie nodded, unable to say another word.

"This…this is unprecedented. I mean, I know that they can telepath with other pack members, but I've never heard of a wolf communicating that way with anyone outside the pack. Let alone a vampire." Xavier took her hands in his and led her over to one of the stools, urging her to sit down. He settled himself on the edge of the table.

"Seeing his blood memories is especially interesting because of your particular gift for shielding. I've never met another vamp that's been able to shield themselves from the blood memories of humans, except for Emperor Zhao, but he's thousands of years old. Then of course there's the fact that vamps can't read the memories of werewolves. Astonishing!"

"I'm scared, Xavier," Sadie whispered through quivering lips.

"You mean of what you saw in his memories?"

"No." Sadie let out a slow breath and pushed her hair off her face. "That wasn't the scary part. Actually, it made me have more sympathy for the guy, believe it or not."

"Then what about this is frightening you?"

"Why?" Sadie leveled a pensive look at her friend and her voice dropped to a whisper. "Why him and why now?"

"Have you told anyone else about this?" Xavier arched one white eyebrow at her. "Because I think you should speak to Olivia."

"No. I don't want to drag her into this. She's got enough crap on her plate at the moment. Besides, we don't even know what's happening." Sadie swiped her eyes and let out a sound of frustration. "This is crazy, Xavier. You and I both know there's only one reason a vampire would telepath with anyone other than their sibling, progeny, or maker."

"Bloodmate," Xavier whispered.

"Yup." Sadie nodded and let out a sound of disbelief. "Werewolves and vampires have been enemies since the beginning of time, and the treaty has only stayed in place so far because we mostly all stick to our own territories. Killian and I can't be bloodmates. That simply *cannot* be possible."

"Well, my dear girl, if there's one thing I learned the night I was turned"—he squeezed her hands in his and gave her that gentle smile—"it's that anything is possible."

"Can't you make some kind of elixir or potion or something? Anything. Maybe a glamour potion for vampires, you know?" Even as she said it, she knew how dumb an idea it was. "Make me forget or make me not want to be near Killian."

"No." Xavier laughed softly and shook his head. "I think we're getting ahead of ourselves. Like any good scientist, I will need more data before making any kind of decision about what we're really dealing with here. You've had a big night, and the first item on your agenda should be getting some sleep. Perhaps in the evening things will be clearer for you. Besides, when Maya and Olivia bonded with their mates, didn't they stop telepathing with the rest of the coven?"

"Yes." Sadie nodded furiously.

"Have you tried contacting Trixie or Suzie?"

"Oh my God. Of course!" Sadie rolled her eyes and put her face in her hands, feeling like an idiot. "No, I haven't. Jeez. I seriously have my head up my ass."

"Not at all." Xavier laughed and patted her arm lovingly. "But that must have been one heck of a kiss."

"Oh please." Sadie lifted her head and shot her dear friend a disapproving look, doing her best to deny it. "It wasn't the kiss."

"Okay, then." Xavier peered at her over the rim of his glasses. "Try contacting Trixie."

"She's probably sleeping." That was a lie. Trixie was in all likelihood still awake. Sadie didn't attempt to telepath Trixie because she was terrified she'd be met with silence. What if that happened? What if she reached out to Trixie and Suzie, and no one answered? "I don't want to wake up Trixie. You know how cranky she can

be, and poor Suzie has been working like crazy at the
Presidium. I'm sure they're both fast asleep."

"Sure, sure." Still laughing, he waved her off and
flew over to the left side of the room. A second later the
wall slid open to reveal floor-to-ceiling shelves littered
with various and sundry items. Xavier grabbed something off the shelf before flying back to Sadie. "Here.
Put on this watch monitor, and let's see if I can gather
some data to help us out."

"I'll take all the help I can get." Sadie held out her
arm and Xavier strapped on what looked like a watch.
The sturdy, black rubber strap fit snugly around her
wrist, and the smooth glass face had a digital screen with
couple of symbols and a number at the center. "What
is it?"

"It's a special monitor. This little gadget is reading
different blood and enzyme levels through the surface of
your skin. That number there is your body temperature.
It's right at eighty-eight point six. Exactly ten below
the human norm, but right on the money for a healthy
vampire like you. When you feed, it will rise by ten to
twelve degrees, but a vamp's body temp never goes
above one hundred. Any higher than that and we run the
risk of combustion, as you know."

Sadie nodded. There were certain rules you learned
early on as a young vampire.

Don't go in the sunlight.

Don't get stuck with silver.

Avoid getting a stake in the heart.

No messy human killings.

And never *ever* feed on werewolves.

Taking in some werewolf blood could make a

vampire high, but too much would be like taking a walk in the sun. *Boom, baby.* Sadie shuddered. She'd almost had that happen when she fought with that werewolf so many years ago.

"Sadie?" Frowning, Xavier pushed his glasses onto his head. "How much of Killian's blood did you ingest?"

"Not much. Only a few drops, I think." Sadie rubbed the smooth surface of the device with her thumb. "I didn't mean to do it at all. I scraped his lip accidentally. Why?"

"Your body temp should be higher than that. Even with only a few drops in your system, I would expect your body temperature to have risen and stayed that way for a while. Wolf blood is far more potent than human and usually takes longer to digest." He shrugged and waved the thought off, which did nothing to ease the sense of foreboding that crept up Sadie's back. The word whispered in her mind again. *Bloodmate.* "Well, no matter. You said there was only a little. Anyway, off you go. If you have any more run-ins with our werewolf friend, bring me the monitor afterward so I can upload the data."

"Well, if I have anything to say about it, I won't be seeing him again anytime soon." *Liar, liar, pants on fire*, she thought as Xavier gave her a doubtful look. "I mean it."

"I know you do. Now you need to stop jumping to conclusions and go back to your apartment and get some sleep."

"Sleep?" Sadie let out a nervous laugh. Nope. The last thing she wanted to do now was sleep. "I'm too wound up to sleep."

"I'm sure everything will look different after you've had some rest. I would encourage you to steer clear of young Prince Bane." He gave her a knowing smile. "But if you find yourself *accidentally* in a situation with him, this little gizmo will track any physical changes you experience."

"It was probably just a fluke." Sadie didn't want to mention that she'd promised to go with Killian to his club. She should call the guy and cancel, but like everything else with the wolves, her actions weren't just about her. She had to take their race relations into account. "When I see him again, I'll be sure to keep my distance. Thanks, Xavier."

"You are most welcome, Sadie girl." He flew up and brushed a kiss on her cheek. The fluttering above them grew louder and he chuckled. "She's like a daughter to me," he shouted. Dropping his voice to a whisper, he said, "Bella gets jealous."

Promising to return with the device in a couple days, Sadie ran through the tunnels back to her apartment beneath the nightclub. Once inside, she let out a sigh of relief, the familiar, comfortable space putting her at ease. Grabbing some blood from the fridge, Sadie heated it in the microwave and drank it in a few greedy gulps.

She rinsed out the glass and placed it in a drying rack on the counter. Her brow knit together when the unexpected sensation of hunger gnawed at her gut. She needed more, which was not the norm. After downing two more full glasses, Sadie finally felt satisfied. Shaking her head at her unusual moment of gluttony, she stripped off her clothes and made her way into the bedroom.

Normally bottle feeds, as they were called, were more

than enough to satisfy Sadie's hunger. She only hunted and fed from humans once a month or so. Bottle feeds hadn't been a possibility when she was turned, given the technology of the time, so she'd had no choice but to take part in live feeds. And live feeds came with blood memories. Since she didn't want to carry around other people's memories—many of which were unpleasant—she taught herself to put up a mental shield and block them out. After that, feeding became a far less tiresome task.

Sadie didn't need a stranger's frightening memories…she had plenty of her own.

She shuddered as the screams from that night filled her head. Shoving away the ugly and surprisingly vivid memories from her last night as a human, Sadie shifted her thoughts to Killian. Peeking into his mind may not have been planned, but it was extremely educational. The prince had far more layers to him than she'd given him credit for. Killian Bane wasn't the vapid playboy she pegged him for, and that revelation made him even more attractive.

Crap. Why couldn't he have been a total jerk?

Tossing her clothes into the hamper, Sadie went into the spacious bathroom and turned the knob. Moments later, ten shower jets sprayed into the massive standing shower, steam filled the space, and Sadie let out a sigh. This was her favorite room in the apartment, the multi-jet shower her big splurge.

After a long and lazy shower, Sadie toweled herself dry and was about to reach for her pajamas when her phone buzzed loudly from the pile of clothes in the hamper.

"Shit." She looked at herself in the mirror above the black lacquered dresser. "Some grown-up you are. You're acting more like some stupid teenage girl."

After digging through the clothes, she pulled the phone free and swore loudly when she saw the text message.

> This is Della with the City Cleaning Service staff. We are outside the entrance of The Coven nightclub. You have us scheduled for six. Do you need to reschedule?

"Damn it." With everything that had transpired, Sadie had completely forgotten about the new cleaning crew.

She frantically texted back saying that she would be right up. After pulling her clothes on with vampire speed, Sadie raced upstairs to let the new cleaning crew in. Too bad she couldn't tell them the truth. *Sorry I'm late, but I'm a vampire who has developed a dangerous obsession with the werewolf prince, and I've got my head up my ass.*

Sadie threw the bolt locks on the enormous doors of the club and pulled them open, using the door as a shield from the harmful rays of sunlight. The four-woman crew filtered into the club, armed with various cleaning supplies. She didn't miss the nervous sidelong glance from the older woman at the end of the group or the quick sign of the cross she made over her ample bosom. Sadie rolled her eyes. Great. Just what she needed, a superstitious religious nut in an old church that now operated as a house of sin.

Closing the door tightly behind them, Sadie followed

the crew inside and gave them instructions of where and what to clean. Knowing she wasn't going to get any sleep, Sadie went into her office in the back of the club. Truthfully, she could have slept. She didn't want to.

For the first time in two hundred years, Sadie was afraid to sleep.

Aside from telepathy with their bloodmates, Olivia and Maya had done one other thing that vampires *never* did. They dreamed. And vampires don't dream. The sleep of a vampire is a shroud of leaden silence and utter darkness, and even though Sadie would probably regret it later, she was going to avoid sleep at all costs.

If she allowed herself to sleep and entered the dream-scape, then she would no longer be able to fool herself. Dreaming of Killian Bane would seal both of their fates and confirm what she already suspected.

Chapter 6

KILLIAN HAD BEEN STARING AT THE BLUEPRINTS FOR twenty minutes without actually seeing them. Barely hearing the buzz of saws and hammering by various workers who were busy putting the finishing touches on the construction, he realized his thoughts were totally and completely preoccupied with Sadie and their brief, albeit sensual encounter last night. He cursed under his breath and ran a hand through his hair, struggling to make himself focus on the task at hand.

But that didn't stop him from looking at his watch for the tenth time in as many minutes. It wouldn't be long until sunset when he'd see that dark-haired beauty again.

She had turned him into one horny bastard.

In the light of a new day, and with the heady sensations from that kiss not at all faded, the voice of reason grabbed him and tried to shake some sense into him. Dreams or visions or whatever the hell they were, Killian simply could not allow himself to pursue any kind of relationship with Sadie. Aside from the fact that his father would lose his ever-loving mind, how could Killian rule his people effectively with a vampire for a mate? Part of his job as prince was to produce an heir, or preferably heirs, to the throne. There would be no offspring with Sadie. Even if by some fluke of nature they did conceive a child, his people would never accept a hybrid child as a future leader of the Werewolf Society.

With his brother gone, Killian was the only acceptable heir to the throne, and he'd never felt the weight of that impending responsibility more than he did right now. Killian let out a slow breath, his lips pressing together in a tight line. The encounter with Sadie was totally inappropriate. Mark or no mark, he would have to be sure nothing like that happened again.

Killian pushed the disconcerting thoughts aside and refocused his attention on the blueprints. The club was coming together, and if they stayed on schedule, the Loup Garou would open next month. He smirked and ran his finger over the club's name, printed in bold blue letters at the top of the paper. Olivia had rolled her eyes and her mate, Doug, actually laughed out loud when Killian told them the name he'd selected. That was the extent of their grumblings, and Killian had to admit he was more than a little surprised that the czars were so welcoming of his new business venture.

He glanced at his watch. Again. It was close to three thirty and the sign company still wasn't here. They were supposed to hang it today, and if they didn't get a move on, they'd run out of daylight. It was a bit early to put the sign up, but with luck it would help build buzz in the few weeks leading up to the club's big opening.

"Mr. Bane?" The portly contractor emerged from the back of the club, hitching up his pants while he approached and looking even more nervous than usual. Wiping sweat from his brow, he handed Killian a piece of paper. "I dunno how this got back there, but I found it in your office. Someone must have slipped it under the door. I run a tight ship, Mr. Bane. I know none of my guys put it there."

Killian took the paper and felt tension settle in his neck when he saw the familiar handwriting. Anger fired through him as he read the anonymous message.

We don't want your kind in this city.
   Take your pack of animals and go back to where you came from.
   Mark my words—if you open this club, it will be the last thing you ever do.
   Blood will run.

"I know it's none of my business, Mr. Bane, but you should really take this to the cops." Mike laughed nervously and looked over his shoulder at Ivan, who was sitting across the room and staring at the human. "Anyway, we finished up in your office. You wanna have a look before they start painting? My guys are gonna put in the rug tomorrow, and then that interior design lady can do her thing."

"Thanks, Mike. I appreciate your concern but this is just probably someone's idea of a sick joke." Killian caught Ivan's eye briefly. *Another fucking note, and this one threatens actual violence against us.* Ivan and David had been taking turns running perimeter sweeps, and in between they hung around like the dutiful security team his father insisted he have. Killian thought having them was overkill, but based on notes like this, maybe not. "I'll be back there in just a minute, but tell your crew to go ahead and start painting."

The older man grunted his understanding before waddling back to Killian's office. Ivan's emotionless gaze clocked the contractor as he passed by, and Killian didn't miss the nervous tension in the human's body language. Waving Ivan over, Killian chuckled and shook his head. *Why do you scare the poor old guy like that?*

What? Ivan hoisted himself from the chair and crossed to the prince. *All I did was look at him. It's not my fault most humans are afraid of their own shadows.*

"What do you think? Are these threats credible?" Ivan closed the cover on his iPad and positioned himself at the end of the worktable. "That's the third note in the past two weeks, Killian, and this time whoever it was actually got inside the building. My money is on the bloodsuckers."

"I haven't picked up any vamp scents." Killian looked past Ivan and spotted two construction workers coming out of his office. "Have you?"

"No, but who else would send notes like that?" Ivan's eyes glittered and his jaw muscle flickered. "Tonight I'll be doing background checks on every human on Mike's crew. I should have done it before, but to be honest, I didn't really think we had to worry. I was obviously wrong."

"You think it's the work of familiars, don't you?" Killian said what he knew Ivan suspected. Familiars were among the select number of humans who actually knew about the existence of vampires. "Damn it."

"Probably." Ivan snagged the paper, and the lines between his eyes deepened. "Shit's getting real, Killian. Are you sure you don't want to reconsider? We can still go home."

"No fucking way." Killian took the paper back, folded it, and stuck it in his pocket. "I'm not gonna get scared off by some prejudiced vampire who's too big of a pussy to put his name on these notes."

"Understood." Ivan watched Killian intently, obviously mulling over what he was going to say next. "Are we going back to The Coven tonight?"

"No." Killian shook his head and kept his gaze on the blueprints. He could feel Ivan's inspecting gaze on him, but Killian maintained a casual tone in his voice. "I don't plan on spending any more time there. After Ms. Pemberton gives me her professional feedback on the Loup Garou, my business with her will be finished."

"Oh really?" Ivan asked with more than a little skepticism.

"Yes, really." Killian stood to his full height and leveled a serious gaze at Ivan. It may not have been an outright challenge, but Ivan's meaning was clear. "Do you have a problem with that?"

"No, sir." Ivan's jaw clenched. "Definitely not."

"Good." Killian kept his tone even and controlled. "If the Loup Garou is going to open on time, I have to keep my eye on the ball. As it is, the damn sign company isn't here yet. I need to simplify my life to maintain my focus. I have to minimize the distractions."

Well, get ready for another one. David's voice cut into Killian's mind with a weary tone. *We have visitors.*

Killian's brow furrowed when he met Ivan's quizzical expression. Clearly David had spoken to both of them. Killian was about to ask David what the hell he was talking about when a high-pitched, familiar female voice echoed through the space. "Killian Bane, you get your fine-lookin' ass over here and give me a kiss."

Son of a bitch…Christina.

Christina Wolcott was the general's daughter, and if the king had anything to say about it, Killian's future mate and the mother of his children.

The look of shock on Killian's face must have been comical because Ivan had to turn away to keep from laughing out loud. Waving a quick hello to Christina, Ivan made a beeline for the back of the club. Killian couldn't blame the guy. He wanted to hightail it out of there too.

Squelching a groan, Killian put on the biggest smile he could muster before turning around to greet his surprise visitor. Dressed head to toe in one designer dud or another, she certainly looked like she belonged in Manhattan as opposed to the wilds of Alaska. Her long honey-blond hair was perfectly coiffed and framed her lovely oval-shaped face. Everything about Christina screamed money and high society, and he'd bet a million dollars she spent at least an hour a day primping. Flanked by her two best friends—and high-ranking she-wolves—Christina stood in the vestibule of the club with her manicured hands clasped in front of her and a come-hither look on her face.

David stood behind the women with an apologetic look. *I'm so sorry. She insisted on coming in.*

Not your fault. Killian glanced at David briefly. *I think it's a safe bet that I have my father to thank for this little surprise.*

"Well?" Christina asked in that breathy trying-too-hard-to-be-sexy voice. "Are you going to say hello to me or not?"

"Of course." Killian widened his smile and strode toward her before taking her hand in his and kissing it with all the formality he could muster. They'd known each other their entire lives. When they were teens, he'd even stolen a kiss or two, but he'd quickly discovered she wasn't for him. Christina was beautiful, educated, and from the right bloodline, and yet kissing her had elicited about as many sparks as making out with a melon.

He dropped her hand more quickly than he should have, and a look of disappointment flickered briefly over her face. Part of him felt guilty. She wasn't a bad person... She just wasn't for him. "It's always a pleasure to see such lovely ladies, but I'd be lying if I said I'm not surprised." He tilted his head and smiled at her companions. "Linda and Diana, good to see you."

The two women, dressed in outfits similar to Christina's, nodded wordlessly. They reminded Killian of drones. No personality and no voice of their own. All they did was buzz around Christina, their queen bee.

"Haven't you gotten formal?" Christina brushed her hair off her shoulder before swatting his arm playfully and walking past him, farther into the club. "I can see that all this time in the city has fine-tuned your social skills. Just as well; you'll need them once you're king. I can understand now why your father hasn't dragged you back to Alaska." Turning slowly, she surveyed the space as though she were a prospective buyer for the club or something, and every warning bell in Killian's gut fired. "You've been a busy boy."

"I've wanted to run my own club for a while. I stumbled across this space after my visit to the city last year and couldn't resist the opportunity." Killian held his hands behind his back and sidled over to Christina.

He cast a look at Linda and Diana that made it clear he wanted them to stay right where they were. "So, what brings you to the Big Apple? Business or pleasure?"

"A bit of both." Christina sighed. She smoothed the lapel of her cream-colored silk jacket and adjusted the gold chain of her shoulder bag. Her blue-eyed gaze clapped onto his and she inched closer, invading his personal space, which made him remarkably uncomfortable. "I've been wanting to take a little vacation. When I visited with your daddy last week, he told me about your adventures here in New York. Well, I have to tell you, I was green with envy. After all, the shopping in Manhattan is second only to Paris. For goodness' sake, the girls and I flew in this morning and we already did some damage at Saks. We haven't even checked into our hotel yet."

"I see." Killian kept his voice light, fighting the urge to growl his displeasure. He made a mental note to call his father and *thank him* for such a wonderful *surprise*. "Taking a vacation in the city and shopping definitely falls under the category of pleasure. You shop like a pro, and if there were an Olympic category for it, you'd have the gold medal." Yet another reason he felt zero attraction to Christina. "Where does business come into play?"

"That's where you come in, Killian." She giggled and trailed one pink fingernail down his shirtsleeve. "You and your club. Well, *our* club."

"Our club?" A sense of dread curled in his belly. "What are you talking about, Christina?"

"Yes." She flashed a red-lipped smile before traipsing away and looking around the space some more. "Our club."

Fury swirled in Killian's chest when he realized what she meant.

"You're the other investor," he said in a barely audible tone.

"I am. Well, my daddy is." Christina let out a sigh. Smiling, she turned around on spindle-like stiletto heels and captured his now-furious expression. Either unaware of or unconcerned by his reaction, she closed the distance between them, her smile deepening. "That makes you and me partners." She lowered her voice while her eyes drifted over him. "In business if not in the bedroom…at least not yet."

Too furious to say a word, Killian stared at Christina through the glowing amber eyes of his wolf. He didn't give a holy hopping shit if one of the construction workers emerged from the back and saw it. Christina's manipulations didn't shock Killian, but his father's involvement in this trickery was unforgivable.

"I'll buy you out," he growled. Killian inched his large frame closer so that he towered over her petite form. "This is my place, and the investor was supposed to be a silent partner. That was the deal."

"Things change, Killian." Christina shrugged. "Speaking of which, I think we should change the name. The Loup Garou seems a tad obvious, don't you think?"

"I think it's my club and I'll decide what to name it." Killian kept his voice quiet but firm. "You may be an investor, Christina, but I still hold the controlling interest. This is my place."

"That may be true, Killian," she sang in a deceptively sweet voice. "But if my daddy withdraws his funding, you won't have a club to name. Will you? From what I hear, you put every penny you had into this little invest-ment." Before he could tell her to stick it, she yelped and glanced at the gold Rolex on her wrist. "Would you look at the time? I have to be going."

Killian gritted his teeth when she kissed him on the cheek, and she brushed past him to the door where Linda and Diana were chatting with David. Killian's mind raced. How the hell was he going to get out of this mess? Sucking in a deep breath, he shifted his eyes back to their human state, but he kept them fixed on the meddlesome she-wolf.

"We're staying at the Ritz, Killian." Christina stuck her nose in the air and gave him a wicked grin. "Why don't you and the boys come pick us up around nine?"

"For what?" His body hummed with anger and frus-tration, and he barely got the words out.

"Your daddy tells me you've been spending quite a bit of time at that *place*—The Coven? I suppose it's wise to have a solid understanding of the *competition*." Her lip curled with disgust, making her feelings about vampires quite clear. "I believe some research would do me good. Because unlike what your father told you, I'm not going to be a silent partner. Pick us up at nine and don't be late."

Without another word, she flounced outside. The door slammed loudly behind her.

"Motherfucker," Killian said, slamming his fist onto the table.

"Is she for real?" David asked, moving cautiously toward the prince.

"I think so." Killian ran his hands over his face and let out a shout of frustration. Hands on his hips, he looked at David and Ivan, who'd emerged from the back office. "I can't believe my father did this to me."

"I can." Ivan studied him, his expression serious.

"Me too," David said evenly. "The king just gave you a ball and chain named Christina. He probably figures one of two things will happen."

"Like what?" Killian shouted. "What could he possibly have been thinking?"

"Option one," David began. "You get fed up with her meddling, pack it in, and head back to Alaska. He's got a better chance of getting you mated if you're back there. If it isn't to Christina, you'll find another she-wolf."

"Not happening." Killian shook his head and folded his arms over his broad chest. "What's your other theory?"

"Option two?" David stuck his hands in his pockets and shot Ivan a knowing look. "By forcing you and Christina to spend all this time together, maybe he thinks that the two of you will hook up. Then he gets the future queen he always wanted."

"Also not happening." Killian rolled his eyes. "I'm not remotely attracted to her. And even if I was, this little stunt she pulled would have snuffed it out. Trickery and deceptive behavior are not a turn-on."

"Would it be so bad?" Ivan asked with a shrug. "Christina's hot."

"Then feel free to mate with her," Killian said flatly. "You have my blessing, Ivan."

"Me? That's crazy." Ivan shrugged awkwardly and looked away, making Killian immediately regret his remark. "I'll go patrol outside. Let me know when you're ready to leave, and I'll pull the car around."

Killian let out a frustrated sigh as Ivan headed to the door and out of the club. He seemed to be fucking things up at every turn.

"Yeah, well, you know she's not my type." David let out a short laugh. Killian gave him a wry smile and nodded. "What's your next move?"

"I'm going to play along." Killian glanced to the doors of the club and a smile curled his lips. "Believe me, David. By the time I'm done with Christina, she'll want nothing to do with the club, this city, and—with any luck—me."

"What's the game plan?" David asked with a tone that betrayed his unease with the situation. "If I'm going to be able to do my job, it would be helpful if I knew what you're up to."

"For starters, we're going to do what the lady wants and take her to The Coven."

"Holy shit." David looked at Killian like he'd lost his mind—and maybe he had. "Are you serious? She hates vampires."

"Absolutely. Fighting with Christina will get me nowhere. For now, my best bet is to keep her happy, at least until I can figure out what will make her give up and go back to Alaska." Killian's lips curved as his mind drifted to Sadie. "If Christina wants to do some research and get to know the competition, I'm more than happy to oblige." He slapped David on the shoulder and gave his friend a reassuring smile. "In the meantime, I'm going to have a look at my office, and then I'm gonna call the sign company and find out where the hell our sign is."

Fishing his phone out of his pocket, Killian walked toward the back of the club as David's concerned voice drifted into his mind. *Why do I think the competition you're referring to has nothing to do with the club?*

The sun was setting as Sadie stared at her cell phone and a knot of nerves rumbled in her gut. After what happened at the pool last night, there was no way on earth she was going with him to his club. Being alone with Killian in any way was a really bad idea. Fingers shaking, she punched in a text message and hit Send.

> I can't make it tonight. Something suddenly came up. Sorry. Maybe another time.

Relief wafted over her once the message was on its way, and she stuffed the phone in the pocket of her jacket. About two seconds later, the damn thing buzzed with Killian's response.

> Isn't that the same excuse Marcia used in an old *Brady Bunch* episode to blow off her date so she could go out with another guy? Next thing u know, you'll say u have a date with George Glass, Jan's imaginary boyfriend.

Sadie laughed out loud as she texted him back.

> LOL. Nope. No other werewolf clubs to inspect.

Nibbling her lower lip, she rubbed the smooth surface of the screen and waited for his response. After what felt like forever, his text buzzed through.

Promise you'll come tomorrow.

His handsome face drifted through her mind as she texted back.

Okay. C u tomorrow.

What the hell was she doing?

—◇◇◇—

Normally, when The Coven was this crowded with humans, dancing and spending money like it was going out of style, Sadie would be riding high. Tonight, however, she felt anything other than normal. Part of it was probably because she hadn't slept all day. She'd been too preoccupied with thoughts of Killian Bane.

She could have slept. God knows she was exhausted, but she didn't. Insomnia wasn't keeping her awake—it was fear. Sadie was terrified that she'd dream.

Given everything that happened so far with Killian, she knew that if she slept and dreamed of Killian, it would seal her fate as his bloodmate.

That possibility meant no sleep for Sadie.

She stayed awake all day, keeping herself busy going through the books for the club and placing more booze orders with her distributors. Sleep deprivation aside, she'd also been unable to shake the distinctly woodsy scent of Killian Bane and it flirted along her senses all day. Just when she thought it was gone, the warm enticing aroma would curl around her like an invisible mist, making her weak at the knees. Sadie had hoped that focusing on work and surrounding herself with the noise of the club would scrub her brain clean.

No such luck.

In fact, she could swear his scent was getting stronger as the night wore on. The only saving grace was that, so far, Killian and his crew hadn't shown up. With any luck, they wouldn't show at all. Walking toward the DJ platform, Sadie flicked a glance at the empty red-leather VIP booth and a pang of longing struck her. God help her. In spite of the insanity of it, she still wanted to see him.

I'm such an idiot.

Why? Trixie's voice touched her mind suddenly. *What did you do now? Forget to smile and wave to a customer?*

Oh, stick it. Sadie thought back with a laugh when the familiar sound of Trixie's voice filled her head. After the cleaning crew settled earlier today, Sadie had finally found the courage to try and telepath to Trixie. She'd never been so happy to hear from her friend in all her life. When Trixie's sleepy voice came in loud and clear, Sadie almost wept with relief. She could still telepath with her siblings, which meant there was no bloodmate bond with Killian. The telepathy with him had been a fluke, a side effect from tasting his blood. *I'm just missing the DJ position, that's all.*

Are you sure you're not missing a certain were-wolf hottie and his buddies? That VIP booth does look awfully empty.

Not likely. Sadie shot Trixie a look over her shoulder as she climbed the steps to the DJ platform. She hadn't told Trixie or the others about her little run-in with Killian last night, and if she had her way, she never would. That moment of weakness would stay a secret until the end of time. *How are we doing at the bar? Do we need to pull anything from the stockroom?*

We could use some more vodka, a bottle of Jack, and maybe another case of Michelob Ultra. Trixie flipped a bottle and caught it before pouring three shots. *At the rate we're going, you're gonna need to double next week's order.*

You got it. I'll make a run down to the storage room for you in a few minutes.

Are you ever gonna hire a new busboy? Even a human one would be helpful, because the owner of the club shouldn't have to make product runs.

I know. Trixie was right. They did need to hire more help, and first thing tomorrow, Sadie was going to remedy that particular problem. *You're right...I'll place an ad tomorrow.*

"What's up?" Sadie shouted to Justine over the bone-rattling music. The girl loved tunes that were heavy on bass, and the current choice was reverberating through her chest.

"Hello there, gov." Justine linked the headphones around her tattooed neck and smoothed the long waves of her blue-and-yellow-streaked hair. She was wearing only a white tank top, no bra, and black leather pants, which put her lean, wiry frame on full display. Her green eyes, lined with dark, heavy makeup, stared back at Sadie with unmistakable mischief. "I have a favor to ask you."

"I knew it." Sadie laughed and crossed her arms over her chest. "You want a raise already."

"Nah." Justine leaned closer and smirked. "Was hopin' I could have Sunday night off."

"Nope." Sadie pressed her lips together and shook her head firmly. "I'm sorry, but you can't take it off." Justine's face fell and before she could start begging, Sadie smiled and patted her on her bare shoulder. "You can't take the night off because we're closed on Sundays. Remember?"

"Balls!" Justine smacked her forehead and laughed loudly. "I can't bloody believe I forgot that." She shook her head and flicked a sheepish glance in Sadie's direction. "Sorry."

"What? Do you have a hot date?" Sadie peered out over the crowd and elbowed her DJ playfully. "You do have the best view of the crowd from here, and I was always able to spot the best-lookin' humans. Not that I ever fed in the club," she added quickly. "Because that's a big no-no."

"No worries." Justine held up both hands in surrender. "My handsome hottie is not out on the dance floor. He's kind of shy and sweet. Dancin' in a club ain't his style, gov. Funny thing is, you'd never guess it by lookin' at him. He's a huge bloke."

"A big brute, is he?" Sadie asked with genuine curiosity. Justine was new to their little group and Sadie knew it was in her best interest to get to know her. "Tough guy?"

"Oh yeah." Justine waggled her pierced eyebrow as she put her headphones back on. She gave Sadie a wink. "You might even say he's an animal."

"Right." Justine's remark was not lost on Sadie, and based on the look that werewolf, David, had given

Justine last night, Sadie knew to which *animal* the DJ was referring. She'd also bet a million bucks that's who Justine had been texting with last night. Sadie leaned over, pulled her headphones off her ear, and whispered, "Just don't forget the rules, Justine. You can play with the animals but don't feed on them."

Justine nodded her understanding and gave Sadie a thumbs-up before grabbing the microphone. Sadie descended the stairs and wove her way through the crowd as Justine riled the humans up into a frenzied mob. Glancing over her shoulder, Sadie watched her colorful and talented DJ. Bathed in the flickering lights of the club, she looked like a wild woman, but a glimmer of concern covered her face. Sadie winked, hoping to put her at ease. Who she hooked up with was Justine's own business. Shit. Sadie certainly wasn't in any position to pass judgment on anyone.

Her primary concern was the club, and the last complication The Coven needed was their hot, new DJ bursting into flames from too much werewolf blood or—God forbid—getting so hopped up that she took too much and killed the wolf before dying herself. That would be a clusterfuck of epic proportions.

A vampire having sex with a werewolf was ill-advised.

Bloodlust and physical lust were too tightly linked for most vampires. Although once Sadie learned how to block the blood memories, it also helped dampen the sexual hunger that often went along with them.

At least until last night.

God damn that Killian Bane and his sexy naked body for messing with her head and her routines! All she'd wanted was a relaxing swim, and instead he had her head swimming.

Sadie must have had a scowl on her face, because Trixie's worried voice touched her mind and interrupted her private flogging. *What the hell happened with Justine?* Trixie waved Sadie over to the end of the bar. *You look like you're ready to drain somebody dry.*

I'm fine. Sadie shook her head and pointed to the back hallway. *I'm going to go downstairs and get the booze you need.*

Running her hands through her long hair, Sadie headed for the storage room. She didn't mind making the run, actually. It was nice to take a momentary break from the sounds and scents within the club, especially the thrumming heartbeats of the humans. Even after two centuries, she experienced moments of weakness and the pull of bloodlust could be overwhelming. She suspected it was tugging at her tonight because of her lack of sleep. Wonderful.

Boss. Damien, the club's bouncer and one of Sadie's newest siblings, reached out to her. As always, he was manning the doors of the club and handling the crowd on the street. *We have a pack of visitors again tonight, and this time they brought a few more of their friends.*

Sadie was about to respond and ask how many there were, and that's when it hit her. The thick, pungent scent of wood burning on a crisp winter night curled around her like smoke…*Killian.* Sadie's fangs hummed and erupted as a pang of desire shot through her, warming her normally cool body. Sadie stopped dead in her tracks, barely feeling the humans who bumped into her while jostling past her to the dance floor. Eyes closed, she willed her fangs away and wrestled for control amid the sudden tsunami of carnal need.

Sadie, the wolves are—

I know. Sadie snapped. With her back still toward the door of the club, she squared her shoulders and turned around slowly. *I'm coming.*

Yeah, but he brought—

Trixie, she interrupted with more than a little annoyance, *I said—*

—A date. Trixie sounded as shocked as Sadie felt. *Or do you call the females of their kind bitches?*

Trixie, what are you—every thought was driven from Sadie's mind when she spun around and spotted them—*talking about*?

A beautiful, elegant blond was draped all over Killian like a second skin, and there was no mistaking that this woman, whoever she was, was a wolf. David and Ivan were present, and each of them had a woman on their arms as well. The other two were also she-wolves, and although they were well dressed, they didn't look quite as good as the blond. Figures, Sadie thought with a huff. It reminded her of brides who chose hideous bridesmaid dresses so their friends were guaranteed to look worse than them on the big day.

Sadie's eyes narrowed and locked onto Killian's smug, satisfied-looking face.

He waved his free arm—the one that didn't have the blond clinging to it. That son of a bitch actually had the audacity to wave at her, like it was no big deal that he had showed up at her club with a date. Anger and an odd feeling of possessiveness filled Sadie as she held his stare and stalked over to the bar.

Shaking off the uncomfortable emotions, Sadie chided herself. They had only shared one stupid kiss. He was free to bang cocktail waitresses or heiresses two at a time if he wanted to. Besides, they weren't going to kiss again anyway. Nope. Not gonna happen. Tearing her gaze away from the wolves, she straightened her back and snagged a stack of drink menus off the bar.

"She looks expensive," Trixie said while wiping a glass dry. Jutting her chin toward the group, she shook her head with disapproval. "A chick like that will bleed a guy dry. I've seen broads like that a thousand times in this city."

"I know who that is," Maya whispered loudly, her big blue eyes pinned to the group of wolves at the door. She scurried to the very end of the bar and put herself between Sadie and Trixie. "Given my *condition*, Shane thought it would be smart to study some of the more prominent members of their people. Just in case, you know?" She lowered her voice further, worried that even with all the noise and music the wolves would hear. "That's Christina Wolcott. She's General Wolcott's daughter and, by all accounts, the woman that Killian is supposed to mate with. Girls, you are looking at the next werewolf king and queen."

"Good for him." Sadie gripped the laminated cover of the drink menu and fought the urge to run. "They make a lovely couple."

"She looks like she wrinkles easily," Trixie said with a snort of laughter. "The face and the clothes."

"The Wolcott family is one of the wealthiest families among their people," Maya murmured. "Some people say they're even richer than the royals."

"I'm sure they're perfect for each other. Get the Cristal ready, Maya." Doing her best to seem uninterested in Killian's date, Sadie smiled broadly. "Those ladies look thirsty."

She headed over to greet their guests, knowing that she should have been happy to hear that Killian had a mate. Sadie *should* have been completely thrilled for them, ready to run out and buy the lovely couple a wedding gift or some shit like that. After all, wasn't she the one terrified by the thought of being Killian's bloodmate? Hadn't the mere notion of being mated to a werewolf filled her with pure unadulterated fear? Sure. She should be feeling one hundred and fifty percent relieved.

Then why wasn't she?

Chapter 7

THE SCENT OF THE WOLVES SWAMPED SADIE'S SENSES as she got closer, making her almost dizzy. Even amid the pungent onslaught, she detected Killian's distinct aroma above all the rest. It was richer and almost sweeter than the others, tickling her from the inside out. A pang of desire shot through to Sadie's core, and it took inhuman willpower to keep her fangs at bay.

"Ms. Pemberton." Killian bowed his head and Sadie almost laughed out loud at his professional airs. His glittering eyes latched on to hers and the hint of a smile played at his lips. "We were hoping to occupy the VIP booth again this evening."

"Good evening, Mr. Bane," Sadie said in the most formal tone possible. *Two can play at this game*, she thought to herself. Killian's expression faltered and Sadie had to keep from laughing out loud. Turning her attention to his date, she smiled broadly. What? Did the guy think she'd burst into tears because he showed up with another woman? Guess again, Casanova. "Please follow me."

"It's about time." The Wolcott woman stuck her nose in the air and plastered her admittedly hot body up against Killian. Her busty, curvy form was covered in a barely there pink dress, and a black wrap draped dramatically over her slim shoulders. The woman might be a werewolf and sprout fur under the moon, but even Sadie had to admit that Christina Wolcott was sexy, beautiful, and elegant. No wonder Killian wanted her for a mate.

Christina was everything Sadie wasn't. Most importantly, a werewolf.

"My apologies, Ms. Wolcott." Sadie forced a small smile and didn't miss the look of surprise from not only Christina but Killian as well. "I can assure you we want all of our clients to be well served here at The Coven. If you'll follow me, the VIP booth is right this way."

Not giving any of them time to respond, Sadie turned on her heels and went directly to the VIP booth. Pulling the red velvet rope aside, she waited as patiently as possible for the pack to settle into the massive curved booth. Killian was the last to take his seat.

"Mr. Bane and his friends are regulars here at The Coven, and I'm well aware that they enjoy partaking of bottles of Cristal." Sadie placed drink menus in front of each of the women. She took turns looking each of them in the eye while intentionally avoiding Killian, even though she could feel his gaze on her. "However, I haven't met you ladies before, and I wouldn't want to assume that you'd order the same drinks as your *dates*."

"Well, well." Christina placed her wrap and clutch on the seat next to her while keeping her blue eyes on Sadie. "You seem to know quite a bit about us. How is it that you know my name?" She nuzzled closer to Killian who, to Sadie's delight, actually looked uncomfortable. "Did my Killian tell you about me?"

"No, he's never mentioned you," Sadie said flatly. Christina's smile fell and she sat up straighter in the booth. The two other girls smirked until the woman shot them a look of warning, quickly squelching their reactions. "I'm Sadie Pemberton, and since this is my club, I make it my business to know my customers." Sadie stood taller and arched one dark eyebrow at the group. "Especially my supernatural customers. I find that being prepared and knowledgeable is the best way to avoid *complications*."

"I'll take that under advisement," Christina responded in a voice edged with anger. She snatched up a menu and flipped through it quickly before letting out an exasperated sigh. "Where's the food menu?"

"We don't serve food at The Coven." Sadie widened her grin and dropped her voice low, knowing the wolves would still be able to hear her. "Only drinks."

"That figures. What else would you expect from a bunch of vampires?" Christina huffed and brushed her long, blond hair off her shoulder. "I don't know why you consider this place any type of competition, Killian. We'll be serving food at *our place* and giving our customers much more variety."

"I'm sorry?" Sadie cocked her head and folded her arms over her breasts. Christina must have meant the werewolf club, not that she actually owned it. "Did you say 'our place'?"

"Yes." Christina linked her arm through Killian's and looked at him lovingly, but he kept his serious gaze on Sadie. "When I heard Killian was opening a nightclub and restaurant here in Manhattan…well, I just had to be a part of it." She flicked that stony blue stare at Sadie. "I don't let profitable opportunities pass me by."

"I'll just bet you don't." Sadie locked eyes with Killian for a split second, and an ache bloomed deep in her chest. She hated herself for feeling jealous and getting worked up over a man who couldn't possibly be hers. Glancing back at the bar, she touched Trixie's mind sharply. *Get that Cristal over here now and take their order. I need some air.* "Trixie will be over in a moment to take the drink order from the ladies. If you'll excuse me, I have business to attend to."

Not waiting for any kind of response, Sadie moved swiftly through the crowd, desperate to get away from the wolves. Who was she kidding? She needed to escape Killian, or more to the point, the feelings that being around him evoked. She burst through the edge of the sweaty crowd, barely seeing where she was going as she ran down the hall to the door that led to the storage facility.

Tearing the door open, Sadie trotted down four steps to the small landing before opening another door on the left. She stepped into the cool space and let out a sound of relief when the door shut silently behind her. Surrounded by bottles and boxes, she leaned against the glass door of the temperature-controlled wine case. The smooth surface felt wonderful and helped her fight her way through the intoxicating effect of Killian's scent.

Eyes closed, she tore off her jacket and tossed it onto the floor before undoing the top two buttons of her ruffled white shirt. It had felt as though it was choking her. Even the black leggings she wore and the tall black leather boots seemed tighter than they ever had before. The world was closing in on her. That's how Sadie felt. Like she was being smothered. Smothered by her body's reaction to Killian Bane, and if she didn't get control of it soon, someone or something was going to break. And it would probably be her.

"Hold it together," she whispered.

Focusing on finding her center of gravity, Sadie kept her eyes shut and tried to fixate on the feel of the glass. If only she could get Killian's warm, cozy, inviting scent out of her head! She couldn't. No matter how much she fought it, his distinct male scent had slipped into her body and practically imprinted there.

Sadie froze when a deep, familiar voice interrupted her private moment.

"That's funny; I was just telling myself the same thing."

Sadie's fangs erupted and her eyes snapped open as she shoved herself away from the glass. In a battle-ready stance, she found herself face-to-face with Killian Bane. Silently berating herself for being so sloppy and not picking up on his arrival, Sadie curled her lip back, flashing him her fangs. How the hell did he sneak up on her like that?

"The door was open," he said quietly, pushing the door shut tightly behind him. His sturdy six-foot-tall frame loomed large in front of her, blocking her exit. His dark, wavy hair was swept off his face and the shadow of a beard, one that seemed ever present, covered his square jaw. The jeans, button-down white shirt, and coffee-colored blazer covered his body but did little to hide his well-built form. The one feature she was drawn to the most, though, was that set of intense, almost caramel-colored eyes. "I didn't mean to startle you."

"What are you doing down here?" Sadie retracted her fangs and snagged her jacket off the floor before pulling it back on. "This area is for employees only. It's not for customers, and it certainly isn't for my competitors. Besides, I'm sure your date is getting lonely."

"She's not my date." The muscle in Killian's jaw flickered and he took a step closer before stopping. Even though Sadie knew she should get the hell out of there, she didn't. Holding her ground, she met his apologetic gaze. "Christina is—"

"Your partner." Sadie folded her arms over her chest, feeling the need to steel her resolve any way possible. "And your future wife. Congratulations. She's quite a bitch."

"Sadie," he said softly. "Christina's father is an investor. If she chooses to call herself my business partner, fine. She is not, however, my future wife." Killian continued to move a step nearer, and as he closed the distance between them, Sadie had the distinct impression of being stalked. "My father and mother can toss around that idea all they'd like, but Christina is not the woman I want for my mate." His brow furrowed. "I'm now more certain of that than ever."

"Obviously nobody gave her that memo." Sadie dropped her arms to her sides as Killian's towering frame invaded her personal space. Heat flowed off his body and washed over her in erotic pulses that matched the strumming beat of his heart. It was tempting and teasing her, practically screaming for her to touch him. Clearing her throat, she tilted her head back so she could continue looking him in the eye. Bumping into a stack of boxes, she took a second to realize that she'd backed up as he approached. "The way she drapes herself all over you, I get the impression she has every intention of being your *partner* in every sense of the word."

The muffled music from the club pulsed from above but neither of them spoke. The only sound in the room was the constant, solid pounding of Killian's heart. Sadie's gaze flicked briefly to the bulging vein in Killian's neck, and she suppressed a groan when a surge of desire whirled in her gut. Squeezing her eyes shut, she pressed her lips together in a tight line, willing her fangs to remain sheathed.

"I don't want Christina," Killian murmured. His warm breath puffed enticingly along her forehead and his scent drifted in the air, heightening her desire. "It's not fair to her though, is it? After getting one taste of you last night, no one else stands a chance."

"Really? Coming here with a date is a funny way of showing it."

Sadie forced herself to look him in the face, and the instant she did, she knew it was a colossal mistake. His eyes looked like pools of liquid gold, and she could swear he saw straight through to her very soul. A growl rumbled in his chest and Sadie gasped. His eyes flickered and shifted into the glowing amber eyes of his wolf. The sudden and instinctive change was a glaring reminder of who he was…who they both were.

In a remarkably steady voice, Sadie whispered, "Last night should never have happened."

"The only thing about last night that shouldn't have happened was the way it ended," Killian rasped.

Sadie stilled when his large hand cradled her cheek. Despite her best efforts to resist him, her body quivered uncontrollably as he surrounded her in every way a person could be surrounded. When the heat of his palm seared against her skin, a needy moan escaped her lips.

She sagged against the stack of boxes. Desire curled inside her like smoke, and regardless of the litany of warnings that ran through her head, Sadie's hands found their way to the front of Killian's shirt. She grasped the fabric, still warm from the heat of his body, and pulled him closer. The evidence of his desire pressed against her hip, and images of him in all his naked glory came roaring back into her mind. Sweet Jesus, the man had a body that looked like it had been hand carved by the gods themselves.

"Is that so?" Sadie pulled his shirt loose from his jeans and slipped her fingers underneath before trailing them along the hard planes of his stomach. Arching one eyebrow, she held his heavy-lidded gaze and unsheathed her fangs. "How do you suppose it should have ended?"

"The same way it should end every night from now on," he growled. Killian slid both hands into her long hair. Sadie shivered when his fingertips grazed her scalp. He pressed his hips against her before slipping his thigh between her legs. Sadie gasped with pleasure as he put pressure on just the right spot, and when a moan escaped her parted lips, a cocky grin emerged on his. Killian tightened his grip on her hair and leaned in so his mouth was just a breath away. "Every single night should end with me buried deep inside you."

In a blur of motion, he captured her lips with his and dove deep. The man tasted like cinnamon and sex all rolled into one, and in that moment Sadie knew she could become addicted. The heat of his body seeped through the layers of their clothing and his scent surrounded her, consuming her with fire. Needing to get closer, Sadie slid her hands up his bare back beneath his shirt. She sighed into his mouth when the thick layer of muscle on his back moved beneath her fingers. Licking and suckling his lips, she clung to him and rocked her hips, seeking satisfaction. With every pass, wicked pleasure ricocheted through her body, making her sex pulse with unfulfilled need.

Killian grabbed a fistful of her hair and tilted her head back before breaking the kiss and trailing his tongue down her throat. With her arms wrapped around his waist, Sadie leaned back to give him better access to the hypersensitive skin along her neck. Her fangs bared, she murmured tiny sounds of pleasure as Killian reached down and grabbed her ass with both hands. He lifted his head and that burning gaze latched on to hers as he hoisted her up and carried her over to another stack of boxes before setting her down.

"We should go back upstairs." She was unbuckling his belt even as the words escaped her lips, and he undid all of the buttons on her shirt and pushed it open. Sadie wrapped her legs around him and tugged him closer, just before sliding down the zipper of his fly.

"No fucking way." The words still hanging in the air, his large hands cupped her breasts, the heat from his flesh seeping easily through the black lacy fabric of her bra. "I'm not going anywhere but here," he growled.

Sadie cried out when the hot wet cavern of Killian's mouth covered her nipple. Tiny shocks ripped through her as he suckled. With one hand cupping her breast and the other arm clamped around her waist, he had her anchored to him and his touch. She'd been in sexual situations with humans and vampires countless times before, and yet she'd never felt the kind of masculine, animal strength she experienced with Killian. It was exotic, intense, carnal, and almost feral to be wrapped in his ironclad embrace.

Writhing against him, desperate to get closer, she shoved his jeans down his hips. Killian shuddered against her when her fingers curled around his steely length and she grinned. Killian's grip on her tightened and he flicked her nipple with his tongue, continuing his merciless assault. His hips pumped in slow strokes as Sadie ran her hand up and down the rigid stalk of flesh, massaging him eagerly with every pass. His body temperature skyrocketed and sweat slicked his skin, the hammering sound of his pulse calling to her deepest, most primal instincts.

Just as the bloodlust seemed like it would overcome her, Killian reached down and covered her sex with his hand. Sadie cried out when his thumb found her clit. It didn't matter that there were two layers of fabric between them; Killian pushed all the right buttons, working her into a frenzy with remarkable speed. Sadie tossed her head back and shouted his name as he rubbed her clit in sure, swift strokes. One of her hands pumping his cock, the other tangled in his wavy hair as Sadie held his head to her breast while he nipped, suckled, and massaged her to the brink of orgasm.

The climax coiled deep in her belly, and as Killian pumped into her hand, she knew he was close to the edge too. With the searing, enticing heat of his body pressed against her and with every nerve ending tingling to life, Sadie tightened her grip on him and tilted his head.

"Killian," she said in a ragged whisper. "Let me taste you."

With the peak of climax nearing, Killian lifted his head and captured her stare while rubbing her clit in tiny torturous circles. One word whispered into her mind.

Yes.

Had she heard it or was it wishful thinking? It didn't matter, because any resolve Sadie might have had went right out the window. She wasn't thinking about the ramifications of what it could mean. Hell, she wasn't thinking at all. At that instant Sadie had been reduced to her basest animal instincts, and all she could do was feel.

Her bright, sweet orgasm erupted. At the same time, Killian pumped his hips and his massive body shuddered in her arms as he came. Breathing heavily and with a growl rumbling in his chest, Killian tilted his head to the side, his unshaven cheek scraping along the tender flesh of her breast. With a curse, Sadie dipped her head and sank her fangs into his neck, sending another orgasm firing through Killian's body.

She expected her own pleasure to be heightened as well, but not like this. When the warm rich liquid touched her tongue, Sadie was a goner and her world exploded.

The second climax ripped through her with brutal force, and lights erupted behind her eyes. Sadie clung to him, her body humming with a bone-rattling surge of power from Killian's potent, life-giving blood. Her fingers tangled in his hair and she cradled him against her, reveling in the feel of his bulging, muscular form pressed against hers. Vibrating with unbridled energy and with a flash of unusually potent warmth coursing through her veins, Sadie knew she should stop. But as the images from his blood memories filled her head, stopping was no longer an option.

The city lights glittering like diamonds beneath a moonlit sky.

The hateful gaze of his brother, Horace, as he charged Killian in a battle to the death.

Grief. Anger. Pain. Betrayal. Loneliness.

His heartbeat, strong and formidable, reverberated through both of them, far more than it ever had when she was feeding from a human. Sadie found herself completely immersed in Killian's emotions.

If the watch Xavier gave her hadn't started beeping like a damn fire alarm, Sadie might not have stopped.

Aware that her body temperature was rising with Killian still wrapped around her, she knew she had to stop. Sadie waited for two more beats of his heart, allowing herself to float in the comforting blanket of his embrace before finally lifting her head. She sealed the wound, leaving no trace of their encounter, but his heartbeat still thrummed strongly through her body.

Eyes closed, her bones liquid, she slumped back against some boxes. She barely registered movement as Killian swiftly put himself back in his clothes. His heartbeat still thundered around her and through her, and when she finally opened her eyes, Killian stood between her legs staring at her with an awed expression. Damn it all to hell. He probably regretted what had just happened and was probably going to hightail it out of there—and she wouldn't blame him.

Killian didn't leave. Instead, he grabbed a dish towel from a nearby shelf and tenderly wiped Sadie's hands, removing all evidence of their passionate encounter. The sweet, thoughtful gesture was almost more than Sadie could take. If she looked him in the face, she might dissolve into tears like a stupid little girl.

Eyes closed, she stilled when Killian grasped her hips before running his thumb along the dip of her waist. An involuntary shiver shimmied up her spine from even that small brush of his flesh against hers. Finding her courage, Sadie finally flicked her eyes open and was met with Killian's warm gaze. The reality of the situation settled over her with a sudden wave of embarrassment and shame as she stared into his ruggedly handsome face.

Holy crap. She could not believe what she just did—what *they* just did.

"I'm sorry," she said quickly. Sadie closed her eyes and hurriedly put her bra back in place before buttoning her blouse. Killian's heartbeat pounded like a fucking drum and still rattled through her. "Damn it all. I know better than to do something like this. I am too freaking old to be playing with fire like some kind of youngling vampire."

"Don't you feel that?" he asked softly.

"What? Mortified?" Sadie rolled her eyes and puffed a long strand of hair out of her face before pushing him aside and hopping off the crates. "I'd say I'm in touch with that emotion, *and* your damn heartbeat is still ricocheting around me like a pinball machine." Sadie let out a sound of frustration and snagged her jacket off the floor. Tugging it on, she spun around to face him. "I know it's been a couple of centuries, but I don't remember werewolf blood making me feel like this."

"Sadie." Killian whispered her name almost

reverently and cradled her hands in his before placing them over her own chest. "That's not my heartbeat."

"What are—" Sadie's words stuck in her throat, and her wide eyes searched his as she felt the steady and unmistakable thump of a heartbeat. Slow and clear. The pulse she'd been hearing and feeling wasn't Killian's... *It was hers.* "What the fuck is going on?" Her voice shaking with fear and confusion, she tugged her hands from Killian's and took a step away. She shook her head and squeezed her eyes shut in a feeble attempt to regain her focus. But he was right. Deep in her chest pounded the unmistakable beat of her long-dormant heart. Pointing at him accusingly, she flicked her eyes open and shouted, "Werewolf blood doesn't do this."

No. Killian's mouth set in a tight line and he let out a slow breath. *I don't imagine any other wolf would have this effect on you.* Killian reached out to Sadie with his right hand, and she immediately stepped back. A look of disappointment flickered across his face, but it was swiftly replaced by anger, and his hand dropped to his side. *Then again, you can't telepath with other wolves either, can you?*

Holy shit. It had happened again. Hearing him in her mind wasn't just wishful thinking or her subconscious. It was Killian, and he'd deliberately telepathed to her. If Sadie was still breathing, she would have hyperventilated.

"No. I don't know what you're talking about." Sadie shook her head furiously and pressed her hand over her chest again. She knew the denial sounded as hollow to him as it did to her. Her heartbeat was slowing, to her relief, but that did nothing to stop her from shaking like a leaf. The long-forgotten sensation had her spinning, and if she didn't get out of there and away from him, she was going to pass out. "I have to go."

"You can't run away from me or from what's happening between us." Killian moved quickly and stood in front of the door, blocking her exit. "Ignoring it won't make it go away."

"What *it* would you be talking about?" Sadie threw her arms in the air.

"I'm not sure, but I know enough to know that tonight isn't the end." His lips tilted. "Not by a long shot."

"Well, I *am* sure about what happened and *it is* the end. We hooked up, Killian. We got each other off and I drank your blood. That's it. End of story. A very fucked-up story but still—that's all that happened." Her voice was edged with a hint of hysteria, and there was a good chance one or more of the supernaturals in the club might hear, but she didn't care. The entire time she ranted, Killian stared at her with an infuriatingly calm expression that made her want to smack the crap out of him.

"It was just sex, Killian. Hell, not even full-on sex. We fooled around and your blood made me a little nuts, that's all. It's probably because you're a royal or something." She buttoned her jacket and smoothed her hair off her face in an effort to regain some kind of composure. "Now, get out of my way so I can go back to work and you can go back to your date."

Killian stepped away, and then just before Sadie tugged the door open, he pressed his palm against it and held it shut.

"You like fighting with me, don't you?" Killian's

gravelly voice skittered over her and the sound tickled her from the inside out. Even though he wasn't touching her, she could sense that every inch of his body was rigid, taut, and ready to pounce. "I have to admit, that turns me on. And I do love a challenge."

Sadie was about to tell him to piss off when Trixie's frantic voice and pounding on the door interrupted them.

"Sadie?" Trixie shouted from the hallway. "Are you in there? What the fuck is going on? I've been calling you for, like, ten minutes and Killian's date is freaking out. She wants to know where he is."

The cold finger of fear trickled up Sadie's back when the weight of Trixie's words settled over her. "Oh shit," Sadie whispered.

"You closed your mind to her?" Killian tugged a strand of her hair, and the teasing tone of his voice made her want to kick him in the shin. "I'm flattered."

"Stop that." Sadie brushed his hand away and pointed at him. The man looked devastatingly handsome. Leaning against the wall next to the door, he seemed surprisingly unfazed by getting caught in the storage room like a couple of high school kids. Between the lop-sided wolfish grin and the twinkle in his eye, Sadie had to look away or she might jump his bones. How could a guy look sexy and infuriatingly arrogant at the same time? "This isn't funny, Killian. Not even a little bit."

Struggling to compose herself, Sadie plastered on a smile and gripped the handle tighter, preparing to face her sibling.

"You're right." Killian's large hand covered hers on the doorknob, and his voice dipped to that low, sexy growl that curled Sadie's toes. His thumb rasped over her knuckles, and even the mere whisper of his flesh against hers sent a zing of electricity through her. How the hell had she let things get so out of control? Sadie let out a frustrated sigh and turned to look Killian in the eye. When her gaze clapped onto his, though, he tightened his grip on her hand and every coherent thought went out of her head. Killian dropped his voice to just above a whisper. "Whatever's happening between us isn't funny, Sadie, but it is very real."

"You have to go." Sadie tore her gaze away and stared at the dull, chipped paint on the door. "I'm not interested in playing games with you, Killian, or putting my club or my coven—to say nothing of the treaty—in jeopardy. This thing between us is finished."

Without waiting for him to respond, Sadie yanked the door open so hard that it almost came off the hinges. She was greeted by Trixie, who looked more than a little annoyed at the delay.

"There you are." Trixie threw her hands in the air and shouted, "What the hell, Sadie? I've been telepathing you forever. Why didn't you answer me?" Before Sadie could respond, Killian stepped into view and slipped past a visibly stunned Trixie into the small vestibule. "Holy shit." Trixie looked from Killian to Sadie through wide eyes. "I guess that answers my question."

"Sorry for holding Sadie up." Killian bowed his head in deference to Trixie and winked at Sadie. "Thank you for the informative lesson. You can be sure that anytime I'm in my storage room taking inventory, I'll be thinking of you. As educational as this encounter has been, however, I really should return to my guests."

"Right," Trixie said nervously. As Killian walked

up the steps, she mouthed *Oh—My—God* to Sadie and covered her growing smile with both hands.

As Killian's towering frame disappeared into the club, he whispered wickedly into Sadie's mind. *By the way, you and I are just getting started.*

Chapter 8

IF SADIE HADN'T GONE TO FETCH THE WATER, SHE'D BE dead too.

The pungent aroma of blood had been overwhelming, and the scent of it still clung to her nostrils. It made Sadie's stomach roll as she fought her way through the foggy mist of the early morning. Terrified, knowing they were right behind her, Sadie kept running as fast as she could. Her heavy skirts tangled between her legs and she stumbled. Her heart thundered in her chest and she struggled to catch her breath. She couldn't stop. She could hear them behind her, their feet scraping against the rocky earth and their legs whispering through the grass as they stalked her.

If they caught her, they would kill her.

They would kill her the same way they had slaughtered her parents and her sisters. A sob choked her when the image of her father's bloody face and lifeless eyes came roaring to the forefront. The only people she had in the entire world were gone and she was left truly alone. When her father had moved the family out to the wilds of the Western Territory, Sadie had often felt lonely but she'd never actually been alone.

Until now.

Afraid to look back and weakened by fear, she kept running and almost shouted with relief when she spotted her safe haven through the tree line. In the distance the *familiar hill with its rock formations called to her like a beacon. Buried within the rust-colored rocks and nestled behind the overgrown brush was the tiny cave. Before today, it had been a place where Sadie and her sister would come and play for hours—but not today. This time it would be her saving grace and a place to hide from her attackers.*

They were getting closer. Faster. She had to run faster. Sadie was only a few feet from the entrance to the cave when the sounds of low growls rumbled around her. Pure unadulterated terror filled her from head to toe, and a split second later, he was on top of her.

Something slammed into her back, knocking the wind out of her and sending her to the ground with an audible grunt. Dirt and rocks dug into her palms as she hit the earth. Too terrified to move and sure that death was only a moment away, Sadie squeezed her eyes closed and prayed to the Lord that he would take her quickly.

The weight of her attacker held her to the rocky earth, and his warm breath puffed along her neck. The growling grew louder and scraped at the last shred of sanity she had. The beast was going to toy with her before he tore her throat out.

Just do it, *she screamed.* Kill me already. Kill me just like you killed them.

With strength she didn't know she had, Sadie flipped onto her back and found herself face-to-face with an enormous brown-and-black wolf with glittering amber eyes. The beast loomed over her, his paws on either side of her body. But he was no longer holding her down, and if she didn't know better, she'd swear the wolf was smiling. Just when that crazy thought entered her mind, the animal blurred, as though vanishing in a flash of light. Then with a blast of heat, it shifted in a split second into a man.

A handsome, familiar, and very naked man—Killian.

Kill you? *His deep, familiar voice sliced through to her core. His hands were braced on the ground on either side of her, and he settled his body between her legs.* I can think of far more pleasant activities that we can do in our dreams. Killing you is not on the list.

Killian. *Sadie's memory returned the instant she whispered his name, along with a fair amount of confusion.* Holy shit.

She wasn't the young, naive girl running from her family's killers in the wilds of the Western Territory. She hadn't been that girl in a long, long time. Nope. Sadie Pemberton was a two-century-old vampire and this... was a dream.

Sadie was dreaming for the first time in almost two hundred years, and to top it all off, Killian was in the dream with her. This could only mean one thing, and it confirmed what she'd known deep in her gut all along.

Killian Bane, the werewolf prince and heir apparent to the Werewolf Society, was her bloodmate.

I'll be honest, if I had my way, chasing you in my dreams would end a lot differently than this. *His brow furrowed and the muscles in his chest twitched as he held himself above her and glanced at the old-fashioned outfit she was wearing.* And I would think my subconscious would dress you in something other than that *Little House on the Prairie* getup.

I wasn't running from you. *Sadie rolled her eyes at the ridiculous situation they were in. She hadn't run from anyone or anything in centuries—not until Killian Bane came into her world. In fact, running from him had become a nasty habit, and it was time to cut that crap out. Trying to ignore the fact that he was naked, she folded her arms over her chest and glared up at him.* Would you mind getting off me, please?

See? *Killian pushed himself to his feet, finally freeing her from the weight of his body.* This is a shitty dream. If I had my way, you'd be asking me to get you off... not get off you.

Well, maybe that's because it's not just your dream. *She pushed herself to her feet, and though Killian offered her a helping hand, she refused. She moved to brush the dust and dirt from her skirts, but she was no longer dressed like the girl from so many years ago. Gone were the prairie skirts and the stiff, high-necked blouse. Instead she found herself clad in the black boy shorts and tank top she'd gone to sleep in that night.* That's much better.

I agree. *Killian's firm lips lifted at the corners, and his caramel-colored eyes glinted in the sun.* I vote for this outfit.

Big surprise. *Sadie turned her back on him and tilted her face to the warmth of the sun, letting out a satisfied sigh.* Now would you do us both a favor and put something on? All you have to do is think about what you want to wear and it'll be there. At least, that's what Maya told me.

Killian let out a heavy sigh of sexual frustration mixed with impatience. The sound of it made Sadie's grin widen. The warmth of the sun in the dreamscape felt delicious on her normally chilly skin and brought back far-more-pleasant memories of her human life—of a time long before that fateful morning her family had been slaughtered. The smile fell from her face and Sadie flicked her eyes open to stare at the line of trees that hid her family's home and the scene of their murder.

It worked. *Killian's low, sexy growl slid over her seductively as he sidled up behind her and nuzzled her ear.* I want to go on record that I was not in favor of putting on clothing, especially when all I can think about is taking yours off.

His arms slid around her waist and he pulled her against his rock-solid frame. Her gut instinct was to pull away, to run from the man the universe had chosen for her, and yet she didn't. Sadie lingered there for a moment, letting her hands settle over his where they rested against her belly. She shivered when he leaned down and his warm mouth pressed a kiss to the circular scar on her left shoulder blade.

Are you sure you're a wolf? *A smile curved Sadie's lips, and she elbowed him playfully before stepping away and slipping out of his embrace. She pointed at him, warning him to keep his distance. He'd done as she promised and covered his nakedness with a pair of faded jeans. That sexy, well-muscled chest, however, was still on full display. Sadie tore her gaze from the trail of dark hair that disappeared beneath the waistband of his jeans and turned to face the woods in the distance.* You act more like a horndog.

Only around you. *Based on the tone of his voice, she knew that a wolfish grin covered his face.*

I bet you say that to all the girls. *Sadie rolled her eyes and glanced over her shoulder at him, trying not to smile at his infuriatingly charming ways.* But as you know, I'm not like all the other girls you've met. Your wolfish wiles aren't going to work on me.

Well, now that you've effectively ruined the moment, can you tell me what's going on? *Killian moved in on her right side and hooked his thumbs in the pockets of his jeans.* I've dreamed before, but it's never been this real. I certainly haven't had this kind of awareness or control in a dream before. This seems impossible.

That's because it's not a regular dream. *Sadie shifted her weight and glanced at him before gathering her courage to tell him what she knew to be true. She had to tell him they were bloodmates, but doing it in person would certainly be a better idea.* It's a dreamscape. I've never been here before either. Actually, I haven't dreamed in almost two hundred years.

You said that Maya told you about this dreamscape? *Killian seemed genuinely curious about their unusual shared dream experience and not the least bit bothered by it.* So that means she's been here before.

Yes. She and Olivia have both walked in the dreamscape. *Sadie cleared her throat and nodded toward the tree line.* This is actually a memory. Or part of one, anyway. At least, that's what I think it is.

It's your memory, isn't it? *Killian asked hesitantly. Sadie nodded silently and she could feel his eyes on her.*

Yes. *Sadie struggled to keep her voice even.* It's the morning I was turned.

Tell me what happened. *Killian's voice softened at the same moment his hand settled on her lower back.*

My family had settled out west in what you would now know as Arizona. It was the early eighteen hundreds. *Staring at the azure sky, she fought to keep her emotions in check.* It was desolate back then, still a few years before the mining rush. *Her voice sounded faraway, as though someone else were telling the story.* My little sister and I didn't want to go live in such a desolate place, and neither did my mother, but Papa wouldn't listen. He kept saying it was where he would build his fortune. In addition to being one hell of a good tracker, my father was also stubborn. He'd been getting into it with some of the local Apache tribesmen—fights over land and who had the right to hunt on it. Anyway, I guess he got into one fight too many and pissed off the wrong Apache. *Her voice shook, and even though tears threatened to come, she managed to keep them at bay.* My family was slaughtered, and if Olivia hadn't shown up, I would have died right along with them.

I'm sorry. *Killian's voice floated over, gentle and strong.* I can't imagine how awful that must have been.

It was. *In spite of her efforts to remain strong, she found herself leaning into Killian's steely embrace. His arm slipped around her and he pulled her gently against him, their hips bumping until finally settling against one another.* Then why did I dream about a wolf chasing me? I mean, why wouldn't I dream about the Apache? Why you?

I don't know. *Killian kissed the top of her head.* This is not my area of expertise. What else do you remember about that day?

I went to fetch the water. *Her voice was barely audible. As she spoke, the tree line in front of them vanished, revealing the tiny log cabin her father had built. Both of them stilled as a scene began to unfold with every word that Sadie uttered. It was like watching a movie of her past in Technicolor.* It was early, really early. The sun was barely up and it was still kind of chilly. I couldn't sleep so I decided to get the water I knew Mama would need for cooking breakfast. I didn't mind, though—

Sadie stopped mid-sentence and Killian's grip tightened around her when they watched a young woman emerge from the cabin with a bucket in her hand. The two of them observed in silence as a young Sadie, clad in the same clothes she'd worn only moments ago, hummed tunelessly and disappeared into the woods on the other side of the clearing.

Go on, Sadie. *Killian held her tighter but Sadie continued to shiver.* What happened next?

There were screams. *Sadie's voice wavered and the image of the house was instantly shrouded in darkness, but it did little to drown out the sounds of terror.* My mother and sisters. I—I heard a gunshot and then…nothing.

The sounds Sadie described ricocheted around them vividly as fog rolled across the field, momentarily hiding the scene from them. With those terrifying noises filling the air, something deep inside her chest ached.

Loss. Pain. Helplessness.

The sounds faded with the lifting fog, and they watched as the young human version of Sadie emerged tentatively from the tree line. The door of the cabin was wide open and the lifeless body of her father lay just outside, the shotgun about a foot away.

I smelled blood. *Sadie's stomach churned as it had that morning when the pungent coppery aroma filled the air.* I wanted to run, to scream, but I couldn't move. I was so scared, Killian. I—

The distinct menacing growl of wolves rumbled around them in the dreamscape, and Sadie watched in horror as three of the largest wolves she'd ever seen emerged from the cabin. The pack was led by a large black male with a thick, stocky body, and right behind him were two smaller but equally vicious-looking wolves.

The leader stepped over her father's body, and baring a mouthful of sharp teeth, he stalked slowly toward her. His slow, methodical gait reminded her of a horror-movie villain. Jason and Freddy never ran after their victims; they seemed to know their prey had no way to escape. Young Sadie, with her eyes and mouth wide, stood motionless and seemingly frozen in time as the three beasts advanced.

Oh my God, *Sadie whispered.* The Apache didn't kill my family, Killian… Werewolves did.

Killian's grip on her tightened, but he said nothing as the truth continued to unfold before their eyes.

Sadie wanted to launch herself over there, to eviscerate the beasts that slaughtered her family. Just when she was about to fly over, the wolves burst into a run. The young girl screamed and ran from the animals, but she was no match for these supernatural stalkers. In a blur, the black one leaped onto young Sadie's back and clamped his massive jaws onto her left shoulder.

The girl's screams shot through the dreamscape, and at the same instant, white-hot pain seared through Sadie's body. Her back arched and she cried out in unison with her human self from all those years ago.

She would have tumbled to the ground if Killian hadn't kept her safe in his ironclad embrace.

Blinded by tears, Sadie writhed in agony and clung to Killian. Pressing her cheek to the warmth of his chest, she forced herself to open her eyes and watch the rest. The other two wolves stayed back as the black one let out a triumphant howl. With another cringe-inducing shot of fire sizzling down her back, Sadie waited for the other two wolves to join in the brutal attack.

A blur of red and brown whisked across the clearing like a bullet, immediately followed by a series of growls, yelps, and whimpers. One minute the wolves were there and about to attack. The next, all three lay motionless on the ground, and in a glimmer of light, they shifted into their human forms. A tall woman with long, curly red hair strode over to Sadie and squatted next to her.

Olivia, *Sadie murmured.* Oh my God.

Olivia sat down and lifted the girl's head into her lap. Leaning close, she looked the barely conscious girl in the eye. A gust of wind whisked through the dreamscape, and with it came the familiar sound of Olivia's comforting voice.

When you wake up, you will remember nothing of the wolves. Your family was slaughtered by a group of Apache warriors who were attacking settlers in the area. Everyone was killed except you.

With Killian's strong arms wrapped around her and with the steady beat of his heart thrumming in his chest, Sadie gasped and watched as Olivia bared her fangs, changing Sadie's life forever. The scene vanished and the tree line shimmered back into focus, leaving no trace of the events they'd witnessed.

Olivia lied to me. *Sniffling, Sadie swiped at her tears as Killian loosened his hold. Stopping just short of actually releasing her.* She glamoured me and *then* she turned me. Why would she do that? What was the point?

I'm sorry, Sadie. *Killian's fingers curled over her hips as he stared down at her through a serious gaze edged with shame.* My people were responsible for the death of your family.

Talk about star-crossed lovers. *Sadie rolled her eyes and let out a curt laugh before slipping out of his embrace. Hands on her hips, she walked a few steps away from Killian. She let her head fall back, staring at the blue cloudless sky.* Like we weren't screwed enough already? *Sadie spun around and threw her hands in the air.* The universe has a twisted fucking sense of humor. So apparently my family was slaughtered by a pack of rogue werewolves, and then the gods or goddesses or whatever decide to tie my fate to one. On what planet does that make sense?

What are you talking about? *Killian's eyes narrowed.*

Well, why should I be the only one to have the shock of my life? *Sadie clapped her hands and gave him a sarcastic thumbs-up. Taking one step closer with every point, her voice bordered on hysterical. Since she felt crazy as a loon, that was no big surprise. To his credit, Killian said nothing and remained the strong, steady guy he always was.* I think it's about time to let you in on the fun. You want to know why I can hear you telepathically? Or how I got your blood memories when we aren't supposed to get memories from werewolves? Or why the hell you and I are in the damn dreamscape when vampires aren't supposed to dream?

Okay. *Killian held his hands at his side and held her gaze. He was the calm to her storm of crazy.* Tell me.

Killian Bane, you and I are bloodmates. The universe in all of its wisdom has paired the two of us up. If we commit to the bloodmate bond, then I become a day-walker. *Sadie smiled broadly and shouted furiously.* I don't know what the fuck the universe was thinking.

What the hell are you gonna tell your old man? "Hey, Dad. Guess who's coming to dinner?"

"No, sorry, Your Highness. I'm not a well-manicured she-bitch, but a leather-wearing vampire." Somehow, Killian, I doubt they'll be throwing us a party.

Hands on her hips, Sadie stared at him, daring him to come back with one of his smart-ass comments. Yet none came. A smile emerged on that handsome face, and those gorgeous caramel-colored eyes drifted over her from head to toe. Despite the load of crazy she'd just dumped on him, the man was looking at her like she'd given him a million dollars.

Now it all makes sense... That's why you bear the mark. *Killian's voice, barely above a whisper, shimmied around her. He reached out with lightning-fast reflexes and linked his arms around her waist. Sadie let out a gasp of surprise and pleasure as he tugged her against his towering form.* I've dreamed of you for years but I never saw your face. All I saw was the mark.

What mark? *Sadie swallowed hard and her voice was barely above a whisper. His body tensed with what she could only hope was desire, the same desire that fired through her mercilessly.* What? You guys mark your women or something? Tattoo them?

No, *Killian whispered. He trailed his fingertips up*

and down her spine with a slow, deliberate stroke. Since I was a boy, I've dreamed of a woman who bore the mark of the moon. *She stilled beneath his touch. Killian persisted, and Sadie knew there was no turning back. Whispering in her ear, he dragged his hand lightly up her back until his fingers settled over the spot on her shoulder. He traced the dark circle with his thumb as he touched her mind with his.* It's you, Sadie. You bear the mark.

This is crazy, *she whispered through trembling lips.* That can't be true. It's just a scar, Killian. I got it the night I was turned. *Sadie's mouth snapped shut as more pieces fell into place.*

You mean when you were bitten? *Killian brushed his warm, firm lips across Sadie's forehead and his hand splayed along her lower back. The heat of his touch practically branded her as his with each passing second.* Bitten by a wolf.

I'm not a werewolf. *Sadie tilted her chin defiantly and tried not to pay attention to the way her body was responding to his.* I'm a vampire.

Perhaps. But it would seem, Sadie Pemberton, that you are destined to be much more.

Sadie was about to pepper him with denials when a bone-shattering rumble pounded through the dreamscape like thunder. The ground beneath their feet shook, and with a rush of wind, Killian vanished before her eyes.

Sadie launched out of her bed in one giant leap. A moment later, she found herself standing on the other side of the room. Body tense and her skin still humming from Killian's touch, she caught a glimpse of her reflection in the mirror that hung on the far wall.

Her long, dark hair was all over the place, and the mascara she'd never removed from the night before had smudged into dark circles. She looked like a crazy, raccoon-eyed nut ball. Awesome.

A pounding on the front door of her apartment startled her and made yelp. *Yup. She was losing it.*

"You." Sadie pointed at her reflection. "You're a hot mess."

Making her way through the messy and often-neglected living room, Sadie wiped at the mascara under her eyes. Checking her reflection in the guitar-shaped mirror by the door, she made a sound of disgust, knowing this was as good as it was going to get.

Tugging the door open, she found herself face-to-face with Trixie and Maya. They gave each other knowing looks before turning back to Sadie. The jig was up; they'd obviously figured out what Sadie had only just accepted. She and Killian were bloodmates and pigs were officially flying.

"Come on in." Letting out a sigh, Sadie stepped back and opened the door wide for her nosy but well-meaning siblings. Shutting the door, she walked past both women who made themselves comfortable on the large, black-leather sectional sofa. Going right to the fridge, Sadie pulled out some of the microwavable stock and held it up. "You hungry?"

"How can you think of food at a time like this?" Maya asked incredulously. Wearing a pink tank top and yoga pants, her blond hair tied up in a ponytail, she sat cross-legged on the sofa, looking at Sadie like she'd

totally lost it. "You find out you have a bloodmate who
is a werewolf—"

"A werewolf prince, no less," Trixie interjected.
Perched on the arm of the sofa, she chomped on a piece
of gum and cracked her ring-studded knuckles. "Don't
forget the royal part."

Sadie shook her head and popped the cup of blood in
the microwave.

"Right," Maya said quickly. "He's the freaking heir
to the throne too. Trixie told me last night that you and
Killian were fooling around in the storage room."

"She did, did she?" Sadie leveled a look at the pink-
haired punk rocker.

"Oh, right." Trixie rolled her eyes and laughed.
"Like I'm not gonna tell Maya about that? Puh-lease.
The whole hallway reeked of sex anyway. It's not
like she wouldn't figure it out for herself if she went
down there."

"We didn't have sex." Sadie knew how lame her
denial sounded, and based on the looks on their faces,
so did her sisters. Pulling her mug from the microwave,
Sadie did her best to act like this whole development
wasn't the big, fat, weird deal it actually was. "We
fooled around a little."

"That's semantics. Plus, let's acknowledge the
fact that you can't telepath with me, Suzie, Pete, or
Damien anymore," Trixie said in a quiet voice edged
with sadness. She shrugged and looked sheepishly from
Sadie to Maya. "Another one bites the dust."

"It's true." Sadie took a sip and went into the living
room with her sisters. Sitting on the sofa next to Maya,
she pulled her feet up under her and settled in for what

she suspected would be a long talk. "I can only telepath with Killian and last night…"

"You walked in the dreamscape with him, didn't you?" Maya asked with wide blue eyes. She clasped her hands together and seemed genuinely excited for her sister. "How was it? Was it scary? Mine were super scary at first but then…well…you know. Being there with Shane made it okay, I guess."

"That's got to be so weird." Trixie slid off the arm and lay back on the empty side of the sectional sofa. Propping her pink-haired head up with her hand, she kept her steady gaze on Sadie. "You haven't dreamed in, like, two hundred years. I've only been in the dark sleep for about thirty years. How was it? Do you remember? I mean, was it like the dreams you had when you were human?"

"No." Sadie rubbed her thumb on the smooth ceramic mug. "It was weird at first. Bright. Loud. Vivid. But once I realized what was happening, it was all so real. Mine wasn't even a dream, really. Not exactly." Sadie wondered just how much she should tell her sisters. Given the no-no of feeding on wolves, she decided to leave out the part about getting his blood memories and to focus on her own instead. "It was more like a memory."

"So was mine," Maya said quietly. "It was from the night I was turned."

"Me too."

"You saw the Apache attack your family?" Trixie asked with a mixture of fear and awe. "That had to be torture."

"No. The Apache didn't do it." Sadie gripped the mug

tighter as the reality of what Olivia did came roaring into focus. "Werewolves did."

"Holy crap cakes." Trixie sat up and looked as freaked out as Sadie felt. "This keeps getting weirder."

"I don't get it." Maya adjusted her position on the couch and looked from Sadie to Trixie. "Olivia said it was the Apache. I mean, didn't she find you dying in a field or something?"

"Yes, but she glamoured me." Sadie nodded. "I saw the whole thing. Olivia killed the three wolves that attacked me and then glamoured me so that I'd think it was the Apache. *Then* she turned me."

"Wait a second." Trixie snapped her fingers and pointed at Sadie. "If you were attacked, that means…"

"I was bitten by a werewolf."

"No. Way." Trixie's hands flew to her mouth before she pointed at Sadie. "That's why Killian can be your bloodmate."

"We're getting ahead of ourselves." Sadie drained the rest of the mug and hopped off the couch. "I have to go talk to Olivia."

"You should totally talk to Olivia, but…" Maya rose from the sofa and followed Sadie into the kitchen. "What about Killian?"

"What about him?" Sadie rinsed out the mug and stuck it in the drying rack.

"Does he know what all of these things mean?"

"Yes." Sadie leaned against the counter and leveled a serious look at both of her siblings. "But it doesn't matter."

"What are you talking about?" Maya folded her arms over her breasts and seemed genuinely upset. "Killian is your bloodmate and you think it doesn't matter? Trust me, Sadie. It matters. After Shane and I bonded—"

"That's you and Shane. I'm happy for you guys and for Olivia and Doug. But Killian and I can't be… 'Killian and I,'" Sadie said, making air quotes. "He's a werewolf, and we all know that the only way for true bloodmates to bond and become daywalkers is for both of them to be vampires. In Killian's case, that's kind of impossible. So, there you go. No blood bond means no bloodmate, and that means no problems."

"I dunno," Trixie said slowly. She scrunched up her face and shook her head. "I think you're oversimplifying it."

"Well, I don't. So, Killian and I have the hots for each other? It's no big deal. We'll just have to steer clear of one another." Sadie walked toward the front door. "Tonight is our only night off all week. Don't you two have other things you'd rather be doing than getting caught up in this drama?"

"You know we're just worried about you." Trixie gave Sadie a friendly punch on the arm and gestured to Maya. "Come on, girl. I'm surprised your man Shane isn't hovering out in the hallway waiting for you."

"I know you're worried, but everything is going to be fine." Sadie opened the door and gave each of her sisters a good, long hug. "Come on, what did you think was going to happen? Killian and I get married and rule the Werewolf Society as king and queen?" Sadie scoffed out loud, but deep inside a tiny voice whispered, *Yes*. Clearing her throat and shoving aside the impossible thought, she shooed them out the door. "Off you go. I have to get myself together so I can go speak to Olivia."

Shutting the door tightly, Sadie leaned against it and whispered, "She's got some serious explaining to do."

Sadie snagged her phone off the counter and quickly sent Olivia a text asking to see her tonight. A reply came quickly and confirmed Sadie's request. Stripping her clothes off and heading for the shower, she wondered if she could scrub away her desire for Killian the way she could that old mascara.

Yeah. Not so much.

Chapter 9

TODAY, KILLIAN HAD GIVEN THE TERM "SLEEPING IN" a whole new meaning. He'd practically slept the entire day away, and if Ivan hadn't stepped in at the construction site, nothing would have gotten accomplished. When Killian called Ivan to thank him, the guy refused to take the compliment and reminded him that even the boss needed a day off. The truth was that even with all that sleep, Killian didn't get a whole lot of rest. Not that he minded. He'd learned more about Sadie Pemberton in that bizarre dream experience than he had in the entire year he'd been in this damn city.

After he woke up, Killian was certain of two things.

One. Sadie wanted him as much as he wanted her.

Two. She would eventually, after much wooing from him, become his wife.

Killian surveyed the waiting room of the Presidium's main offices and found himself impressed by the slick, modern design of the space. Vampires had a reputation for being old-world creatures stuck in centuries past. Clearly that wasn't the case for the Czars of New York City.

If Killian didn't know better, he would think he was in the waiting room of a high-powered law firm in a Manhattan high-rise, as opposed to the underground offices of the vampire headquarters. The burgundy and beige tones were warm and welcoming, and the leather sofa he sat on was as soft as butter. He glanced at the coffee table in front of him and couldn't help but smile at the stack of magazines that ranged from *Us Weekly* to *Forbes*.

"Can I get you some coffee or a glass of water, Mr. Bane?" Suzie asked. The czars' secretary was clearly a new vampire and looked like she was fresh from a farm. With her fair skin, wide eyes, and pale blond hair, she was the epitome of the girl next door. Definitely not the traditional sort of vampire, at least not what most humans would expect. "Olivia and Doug should be finished with their previous appointment momentarily."

"No, thank you." Killian gave the girl a friendly smile, hoping it would ease her anxiety. Suzie was the most skittish vampire he had ever met. No wonder Olivia had the girl working here in the offices and not more connected with the human world. "I'm fine for now."

The girl nodded and sat at her desk again. She began typing something on the computer keyboard, and even out of the corner of his eye, he could tell she kept looking over at him. He couldn't help but feel sorry for her. For her sake, he hoped that Olivia would call him in sooner rather than later. Suzie was obviously uncomfortable having a werewolf in her waiting room.

A second later the door across the room swung open, and Olivia Hollingsworth stood in the doorway. Her curly red hair flowed over her shoulders and her intelligent green eyes zeroed in on him instantly. Treaty or no treaty, Killian knew that she still didn't trust him and probably kept him close just so she could keep an eye on him. She wanted to improve relations between their races as much as his father did, but she was wary. Given what had happened to Sadie and her human family, he completely understood why.

"Come on in," Olivia said with a wave and a small smile. "Suzie, why don't you head out? It's almost sunset, and you've been working like a dog. Seriously, girl. I order you to go outside and live a little."

"Okay, Olivia," Suzie said quietly.

Killian rose to his feet and crossed the room to shake hands with the czar. He could feel the secretary's eyes on him the entire time. Based on Olivia's tense body language, she'd picked up on the girl's concern too. Unable to ignore Suzie's staring, Killian dropped Olivia's hand and turned slowly to face the young vampire.

"Is there something I can do for you?" he asked politely.

Suzie rose to her feet and opened her mouth like she wanted to say something. Killian gave her his most charming smile, hoping it would make her feel more comfortable. A moment later the girl shook her head, snapped her mouth shut, and sat down before turning back to her computer screen.

Killian gave Olivia a quizzical look. The czar shrugged and said, "Don't ask me."

She ushered him into the conference-style meeting room before closing the door and offering him a seat. It looked like any other office conference room except for the notable lack of windows and a few children's toys that sat in a box in the far corner of the room. A reminder of the unique child Olivia and Doug were raising.

"Doug is tied up with another engagement, so why don't we go ahead and get started." Sitting in the seat across from him, Olivia smiled and folded her hands on the table. Dressed in a sleek black suit, she looked like a powerful CEO, and for all intents and purposes she was. "What can I do for you, Your Highness?"

"You can start by calling me Killian."

"Understood." Olivia gave him a small smile. "I'm not a big fan of titles, and neither is Doug." Leaning back in the leather chair, she said, "So, *Killian*, what brings you to the Presidium?"

He removed the anonymous notes from his jacket pocket and slid them across the table to the czar. Killian sat quietly while Olivia read through the notes, and with each one, her expression grew more furious.

"When did you get the first one?" Olivia asked tightly, her eyes still fixed on the notes.

"A couple of weeks ago. You would think that if one of your people had real issues with a werewolf business in the city, they would have voiced their concerns a few months ago when we started renovations on the club."

"True, but word about the Loup Garou didn't really get out until recently." Olivia flicked her gaze to his briefly before flipping through the notes again. "I intentionally kept it under wraps. I figured the less buildup about it, the better off we'd be, and I'd hoped that people would be less likely to cause trouble once your place was up and running. I didn't even discuss it with my coven. Actually, the rumblings that I've been hearing started *after* you and your pack began to frequent The Coven's VIP booth."

"I see." Killian's mouth was set in a tight line. "What rumblings would you be referring to?"

"The vamps that live in this city are freaked out by the idea of a pack of werewolves setting up house here."

She rolled her eyes. "Darius and his vamps came in here earlier tonight and chewed my ear off about you and your pack. Actually, it's not even all vamps. Just the older ones like Darius. The ones who remember the war seem to be bitching the loudest, but they'll get over it. Change is a part of life, even for us vampires."

"Yes." Killian kept his sights on the czar, watching for any change in her demeanor. "Sadie was more than a little surprised to hear that I was opening a business here."

"I'm sure she was," Olivia said through a laugh. "Your club will certainly compete for the supernatural clientele who visit this city, to say nothing of the humans." She placed the letters on the table and sat back in her chair while holding his stare. "I have to admit, I'm relieved you brought these notes to my attention. In my experience, wolves tend to be...*confident*."

"You mean arrogant."

"Tomato, to-mah-to." Olivia lifted one shoulder. "You're an alpha. It goes with the territory."

"True." Killian sat back and folded his hands in his lap. "However, given the delicate nature of our race relations, I thought you'd want to know about this. I'm not concerned about my safety. That's not why I brought these notes to your attention."

"Okay, then." Olivia arched one red eyebrow and smirked. "Why did you tell me?"

"My father isn't the only one who wants to build better relations with your people." He paused for a moment and said, "I want you to trust me. If I kept this to myself, that wouldn't be very trusting, would it?"

"No," Olivia said quietly. "I don't suppose it would."

Her eyes narrowed and she pulled a phone out of her pocket before texting something. "I think it would be a good idea to have Xavier run some tests on the notes. He's our resident inventor slash mad scientist. He can look for trace evidence and perhaps give us some idea of who's behind them. I have a few vamps that come to mind, but before I start pulling people in for questioning, it would be wise to have evidence of some kind. How does that sound?"

"Perfect." Killian went to stand up but stopped himself and settled back into his seat. "There is one more thing."

"There usually is." Olivia's lips tilted and her green eyes twinkled.

Killian held his breath for a moment and studied the czar, knowing he shouldn't say what he was about to say, but he did it anyway.

"I plan on taking Sadie for my mate."

To his surprise, Olivia burst out laughing. "Are you serious?"

"Dead serious." Killian kept his tone even and his expression calm. He and Sadie had a hell of a road ahead of them, and getting Olivia on their side sooner rather than later seemed like a smart idea.

"You aren't kidding, are you?" Olivia's smile faded. "That's a bold statement, not to mention kind of insane."

"Maybe." Killian shrugged. "But it's the truth. I realize you aren't her mother, but you are her maker and the czar of this district. Given the tension that lingers beneath the surface between our people, I thought it would be a good idea to lay my cards on the table. I wouldn't want there to be any misunderstandings about my intentions. After all, the mixing of our races is not exactly…commonplace."

"Fair point." Olivia's smile faded. "Well, Your Highness, what exactly are your *intentions*?"

"For starters, I'll be getting to know Sadie, and the best way to do that is to take her out on a date or two. I wanted to arm you with the facts before rumor and innuendo could create drama that none of us need."

"I appreciate the courtesy, but have you spoken to Sadie about any of this?" Her eyes narrowed. "How do you know she's even interested in you?"

"I can assure you that she is…interested." Killian leaned back in his chair and held the czar's gaze. "Or maybe 'intrigued' is a better word. Any way you want to describe it, the bottom line is that I will be getting to know her better. Much better."

"Hang on." Olivia raised one hand, stopping him from continuing as her laughter faded and she let out a slow sigh. She settled both elbows on the armrests of her chair, and her mouth was set in a tight line. Her voice dropped low and she said, "Getting involved with any vampire would be a challenge for you, and Sadie's not just any vampire. Let's just say her past is *complicated*."

"She already knows that," Killian said quietly. "At least, she does after last night."

Olivia stilled and those emerald eyes narrowed. "Go on."

"Last night, Sadie and I walked in the dreamscape. Actually, it was more like a memory." Killian folded his hands on the table and leaned closer, knowing he held the czar's complete attention. "To be more specific, it was Sadie's memory."

"Holy hopping horseshit," Olivia said, none too delicately. "She dreamed about the night she was turned?"

"Yes," Killian said quietly. A glimmer of anger fired
up his back when he thought about the way Olivia had
lied to Sadie all these years. "And you can imagine how
surprised she was to see a pack of werewolves instead
of some Apache warriors. You lied to her."

"You're damn right I did." Olivia's voice was quiet
but edged with steely strength. "I had my reasons,
and while I'm sure she's totally fucking furious with
me, she'll understand once I explain it to her." As she
leaned back in her chair, her sharp green eyes studied
him closely. "So, you and Sadie are bloodmates?" She
pointed at the door. "I'll bet a million dollars that's what
Suzie was tweaking out about before."

Killian gave her a quizzical look.

"My assistant, Suzie, has some psychic ability, but
the poor kid hasn't gotten a handle on it. It didn't even
manifest until after she was turned. Anyway, she probably saw that you and Sadie are supposed to hook up."
Olivia pressed her fingers to her eyes briefly before
dropping her hands. "Yet another conversation I'll be
having later tonight."

"I'm surprised that you aren't more upset by this."
Killian's brow knit together. "I just told you that a
member of your coven is meant to be the mate of a
werewolf, and you seem more worried about managing
the psychic episodes of your secretary."

"Sorry. First of all, Sadie is two centuries old and can
handle herself. Suzie was turned within the past couple
of years, and vampire or not, the girl is afraid of her
own shadow." Sitting back in her seat, Olivia crossed

her legs and kept her steely stare on him. "Killian, you have to understand that weird shit has been going on around here for the past couple of years. It's not like you're dropping this news on some stodgy vamp who never colors outside the lines. I am a three-hundred-year-old *vampire* who recently gave birth to a little girl who is a human-vampire hybrid. So a werewolf prince hooking up with one of my progeny isn't exactly the craziest incident we've experienced in our little corner of the world."

"Point taken." Killian tilted his head and smiled.

"That's not to say this situation with you two won't be complicated. If things progress and you really do end up mating with Sadie, then I will definitely have to inform Emperor Zhao. That being said, some developments fall under a need-to-know category—like this one." Olivia's tone grew more serious. "Have you told your father yet?"

"No." Killian didn't miss the hint of a smile on the czar's face. "Like you said—need-to-know basis."

"Right." Olivia's tone lost all humor. "I'm sure he'll appreciate that you came to me about this before you went to him. Listen, if you and Sadie *do* decide to commit to each other and honor the bloodmate bond, the next conversation you have to have is with your father—and the sooner, the better. While he wants to improve relations, I can't imagine this is what King Heinrich had in mind. If you were to mate with Sadie, the impact would be far more serious and have wider-reaching ramifications for the Werewolf Society than for ours."

Killian was about to respond when the sound of the door opening behind him caught his attention. He didn't have to turn around to know who had arrived. A smile curved his lips. He didn't miss the somewhat amused expression on Olivia's face when Sadie came into the room.

"You have got to be kidding me," Sadie said with pure exasperation.

Killian spun his chair around, and the instant he clapped eyes on her, he got the wind knocked out of him. The woman was stunning. He'd known that the first moment he saw her, but he'd never seen her quite like this—clad in a white T-shirt, faded jeans, and black combat boots and with that gorgeous face free of makeup. With her long, dark hair swept up in a ponytail and a few stray strands drifting along her cheek, she looked absolutely beautiful—pure, innocent, and young. Killian's smile faltered. He'd never realized just how young she must have been when she was turned. Eighteen? Twenty? Dressed casually and outside the buzzing energy of the club, she didn't look much more than a girl.

"What a lovely surprise," he said softly, rising to his feet.

"That's one way to put it." Sadie shot Killian a furious look.

"Sleep well?" Killian teased.

"Zip it, Prince Charming." After giving him a withering look, Sadie turned her attention to Olivia. "What's going on, Liv? I thought we were going to have a chance to talk."

"Yes. I'd say I'm a little late with one talk in particular." Olivia rose from her chair, strode across the room, and took Sadie's hands in hers. Killian watched with rapt attention while the czar, the leader of all of the vampires in the Northeastern Territory, turned into the maternal spirit she inherently was. "Sadie, I owe you an apology. I'm sorry I lied to you about what happened the night you were turned. You have to understand that it really was for your own good."

"You told her?" Sadie looked at Killian like she wanted to kick him in the nuts, and he realized he'd overstepped his bounds. "You might be my bloodmate, Killian, but that doesn't give you the right to butt into my business."

Yup. Way overstepped his bounds. Shit.

"Don't get pissed at him, okay?" Olivia brought Sadie over to the small love seat along the back wall of the conference room. Pulling her down onto the cushions next to her, Olivia continued. "I had to do it, Sadie. The treaty with the wolves was just coming into play and the war was finally settling down. If I turned you and allowed you to keep that horrible memory of what that rogue pack did to you and your family, you would never have been able to settle into your new life as a vampire. It was, whether you believe me or not, for your own good. I wanted you to be safe."

Silence hung heavily in the room while Sadie stared intently at her maker. In the span of only a few minutes, Killian saw a range of emotions flicker across her face. Anger. Hurt. Confusion. Sadness. Sadie's shoulders sagged and she shot a glance in Killian's direction.

She loves you, Sadie. Killian knew he should stay out of it but he couldn't help himself. The pall of sadness hanging over Sadie tugged at his heart and made him feel helpless. He could handle anything other than this. His father's disappointment, a flock of hungry vampires, anything except watching Sadie suffer. *Olivia did what she did because she wanted to protect you... It's a feeling I'm starting to get familiar with.*

Sadie straightened her back when Killian's mind met hers, and to his relief, she didn't shut him out. Her dark, almost ebony stare met his, and in that split second he detected a glimmer of hope.

Somehow, some way, everything would work itself out. A smile tilted his lips as he thought of his mother. That was her favorite saying. Any time he'd worry about something, she would pat his arm and say, "*Don't worry, my boy. Everything has a way of working itself out.*"

"I'll be honest, Olivia. I'm pissed at you for lying to me, but the reality is that if not for you, I'd have died— really died—a long time ago." Sadie looked at her maker through large, dark eyes. "I can try to understand why you made that decision, but given that I had already been bitten by a werewolf, weren't you afraid of trying to turn me?"

"Absolutely, but you definitely would have died if I didn't at least try." Olivia brushed a strand of long, dark hair off Sadie's forehead and cupped her cheek. "I couldn't leave you there to die alone like that. You were so young, so fragile and innocent. How could I just walk away?"

"Did Sadie's turn go normally?" Killian interjected. He folded his arms over his chest and kept his intense gaze on Sadie. "I thought that when a vampire is turned, much like when a human is turned by one of my people, any scars or wounds they had as a human vanish. But Sadie has a scar. The one on her shoulder that looks like a full moon."

"It took two days, like it does with most vamps. After the turn Sadie remained, shall we say, *sensitive* to the presence of werewolves." Olivia smiled and squeezed her progeny's hands. "You always had a sixth sense about it if any were around. Nothing specific or anything, but your hunches always gave us a heads-up."

"My scar tingles sometimes." Sadie looked at Killian with something akin to acceptance. "The scar where I was bitten."

"Your blood was some of the most potent I've ever tasted." Olivia sat back on the sofa and let out a tired sigh. "When I drained most of it for the turn, I got seriously high. It wasn't that different than feeding straight from one of Killian's people. Anyway, the only other unusual side effect was that scar you retained on your shoulder."

"There's one thing I don't understand," Sadie said, tearing her gaze from Killian's.

"What is it?"

"You ended up putting the treaty in danger anyway by killing those wolves when you saved me. Why bother changing my memory if you killed them?"

"I didn't kill them." Olivia glanced at Killian before turning back to Sadie. "Not then, anyway. That night I knocked them out, only wounded them. I didn't kill them until a few nights later. Truthfully…*we* killed them a few nights later."

"Oh my God." Sadie's eyes grew wide with tears. "The pack we fought…just a few nights after I was turned. *They* were the same pack who killed my family."

"Yes." Olivia nodded and patted Sadie's knee before giving it a squeeze. "I took you to an abandoned cabin while you were in the transition sleep. It wasn't far from where you lived with your family, and unfortunately they tracked us there."

"So you killed them after all?" Killian asked.

"You're damn right I did." Olivia shot him a deadly look and sat up straighter in her seat. "I gave them a chance to escape with their lives, but that wasn't enough. They came back for revenge and they sure as hell got some."

"N-no one ever found out about that, did they?" Sadie asked quietly.

"No." Olivia shook her head adamantly. "That area was virtually uninhabited at that time, so we were able to sweep it under the rug. I was worried that the second encounter with them would trigger something in your memory. But it didn't. It sure made you want to stay far away from wolves of any kind though."

Sadie flicked her gaze to Killian's and he touched her mind with his. *Not all wolves, I hope.* To his delight, the hint of a smile played at her lips before she looked away.

"So no one ever knew," Olivia said firmly. Turning a stony look in Killian's direction, she rose to her feet. "At least until now. Am I going to have to worry about this revelation being *accidentally* leaked to the king?"

"If you ask me, Olivia," Killian murmured. "You shouldn't have let them go the first time around. After what I saw in that dreamscape, those men deserved their fate. Attacking an innocent family and slaughtering women and children is an act of cowardice. Men like that have no honor and bring nothing but shame to my people. Besides, it's ancient news. It has no bearing on current or future events."

"Good." Olivia crossed her arms over her chest and

arched one eyebrow. "I'm glad you agree." Turning to Sadie, her tone softened along with her rigid posture. "I really am sorry, Sadie. To be honest, I'm relieved you finally know the truth."

"Yeah, well, the truth isn't all it's cracked up to be," Sadie murmured. Rising to her feet, she shrugged and suddenly looked remarkably uncomfortable. "So, Killian told you about…us…I mean…the bloodmate thing."

"Yes." Olivia seemed to be suppressing a smile. She nodded as she moved past Sadie toward the notes she'd left on the table. "Actually, given your history and what happened on the day you were turned, being mated to a werewolf doesn't seem all that weird."

Killian stilled and clapped eyes with Sadie as a few more pieces to their bizarre puzzle fell into place. The universe seemed to be doling out information one crumb at a time, and he had just snagged another one.

"Of course…" Killian murmured. His brows knit together and he met Olivia's curious green-eyed gaze across the room. "Sadie must have retained some of our DNA in her bloodstream, and maybe that's why we're so *compatible*. When a human is bitten by a wolf, their DNA is altered, just like when a human is turned into a vampire."

"Sadie's blood is registered with the Presidium archives, like that of all vampires is, but her blood wasn't tested—only logged."

"Can your friend Xavier run blood tests in his lab?"

"Interesting." Olivia's eyebrows flew up and she nodded slowly, understanding where Killian was going with it. "We could have him test her blood and check for any signs of werewolf DNA. It would explain a lot," she murmured with a pointed look in Killian's direction. "I can't imagine your father, not to mention your people, would be interested in having a vampire for their queen. Maybe if Sadie still has some werewolf DNA in her bloodstream, everyone would be more willing to accept your *situation*."

"They have nothing to do with this," Killian bit out. "My life is my own and no one else's."

"Excuse me." Sadie raised her hand and cast an insulted look at Killian and Olivia. "How about me or my life? Did anyone ask me if I'd like to be studied like some kind of lab rat, or if I'm even interested in hooking up with Killian and being queen?" She threw her hands up. "What am I talking about? You don't even want to be king."

"Oh please." Olivia rolled her eyes and snagged the notes off the table. "You're being dramatic. All you have to do is let Xavier draw some blood. And as far as hooking up with Killian?" The czar smirked and waved one hand dismissively. "Let's just say, I have a feeling it's not an outrageous suggestion. You forget, my friend, I've already been through the bloodmate bonding. I'm well aware of the intense physical attraction that comes with it, and you can't ignore it. You have to face this and figure it out."

"It *is* intense." Killian winked at Sadie. "Nothing gets by your maker, does it?"

Hands on her hips, Sadie's eyes narrowed with the fiery determination that Killian so adored. Good God, this woman was hot, and in spite of her anger, he was remarkably turned on. *You know you're gorgeous as hell when you get angry?*

"Cut that out!" Sadie let out a sound of frustration, and her hands curled into fists at her side. "I'm not kidding, Killian."

"I'm sorry." Raising his arms in the universal sign of defeat, he gave her the most apologetic look. "Really, I am." Dropping his hands to his side, Killian lowered his voice. "But I can't help myself, because it's true."

"What is?" Olivia asked with mild amusement.

"How gorgeous she is when she's angry," he said, giving Sadie a wink.

"Damn it, Killian." Sadie pointed at him, and even though she did her best not to smile, the hint of one glimmered in her eyes. "You may be the only one I can telepath with now, but that doesn't give you the right to invade my thoughts every two seconds."

Sorry. He shrugged.

"Killian!" Sadie shouted with a laugh.

"Okay, okay. I'll stop."

"Oh Lord." Olivia sighed. "I can tell the two of you are going to have one hell of a time figuring this all out. In the meantime, you need to go see Xavier. Sadie, since you're going there anyway, you can take Killian with you." She reached across the table and handed the papers to Killian, but kept her sights on Sadie. "He needs to bring these notes to Xavier for analysis, and he doesn't know the way. Doug and I have another appointment that I can't be late for, so you can take him."

"What about Suzie?" Sadie asked quickly. "Why doesn't she take him? I can go see Xavier another time."

"Are you serious?" Olivia all but laughed out loud. "That poor girl is still afraid of her own shadow, and you expect me to send her on a walking tour of the Presidium with a werewolf? Besides, I already sent her home. And before you ask, no, I'm not getting Trixie or Damien." Olivia slipped her hands into the pocket of her slacks, and a smile bloomed. "Besides, you and Killian obviously have a lot to talk about. So that makes you the perfect escort. No time like the present. Go on."

"We can talk and talk and talk until the next full moon and he turns furry but—"

"Actually," Killian interrupted. "We don't need a full moon to shift. Just the *desire*."

"Whatever." Sadie sighed. The innuendo in his words wasn't lost on her. "As I was saying, all the talk in the world won't change the facts. I'm a vampire. Killian is a werewolf. We aren't exactly compatible biologically, socially, or politically. Then if that's not enough, bloodmates only bond if both are vampires, and Killian can't be a vampire because werewolves can't be turned. So the way I see it, this whole bloodmate deal between us is a nonissue. I'll admit there's an attraction. *But*, we are both grown-ups." She sent a narrowed glance at Killian. "Well, one of us is, anyway, and I'm more than capable of keeping my hormones under control. So as long as Prince Charming here keeps his paws to himself, the problem is solved."

"Fine by me," Killian murmured.

Fully aware he was pushing her buttons, to say nothing of the levels of propriety in front of the czar, Killian continued. He closed the distance between them slowly, but Sadie didn't retreat. She held her ground and met his challenging stare with one of her own. Her simmering brown eyes were filled with more than anger, and beneath her fury he sensed lust. A smile curved

Killian's mouth as he inched close enough to touch her. Sadie wavered slightly, even though her feet remained planted firmly in one spot. His gaze danced over her perfectly crafted features.

Keeping his urge to touch her chained beneath the surface, he whispered, "And by the way, Ms. Pemberton, you aren't the only one who can show a little self-control. I make you this promise, with your maker here as a witness. I will not touch you from this point forward *unless* you tell me to." Leaning closer still, her body scant inches from his, he growled, "And we both know you will. It's only a matter of time."

Sadie's eyes widened in shock before her mouth snapped shut with an indignant yelp. Without waiting for her to formulate any kind of retort, Killian turned to Olivia. She looked more than a little amused by the previous exchange.

"Thank you for your help with this, Olivia." Killian shook the czar's hand and turned to Sadie. "Shall we?"

Without a word, Sadie spun on her heels and threw open the door, leaving in a silent furious blur. Killian smoothed the lapels of his jacket and bowed his head to Olivia before following Sadie out.

"Good luck, Your Highness!" Olivia shouted after him. "You're going to need it."

As Killian followed Sadie out into the Presidium's waiting room, he had a feeling he was going to need more than luck.

Chapter 10

THEY WALKED IN SILENCE SIDE BY SIDE THROUGH THE underground stone hallways of the Presidium, and Killian noted the detailed workmanship. Aside from the intricate stone archways, there were beautiful carvings throughout. The cavernous passages were lit with iron chandeliers that had been modernized to electricity years earlier. It was an impressive facility, and a fascinating combination of the past and present. What made it even more intriguing was that the city of Manhattan bustled above with no knowledge of the world that thrived beneath.

"Xavier's lab is just around this corner." Sadie didn't look at him, pointing to a corridor on the left. "I'll make sure you get back to street level, and then you can be on your way. I have work to do and I'm sure you do too. Besides, I have a feeling that *partner* of yours is going to keep you jumping. She seems like a real barrel of laughs."

Killian suppressed the grin that threatened to bloom when Sadie mentioned Christina. Whether or not Sadie wanted to admit it, she was jealous. He wasn't looking to have two women fight over him, and yet he felt a certain amount of satisfaction in knowing that Sadie had Christina on her radar.

"I've known Christina my entire life. She's more like a kid sister than anything else."

"Right," Sadie scoffed. "I've never seen a sister paw at her brother that way. Talk about inappropriate. Anyway, she seems like exactly the kind of woman you should be with. She's rich, well-groomed, and stuck-up. Sounds like a match made in heaven."

"It's true that Christina's life has been one of absolute privilege, and I can assure you that I have no illusions about her motivation. She wants to be queen. There's no mystery there."

"She may not be mysterious, but she's certainly beautiful," Sadie said quietly with a quick look at Killian. "Regal, almost. She already looks like a queen. The duds she had on last night probably cost more than everything I own put together."

"Perhaps." Killian kept his voice low and fought the urge to reach out and tangle her fingers in his. He stuck his hands in the pockets of his jeans instead. They stopped in front of a set of massive stainless-steel doors and Sadie pressed a panel to the left. Desperate to touch her, Killian inched closer and breathed her in. Her spicy, exotic scent filled his nostrils and instantly brought back memories of their tryst at the club last night. There was no sign of the heartbeat she'd miraculously attained after drinking his blood, and she was doing her best to pay him as little attention as possible. He kept his gaze on her.

"Sadie, I promise you that in spite of her best efforts, Christina will not be my queen."

"Why not?" Sadie pressed the panel again and folded her arms over her chest. "Where the hell is Xavier?"

Silence filled the hallway and he felt Sadie's unusual energy humming around him again like music. She bit her lower lip and squeezed her eyes shut as Killian's gaze slid over her delicate, curvy profile. The long, dark ponytail swung temptingly at the middle of her back, right above the delicious dip of her waist. He suppressed a groan of driving need. Damn it all. The only thing he could think about was rubbing the silky strands between his fingers.

"Aside from the fact that I can't stop thinking about you...I don't love Christina and I'm not attracted to her. At all." His hands clasped casually in front of him, he smirked. "You don't have anything to be jealous about."

"Why, you arrogant bastard." Eyes flashing, Sadie spun around and poked him in the chest with one finger, getting right in his face. "I am not jealous. I was simply making an observation."

Killian dipped his head low so that their mouths were scant inches apart. "So was I."

The thick pulse of desire swirled around them and Killian breathed her in, which only served to entice him beyond reason. Sadie's eyes widened and her curvy body wavered ever so slightly, making the thin, cool fabric of her T-shirt brush against him. A growl rumbled in his chest, heat coiling in his gut, and every inch of him hardened to the point of pain. Sadie's lips parted on a sigh, and for a split second, he thought she was going to cave in and kiss him.

The sudden and sharp clanging of a lock slipping open echoed through the cavernous stone halls. The massive steel door slid open, breaking the spell. Sadie blinked and practically jumped away from him, trying to act as though they hadn't been eye-fucking each other about two seconds earlier. Unable to resist the temptation to tease her, Killian reached out and whispered into her mind. *I'd say that round goes to me. Wouldn't you agree?*

Tucking a stray hair behind her ear, she shot back a response with all the spice and sass he loved: *No, actually, I wouldn't.* Sadie narrowed her eyes and flicked them down to the growing evidence of their encounter. Folding her arms across her breasts, she gave him a satisfied grin before walking toward the open door. *I'm not the one with a big hard-on.*

Unable to argue with that true and sexually frustrating fact, Killian buttoned his jacket before following her in. The vampire who greeted them was not at all who or what Killian was expecting. The fellow was only about three feet tall, for one. In addition to a shock of white hair on his head, he had a giant smile on his face that was clearly meant for Sadie.

"Hello, Sadie girl!" he shouted. The smile faltered when he spotted Killian. "I see you brought a friend. You must be Killian."

"Great," Sadie groaned. She shot Xavier a mortified look before walking past the two men into the lab.

"I see Sadie has told you about me." Killian shook Xavier's much smaller hand and gave Sadie a sly smile. If Sadie had mentioned him to her friend, he could only take that as a good sign. "Thank you for your help with this."

"Yes." Xavier chuckled and flew back into the lab. The doors shut silently behind Killian. "Right this way. Olivia texted me that you had some letters that need to be examined for evidence. Correct?"

"What are these letters, anyway?" Sadie asked.

She looked genuinely concerned, seated on a stool near Xavier.

"Threats," Killian said casually. He pulled out a stool on the other side of the table and sat down. He reached over and handed the ominous notes to Xavier. "Looks like a few of your people have their panties in a wad about the Loup Garou opening here in the city." He winked. "People aside from you."

Sadie rolled her eyes and suppressed a smile as she scooted closer to Xavier, peering over his shoulder at the notes. Her reaction, albeit a small one, gave him hope.

"Were they mailed?" Xavier pushed his glasses onto his head. "Dropped off? What? Are there envelopes?"

"No. The first two were slipped under the front door of the club, but this last one, the more threatening message, was slipped beneath the door of my office." Killian leveled a serious look at Sadie. "*In* my club."

"Alright. I'll run an analysis on the paper for trace DNA evidence and see what we come up with. Did anyone else handle these?"

"Aside from you, just me and Olivia." Killian snapped his fingers. "And one human. He's the foreman on the construction at the club. Mike."

"Can you get me a DNA sample?" Xavier popped his glasses back down and perused the note some more. "Hair maybe?"

"How do you suppose I go about that?" Killian asked, running a hand through his hair as frustration started percolating. He just wanted to open his club and do his thing. All of these complications were starting to piss him off. "Not to sound ungrateful, but do you suggest I just walk up to the guy and ask him for a hair sample?"

"I see your point." Xavier looked at Sadie and his white eyebrows flew up. "It seems our friend here could use the glamouring skills of a well-schooled vampire."

"I can't—"

"Sure you can." Xavier elbowed her playfully. "You're great at it, and it really would be a help to me, Sadie girl."

"Xavier." Sadie let out a sound of frustration and looked from Xavier to Killian and back again. "Okay, fine. I'll do it. But that's it. After that, I leave the sleuthing to you."

"Perfect." Killian rose to his feet. "In fact, Mike should still be there. We can kill two birds with one stone, because this will give me a chance to show you around the club. Just like you promised."

Sadie narrowed her eyes. *You're really enjoying this, aren't you?*

I have to admit that watching you squirm is kind of amusing.

"Sadie girl, come on over here. I'll give you a sterile evidence bag." The scientist flew to the other side of the room and waved for Sadie to follow him. "I'll give you a swab too. If you could get me both hair and saliva samples, that would be best."

Killian walked around and perused the rest of the lab while Sadie and Xavier chatted quietly in the back. He could have eavesdropped if he'd wanted, using the heightened hearing of his wolf, but he didn't. He wasn't interested in violating her privacy. If he wanted her to trust him, giving her space was a good place to start.

—∽∽∽—

Sadie couldn't ignore Killian if she tried, and damn if she hadn't been trying since they left Xavier's lab. Xavier had taken the watch monitor from her so he could download the information it had gathered, but she doubted it would shed much light on her weird situation.

While making their way through the Presidium's hallways, she blamed the close proximity to Killian for why she couldn't escape the attraction. It was bullshit. Walking alongside him, with his woodsy scent surrounding her, Sadie knew it wouldn't matter where she was. Killian Bane would always be nearby—the man had gotten in her head and under her skin.

And he knew it.

She'd tried to act like she was pissed at him back at Olivia's office and failed miserably. Pushing him away seemed like the smart choice, and yet he seemed totally unwilling to allow her to get away with it. It was monumentally frustrating to stand her ground when the guy could make her laugh at the most annoying moments. Her father had been able to do that with her mother. No matter how upset Sadie's mama may have been with him, her daddy had a way of getting past it and finding her funny bone. It was charming and disarming, and until Killian, she'd never met a man who could defuse her anger like that.

"The entrance to the subway tunnels is just up ahead." Sadie nodded to a doorway down the hallway on the left. "The sun isn't down quite yet, so we can't go to street level. As much as I love the summer, the shorter nights are a bitch. We should be able to use the subway tunnels to make our way over to your club."

"My club?" Killian's deep voice echoed through

the halls, surrounding her. "There's no underground entrance into my club."

"You sure about that?" Sadie stopped at the black-paneled doorway and pressed the button on the left. "Your Highness?"

"Positive." Killian's eyes narrowed and he peered at her with his usual air of confidence. "Ms. Pemberton."

The door opened silently and a rush of damp warm air came with it, making Sadie's ponytail flutter behind her like wings. She stepped into the tunnel with Killian close behind. The door slid shut, leaving them both in the dimly lit tunnel of the New York City subway system.

"You're awfully cocky for a guy who's new to this city." Sadie hopped off the ledge and onto the tracks. Killian followed and quickly matched her pace. "How can you be so sure?"

"Because we sealed the entrance," he said calmly.

"What?" Sadie stopped short but Killian kept moving. His tall form cut a striking figure even in the dingy, dank subway tunnel. "You closed off the entrance? Does Olivia know that?"

"I don't know." Killian glanced over his shoulder at her briefly before continuing on his way. "It's my club and my building. Ivan and David found the entrance during one of our initial tours of the facility. They picked up a vampire scent. Granted it was old and no vamps had likely been there for some time. The building had been empty for years, after all. Anyway, we thought it would be a good idea to get rid of it."

Sadie watched him saunter along the tracks and shook her head. The guy looked remarkably comfortable and didn't seem to have a worry in the world. He didn't seem fazed in the least that he was deep within vampire territory. She should probably be annoyed, and yet to Sadie's surprise, she found his confidence refreshing.

And sexy.

Drat.

Like it or not, she was undeniably attracted to Killian. No matter how much she wanted to ignore it, she couldn't. She was going to have to deal with her feelings so that she and Killian could get past this *thing* between them. After all, there wasn't any way for them to have a future together.

In a blur of speed, Sadie flew up to meet him. To her delight, he flinched when she landed next to him. His light brown eyes glinted at her and the lines at the corners deepened as he smiled.

"Not bad." Slipping his hands in his pockets, he nodded with approval. "I knew you were fast. You're quiet too."

"Yeah, well. I have to tell you that this is the slowest I've ever moved through these tunnels." She made a sweeping gesture with both arms. "Especially ones like this that are still in use. Can you move any faster? I'd prefer not to get hit by a train, and even though this line doesn't run as often as some of the others, it's still active. No offense, but you're kind of slow."

"Me? Slow?" Killian stopped dead in his tracks and his hand went to his chest, feigning injury. He leaned closer, dropping both arms to his sides, and whispered. "I guess you've never run with a wolf."

Before Sadie could respond, Killian stood to his full height. She took a step back and watched with a mixture of curiosity and awe as Killian's eyes shifted into the glowing amber eyes of his wolf. A low growl rumbled around them and grew louder with each passing second. An instant later a blast of heat shot out of his body, along with a brilliant flash of light. Sadie squinted against the sudden illumination and when she looked back, allowing her eyes to adjust to the lighting, the tall, handsome man was gone. Instead, standing in front of her was a massive brown-and-black wolf with a pair of familiar glowing eyes. He had a thick, stocky build and a mouthful of sharp white teeth—teeth that could tear through a human or vampire with ease.

"Whoa," Sadie murmured and took an involuntary step back. It had been centuries since she'd been this close to a werewolf in wolf form, and her gut instinct was to flee. Looking into those eyes though, Sadie knew she was safe. She licked her lips and folded her arms over her breasts in an effort to steady her nerves. "You're a lot bigger than I thought you'd be."

You're not going to tell me what big teeth I have, are you? Killian's growl stopped short, and his deep, soothing baritone filled her mind. *Because that line is played out.*

"No." Sadie laughed. "Little Red Riding Hood I am not." Rolling her eyes, she pointed to the pile of clothes. "Do you plan on walking into the construction site naked or in your wolf pelt? I can't imagine either of those going over well with the workers."

Shit. A growl rumbled and she could swear she saw a look of annoyance on his furry face when he looked at the pile of shredded clothing. *We'll have to make a detour. I'll have David meet us in the parking garage of my apartment building with some clothes. It's not that far from the club.*

"Your apartment?" Sadie asked skeptically. "I guess. By that time the sun will be down and we can get to the club at street level. I should warn you, we're going to have to use the sewer tunnels for part of the trip."

Sewer tunnels? No thanks.

"Well, we're going to have to use the sewer tunnels to get into the parking garage of your apartment building." Sadie raised both brows and put her hands on her hips. "You're not chicken, are you?"

Hardly. Killian stuck his nose in the pile of clothes and came up with a leather wallet clenched between his teeth. *I am lacking pockets at the moment. Would you mind?*

Nodding her agreement, Sadie swallowed the irrational lump of fear in her throat. She had no reason to be afraid of Killian, and yet as she reached toward his mouthful of teeth, she couldn't stop her body from shaking. Sensing her fear, Killian sat on his haunches and gave her time to acclimate. After a few seconds, he gently dropped the wallet into her hand and then did something far more surprising—he licked her fingers. Sadie stilled as his warm, wet tongue bathed her hand in a sweet, reassuring gesture. *I would never hurt you, Sadie.*

"I know." Gripping the wallet tightly, she met his fiery stare. "I mean I know you wouldn't hurt me intentionally. It's just going to take some getting used to, that's all."

Understood. Killian rose to all fours. *Lead the way.*

"Alright, but I just hope you can keep up." Sadie

winked at him while slipping his wallet into the back pocket of her jeans. "Don't worry. I'll try not to go too fast."

I can take whatever you dish out. Killian growled and shook his furry body, readying himself for the run. He crouched low, a wolfish grin covering his face. *Just say the word.*

Sadie met his challenging stare and found herself more excited than she should be to race a wolf through the tunnels. As in all her other encounters with Killian, nothing was as it should be.

"Go," Sadie whispered.

Bursting into a run, she raced down the tunnel with the typical speed of a vampire. She fully expected him to be a few lengths behind her, and yet again, Killian Bane was full of surprises. She glanced down to her right to see Killian matching her speed stride for stride, a focused and determined look on his adorable furry face.

I told you I was fast. Killian's confident rumble whisked into her mind, and without warning, he picked up his speed, inching ahead of her. *You're holding back, Sadie.*

My mistake. Sadie pumped her legs harder and easily caught up to Killian.

It was energizing to find someone who challenged her, pushed her to go faster and be better. Olivia and the girls in the coven were strong and steady, but no one challenged her. Everyone had their place and a job to do. Until recently, life had been all about following the rules in order to survive. Being with Killian was the exact opposite—it was all about breaking the rules.

A familiar and growing vibration in the tunnel

captured her attention, marking the impending arrival
of an oncoming train. It was coming at them from up
ahead, and based on past experience, Sadie knew they
had less than two minutes until the speeding contraption
came around the bend.

Killian. Sadie touched his mind with a now familiar
ease. *A train is headed for us. There's a utility-room
doorway up ahead. If you shift, we should both be able
to fit in the alcove and avoid the train.*

I see it.

The rumbling of the train grew louder and the
vibrations ricocheted through Sadie's body with bone-
clattering strength. She spotted the lights of the train
along the cement wall, knowing it would round the
bend soon as she leaped into the safety of the doorway.
Killian skidded to a halt, dirt and grime from the subway
floor shooting out from beneath his paws. The light of
the train gleamed over his body, giving him an almost
unearthly glow. Panic welled. He wasn't going to
make it.

"Shift, Killian!" Sadie screamed. "Now! Killian, shift
and grab my hand."

It felt like an earthquake as the train roared around
the bend. Just when she thought Killian was going to
get hit, a brilliant flash of light and heat blasted over
her. The next second, Killian's tall, hard, naked body
was pressed tightly against hers in the confined space.
Sadie's back was pressed up against the metal utility-
room door and her arms were being held over her head,
Killian's hands curled around her wrists. Heat fired over
her and through her, and she couldn't tell if it was from
Killian or the train that was speeding past them.

Holding his heated stare, and with the flickering lights from the train and the ear-shattering noise of its engines surrounding them, Sadie felt like she was being consumed. Neither of them moved as the train, with its seemingly endless string of cars, roared past. She didn't dare move; if she did, it would be so she could lick and suckle at those firm lips of his.

His body hardened against her with each passing second, and the hot length of his erection pressed insistently against her lower belly. His muscular and perfectly sculpted form looked like it had been created by computer magic, not nature. How could nature have created someone so perfect? Everything about this man screamed sex and lust, and trying to ignore her attraction to him was an effort in futility.

The last car whisked past and a swirl of wind curled around them while they remained motionless in the shelter of the doorway. Killian's breathing had gotten notably faster, and his heart thundered through his chest like a jackhammer. He licked his lower lip and his heated, glowing gaze drifted over her face. One of them should move, she thought. She didn't trust herself to do it.

God help her, she wanted Killian more than she'd wanted anyone in her existence.

"That was close," Killian murmured. His fingers around her wrists loosened and his thumb brushed over her palm. Sadie gasped with pleasure from even that tiny whisper of flesh over flesh. "I almost got run over, and wouldn't that have been a memorable first date?"

"You call this a date?" Sadie asked absently.

"It's a start." Killian's chest heaved with effort as

he struggled to catch his breath, and the gentle pressure against her breasts almost made her moan. "I promise our next date will be somewhere cleaner, with less traffic…and aboveground. With no danger of being run over."

Sadie nodded curtly but couldn't bring herself to say anything. Desire hummed in her blood and her fangs vibrated, begging to be freed. She uncurled her fists, expecting Killian to release her. He didn't. Instead he slid his hands over hers, tangled their fingers together, and continued holding her arms over her head.

"Then again," he whispered, "that's exactly how I've felt since that kiss on the roof." Killian pressed his lips to her forehead and murmured, "Like I got hit by a train."

"Killian," Sadie whispered, the needy sound of her voice betraying her as the sex-hungry woman she'd become. Killian tilted his hips and slid his bare thigh between her jean-clad legs, putting pressure on exactly the right spot. A thready moan escaped her lips and she rasped, "This can't go anywhere…"

"Well, you're part right." He grinned and flicked his tongue over her lips while rotating the hard plane of his thigh against her clit. Killian's grin widened when Sadie let out a moan of pleasure. She rode his thigh, shamelessly seeking more. "We can't take this any further *here* because I won't be able to or want to stop. I'll want to bury myself inside you and lose myself in every wickedly gorgeous inch of you. But when I make love to you for the first time, it will be somewhere safe, private, and beautiful, not in a subway tunnel under the city."

Killian kissed the tip of her nose and released her hands before hopping down to the tracks. In a blinding flash of light and a rush of heat, he shifted into his wolf and that mischievous look came over his face. *I want to take my time, and you deserve nothing less than perfection.*

Unable to form a coherent sentence and feeling her flesh buzz with unfulfilled lust, Sadie squeezed her eyes shut and pressed herself deeper against the cool metal of the door. She needed something, anything to cool off her turned-on body. Thank God she'd left that watch monitor with Xavier. Otherwise it probably would have beeped like a damn fire alarm.

Are you coming? Killian's teasing voice slipped into her mind and made her smile.

"Not yet," Sadie sang. She hopped onto the tracks and winked at Killian. "But you can make it up to me later."

Then, without letting him respond, she raced ahead. Moments later, Killian's strong, furred body was running alongside hers with the long, swift strides he executed so easily. Her body was already lost to him, and it was only a matter of time before she gave it to him completely.

She kept reminding herself that as long as she didn't feed on him again, they could explore their sexual attraction and have a little fun. There was no rule against that. But Sadie had to be sure that her bloodlust and physical lust remained separate. Blurring those lines would be a death sentence for both of them.

Chapter 11

AFTER MEETING UP WITH DAVID IN THE PARKING garage, Killian made quick work of getting dressed before they drove over to the Loup Garou. They rode in the back of the limo in silence, and Sadie didn't miss the occasional looks from David. He was friendly enough, and Sadie supposed she couldn't blame him for being wary. To his credit, the guy didn't say anything. Although, based on Killian's body language at certain points, she suspected the men were telepathing. And that was more than a little annoying.

Hey. Sadie, who kept to her corner of the black leather bench seat, smacked Killian on the leg and gestured toward David. *You can still telepath with him and the rest of your pack?*

Yes. Why? Killian looked confused for a second before a look of understanding covered his face. *Right.* He pressed his lips together and let out a slow breath. *You can't communicate telepathically with your coven anymore. Shit. I'm sorry...*

"Hey, Boss!" David shouted from the driver's seat. "Christina has been looking for you all day." He caught Sadie's gaze briefly in the rearview mirror before looking back at Killian. "I think she's kinda pissed. She's been up Ivan's ass all day trying to find you."

Sadie fought the surge of jealousy that reared its ugly head and looked out the window, trying to act like she was totally uninterested. She had a feeling David brought up Christina more for her benefit than Killian's. He could have telepathed that information, so saying it out loud was totally for her benefit. He wanted to see what her reaction would be, so she didn't give him one. The men in Killian's pack probably knew there was more than a business relationship between Sadie and their prince. Shit. The scent of arousal practically clung to both of them, and it was so strong, a human could probably pick up on it.

She tried to calm the swirl of nerves in her gut, tapping her knuckles on the window and watching the New York City nightlife whiz past. Because she and Killian were bloodmates, her coven had been accepting enough of the thought of Sadie and Killian together, more so than she had even been herself. But what the hell would the wolves say about it? Probably nothing good. Wonderful, she thought with a roll of her eyes. She'd hoped to navigate her involvement with Killian without interference from the Werewolf Society. Not likely.

Damn it.

"I know, David." Killian sighed. Sadie gritted her teeth but kept staring out the window. "Christina's been texting me all day."

"Texting you?" David scoffed and turned onto Broadway. "I thought she would have been in your freaking head all day long. The woman is seriously tenacious."

"Yeah," Killian said absently. "You would think that, wouldn't you?"

"You got it, Boss."

Killian? Sensing his unease, Sadie turned in her

seat to face him. Based on the somewhat sick look on his face, she had a feeling she knew exactly what had caused it. *You never heard her today, did you?*

No. Killian shook his head, confirming what Sadie suspected. *Actually, come to think of it, I've only telepathed today with David.*

Good. Sadie tried to suppress a smile and lifted one shoulder before looking out the window again. She knew she shouldn't celebrate the fact that Killian's telepathy was limited because of the bloodmate stuff, but at least she felt like the playing field had been evened. *I'll be honest. I'm not crazy about the idea of Christina, or any other woman, being in your head.*

Neither am I. Killian countered, his sexy baritone tickling her from the inside out. *The only woman I want in my head, or anywhere else on my body, is you.*

Easy there, big guy. Sadie shot a glance in his direction. *Let's take this one step at a time.*

We may not have the luxury of time. Killian's tone changed to one of caution, which made all of the alarm bells in Sadie's head clang in warning. *I was planning to wait before I spoke to my father about what's happening between us, but circumstances may force that discussion sooner rather than later. If members of the society cannot reach me via telepathy...*

Your father? Panic gathered in Sadie's chest and she shot him a warning look. *Killian, this thing, whatever it is, is only temporary.*

No it's not. Killian pressed his lips together and shook his head playfully before looking out the window. *I've already told my sister, Naomi, about you. She's dying to meet you.*

Your sister? I didn't even know you had a sister to tell. Sadie's mental voice squeaked, betraying her nerves. *Jesus, Killian. This is getting out of control. We're not committing to a bloodmate bond—we can't. There's no reason your father or anyone else has to know about our sex life—or possible sex life. Our business is just that. It's our business.*

Sadie. Killian reached across the seat and took her hand in his. The warmth of his flesh swiftly engulfed hers, reminding her of what bathing in the glow of the sun felt like. *You and I both know that what's happening between us is anything but temporary.*

Gathering her hand in his was a remarkably disarming gesture that warmed her heart even more than her flesh. Her belly quivered while she stared into those kind caramel eyes, and she was terrified by her own emotions. Being sexually attracted to Killian was something she could deal with. After two centuries, sex wasn't a big deal. The tug in her chest, however, the one that clenched tighter with each moment of tenderness he displayed, that was another story entirely. The prospect of an emotional entanglement was far more terrifying than being unable to keep her bloodlust in check.

No, we don't, Killian. We have no idea what could or will happen. Actually, that's not true. We do know that your father and the rest of your people would never in a million years accept a vampire for their queen. And that's working under the assumption that I even want to attempt that lifestyle adjustment. Sadie slipped her hand from his grasp and leveled a deadly serious look in his direction. *It took me a long time to accept who and what I am. I'm not going to grovel in front of your parents*

and beg for their approval or something. I'm a vampire,
Killian. That will never change.

I know that. A sad smile played over Killian's lips.
He clasped his hands in his lap and let out a slow breath.
I will respect your wishes. I won't discuss our relation-
ship with my father, if that's what you really want—at
least not yet. However, I do plan on telling him that I'm
relinquishing my place in line for the throne.

Sadie's mouth fell open in stunned silence. For the
first time in her two centuries, she was actually speechless. Killian was planning to give up the throne for her?

The car came to a stop at the curb in front of the club,
and David got out of the car, leaving them alone.

"You don't even know me," Sadie whispered,
her eyes searching his for some kind of explanation.
"Killian, this is crazy."

"No," Killian murmured. "But I know enough to
know that I want to learn more. I want to discover everything there is to know about you, Sadie. From finding
out what music you love to figuring out what makes
you laugh. That smile of yours, the one that lights up a
room—I need to know what I can do to make sure I see
it every day for the rest of my life. I have no interest in
being king if I can't have you for my queen."

Still not entirely sure she'd heard him correctly,
Sadie stared at Killian with pure disbelief. She had a
million questions running through her head, but before
she could ask any of them, David opened the car door
and the sounds of the city flooded the space.

"Let's go," Killian said quietly. "We need to get
those samples from the foreman before he leaves."

"Oh, right." Sadie blinked and shook her head,

having completely forgotten why the hell they had come there in the first place. "The samples for Xavier," she said absently.

Killian offered her his hand and helped her from the limo, which made her feel surprisingly ladylike, even in her torn jeans and combat boots. Sadie was many things—tough, smart, capable, and tenacious—but she never really thought of herself as ladylike or sexy. Yet somehow Killian could make her feel like a desirable woman, instead of a scrappy, independent fighter.

Removing her hand from his far larger one, she captured his smiling gaze and realized that she felt positively delicate around him. How bizarre was that? Sadie could kick butt with the best of them, and except for silver, she was impervious to real injury from weapons. Like most vampires, she was a killing machine and tough as nails. Yet around Killian, she felt almost fragile.

"What do you think?" Killian asked with a broad smile and a sweeping gesture toward the building. "Is it too much?"

Sadie almost laughed out loud because even though he was talking about the sign for the club, she was still thinking about him. Tearing her eyes from his, she turned her attention to the massive signage that hung above the gleaming surface of the building. The front of the club was polished black granite that glittered in the light of the streetlamps, reminding her of a starry night. Hanging above the silver and black doors was an enormous sign that said "The Loup Garou." The scrolled lettering was a brilliant, deep shade of cobalt blue, and looming behind it was the image of a luminous, electric full moon.

Slipping her hands in the back pockets of her jeans,

Sadie nodded her approval and elbowed Killian in the ribs. "Not bad and not at all subtle."

"Does that mean you like it?" he asked, folding his arms over his broad chest as he stood by her side, appraising it along with her. "And for the record, calling your club The Coven isn't exactly subtle either."

"Touché, my friend." Sadie squinted and moved closer to the slick granite that covered the front of the building. Upon closer inspection, she saw a design carved into the stone. She ran her fingertips along the cool surface, and sure enough, there were grooves. She was about to ask him what it was, when lights flickered and the design came to life. "Whoa."

Sadie stepped back to take in the full sight and a smile bloomed slowly across her face. The front of the building no longer looked like some boring, old club in New York City. Instead of glittering granite, the front of the Loup Garou looked like a moonlit forest. Even the doors were incorporated into the design, and instead of plain, old doors, they looked like the entrance to a path through the trees.

"This is absolutely beautiful," Sadie whispered. She barely noticed the humans who were gathering on the sidewalk to check out the stunning artwork. "I can't believe I haven't heard about this from anyone. It's… amazing. I mean, it looks like I could step right into that forest. Jeez, Killian. If the outside looks like this, what the hell does it look like inside?"

"A mess, actually," he said with a laugh. "I wanted to get the outside finished so we could generate some buzz. You haven't heard about it because tonight is the first night I lit it up." Killian inched closer and lowered his voice to conspiratorial tones. "I wanted you to be among the first to see it."

"Me?" Snapping her head toward him, Sadie's heart clenched in her chest as she captured Killian's stare. "Why me? I mean, I'm your competitor."

"You are many things, Sadie," Killian said slowly. "You are smart, beautiful, a savvy businesswoman, a devoted coven member, and tough as steel. I wanted you to see it first. I value and respect your opinion, because unlike most other people in my life, you won't feel obliged to lie to me and tell me you like it if you don't. Your honesty, though it's sometimes painful, is one of your most endearing traits." His gaze flicked over the length of her body so swiftly and surely that she practically felt his eyes on her. Dropping his voice to barely above a whisper, he leaned closer. "Tonight, after David and Ivan are sent on their way, I'll show you what other qualities of yours I *admire*."

Sadie's body hummed and desire burned brighter with each passing second. Terrified she'd lose her head and maul him right there on the sidewalk, she stepped back abruptly and shoved her hands in her pockets again. She moved toward the front doors, her stare affixed firmly to his. "Let's see if what you've got inside is as snazzy as what's on the outside."

Turning on her heels, Sadie almost tripped over her own feet when she spotted David holding the door open. She'd completely forgotten the guy was standing there and likely watching her interaction with Killian. She practically groaned with embarrassment while moving past him and into the Loup Garou.

Once over the threshold, Sadie stopped short. Killian

hadn't been kidding. It was a mess. As she let out a low whistle, the door clanked shut behind them with a sound that echoed through the cavernous space of the club. At the moment, actually, it wasn't a club. It was a construction site that would eventually be a club. The most unique feature of the large, open space was the balcony that ran all the way around the massive room.

"Are you going to have VIP tables up there?" Sadie asked, pointing up to the balcony. "Or will it be solely for dancing and observing other dancers?"

"Both." Killian went to a table at the center of the room that was laden with papers. He waved her over and opened the blueprints before showing her the club concept. "The bar will be over here along the far right wall, and tables will be sprinkled throughout the club, essentially surrounding the dance floor. The DJ booth will be up there, at the center of the balcony and directly across from the main entrance. There are four stairways that lead up to the balcony, as well as two emergency exits that lead out to back stairwells. They empty out into the alleys on either side of the building."

Sadie nodded and inched closer to him. His large hands splayed out on the paper, and she tried not to think about those strong, talented fingers of his. Watching him run his forefinger along the blueprints, she couldn't help but recall how it felt to have those fingers running over her.

While he spoke, Sadie stole a peek at Killian's strong profile. She didn't think she could find him any more attractive than she already did. With the stubble-covered chin and the wavy hair that barely brushed the collar of his blazer, the guy was hot. Add the intense passion and focus he exhibited when talking about his business, and he was downright irresistible. Killian was driven, intense, intelligent, and passionate, and he possessed a confidence that was just a hair shy of arrogant.

"My office is back here," he said, jutting a thumb to his left. Sadie tried not to pay attention to the enticing heat that radiated from his body, but good luck with that. Clearing her throat, she nodded and turned her focus back to his blueprints. "The entrance to the kitchen is in that far left corner. Even though a bank of tables will surround the dance floor, I'm going to have a cluster of tables on the left side. The tables and chairs will be from my family's furniture company. It's all rustic wood and handmade. The walls will be a similar design to the front of the club. I want people to feel like they're in the Alaskan woods at night." Taking a deep breath, he turned and peered at her intently. "So, what do you think?"

"I have to hand it to you." Sadie made a sweeping gesture with one hand and smiled. "This place is going to be unique."

"Unique?" Killian narrowed his eyes and pointed at her. "That's not code for crappy, is it?"

"No." Sadie laughed. "Definitely not. Unique is good. Listen, Killian, there are hundreds of joints in this city, and it's really tough to find a new spin on an old business. You just may have done it."

"So I've impressed you, Ms. Pemberton?" he asked with a lopsided grin. Lowering his head, he murmured, "I'd say that bodes well for the rest of our evening."

David cleared his throat from his position by the door, reminding them both of his presence. Sadie stepped back, increasing the distance between her and Killian, who shot an irritated look at his friend. Killian opened his mouth to say something, but they were interrupted when three humans emerged from the swinging door that led to the kitchen.

"The kitchen is just about done, Mr. Bane." A rotund fellow hitched up his pants while he approached. Since the other two men followed, Sadie assumed the big guy in front was the foreman. "The appliances are installed and in working order."

"Thank you." Killian shot a glance at Sadie. *This is the one.* "Before you leave, I'd like to ask you a question about something. Join me in my office."

"Sure thing." Mike wiped his sweaty brow with a filthy-looking handkerchief from his back pocket. "You guys go on. I'll see you back here tomorrow morning."

The two other men, dirty and clearly exhausted, waved wordlessly before leaving. Sadie didn't miss the nervous energy that exuded from the humans as they went past David and out the door. Perhaps they simply sensed something different about him.

Leaving David to guard the front door, Sadie followed Killian and Mike to the back of the club and into Killian's office. Shutting the door tightly behind her, Sadie turned around and caught Killian's eye as he gave her a slight nod. *He's all yours.*

"So, what's up?" Mike asked. Sweat beaded on his upper lip as he stood in the unfurnished office in between Killian and Sadie. He fiddled with the clipboard in his hands and thrummed his fingers on it nervously. "You're happy with the paint job and the carpeting, aren't you?"

A swirl of excitement curled in Sadie's belly as she

moved closer to the human. Some vampires—Olivia, for example—weren't fond of glamouring humans, but Sadie had to admit that she loved it. It was an intense experience to push her way into someone's mind and peel away the bullshit to get to the core of who they were.

Once she was about a foot away, she met Mike's pale gray stare with hers and pushed her mind into his. Like a hot knife through butter, Sadie entered the human's feeble consciousness with her far stronger one. The instant she linked her mind to his, the man's rotund body went limp. Swaying on his feet and with his mouth hanging open like a fish out of water, Mike drifted into the coma-like state of the glamour.

"You're safe, Mike." Sadie continued talking, keeping her voice soft and melodic, while she removed the specimen bag and tube from her back pockets. "I just need to get some of your hair. Can you pull out some strands and put them in this bag for me? It's okay. You won't feel any pain."

Mike nodded wordlessly and did as Sadie asked. She held the bag open for him and flicked her gaze to Killian, standing silently behind the human. Looming large, he watched with rapt fascination as Sadie worked her magic.

"Thank you, Mike." Sadie sealed the bag and stuck it in her back pocket. "Now open your mouth." Making quick work of getting a saliva sample, she tucked the swab back in the tube and secured it. "That's wonderful, thank you."

"You're welcome," Mike mumbled. The faraway look in his eyes didn't waver, and the man's breathing remained calm and steady.

"I want to ask you a question, Mike." Sadie lowered her voice further and looked past him, her gaze latching with Killian's. A smile curved her lips and that swirl of excitement in her belly ratcheted up a notch as she stared into Killian's heated gaze. "Do you believe in vampires or werewolves? Are you a familiar?"

"No." Mike let out a snort of derision and his meaty body swayed toward Sadie. "That's a lot of crap."

"Good." Sadie winked at Killian. *He's definitely not a familiar.* Placing both hands on the human's shoulders, Sadie met his gaze and pushed further into his mind. "When the door opens, you'll remember being in the office with Mr. Bane. He told you what a fine job you've been doing and that he loves the way his office came out."

"Fine job." Mike sighed, and half a smile cracked his pudgy red face.

Sadie walked backward toward the door, with her eyes set on Killian's. Curling her fingers around the brass knob, she opened the door and said, "Time to wake up, Mike."

The foreman woke from the glamour with a huge grin and spun around to face Killian.

"Thank you so much, Mr. Bane." Mike grabbed Killian's hand and gave him an enthusiastic handshake. The expression on Killian's face was nothing short of amused. "I am so happy that you're pleased. I promise you we are on track to open one month from today. We just have to finish up the main room and the balcony."

"That's fantastic news." Killian clapped the man on the shoulder and gestured toward the door. "Come on, Mike. I'll walk you out."

Now it looks like you're the one who's impressed.

Sadie couldn't help but feel completely satisfied with herself, and there was no stopping the smile on her face as she followed them back out to the front. She wasn't sure which she enjoyed more: the way Killian had looked at her while she glamoured the human, or the fact that she had done something that only a vampire could do. Being a vampire might have certain limitations, but there was no denying the perks.

Killian spoke quietly with David near the door after Mike left, and Sadie lingered by the table with the blueprints. She heard the front door open and close and didn't have to look up to know that David was gone, which meant she and Killian were alone.

"Where'd your friend go?" Her stomach fluttered in anticipation as she heard Killian approach with slow, sure steps. "Did you give him the rest of the night off?"

"Yes." His heavy steps echoed through the room, and he removed his jacket as he strode toward her. He draped it over the folding chair at the end of the table, and that cheeky grin spread across his handsome face. "I believe he has plans to meet up with your DJ."

"So you know about him and Justine?" She pushed aside the papers before hoisting herself onto the table, nibbling her lower lip. "You don't have a problem with it?"

"Why would I?" Killian tilted his head and cast her a confused look. "What he does with his personal life is his own business. I don't care who he sleeps with."

"What about that Ivan guy?" Sadie challenged.

Two steps closer.

"I don't care who he sleeps with either," Killian countered.

"Very funny." Holding Killian's burning stare, Sadie swung her combat-boot-clad feet back and forth and braced her hands on the table on either side of her hips. She gripped the edge of the table in an effort to retain control. She was afraid she'd strip off her clothes and beg him to take her right there on the table. She might be his bloodmate, but shouldn't she play a little hard to get?

"What I meant was, is Ivan as willing to look the other way as David? One of your security team members is banging a vampire. I can't imagine that's following protocol."

While Sadie tried to keep her fangs at bay, Killian walked over and stood in between her legs. She sat up taller but didn't let go of the table, even though the heat of his enticing body was wickedly inviting. She wasn't sure what to do or say, other than hold his stare, so she decided to let him make the next move.

"I don't care about protocol either."

"What do you care about?" Sadie asked bluntly. Arching one eyebrow, she studied him closely and watched for his reactions. "I mean aside from this club. You don't seem to care about much. Not your parents' approval. Not the throne. So tell me, Killian Bane." Sadie lowered her voice to just above a whisper. "What do you care about? What matters?"

"You," Killian murmured. Inching closer, he curled his large, warm hands over her jean-covered thighs. Pulling her legs farther apart, he tugged her butt to the edge of the table. The sudden movement made her gasp. Her hands flew to his waist and clung to him for dear life. Killian's eyes widened in response and his fingers gripped her thighs tighter. Dipping his head low, he brushed his stubbly cheek over hers and kissed her earlobe, his warm breath puffing over her neck. "Getting to know you, Sadie. That's what matters."

A lock of his hair drifted against her forehead, his mouth hovering an inch from hers. The steadily thrumming beat of his heart called to her like a beacon. With the pace of his breathing increasing and the heat of his body surrounding her, Sadie's last ounce of restraint evaporated. In a blur, she captured his lips with hers and held on. Killian's tongue slid between the seam, and Sadie opened to him eagerly. He lifted her legs and tugged her against him as he suckled and plundered.

Breaking the kiss, Killian trailed his lips down her throat. Sadie wrapped her legs around him, holding him to her. A desperate moan escaped her parted lips as her head fell back, giving him unfettered access. Needing to get closer and wanting to feel his flesh against hers, Sadie tugged his shirttails free from his pants and groaned when her fingertips met the skin of his lower back. Cradling her neck with one hand, he lifted his head and kissed her deeply. He rocked his hips against her, and Sadie moaned as the rigid length of his cock found her most sensitive spot.

Heat fired over her skin, sending her desire for Killian over the edge and her bloodlust into overdrive. Her fangs burst free and Sadie gasped, immediately breaking the kiss with Killian. Movement across the room captured her attention and brought everything to a screeching halt. With the fog of lust clouding her senses, it took her a moment to realize they were no longer alone.

Three figures loomed in the shadow of the doorway, along with three pairs of glowing amber eyes. She recognized two of them instantly—the smaller one was Christina and the man to her right was Ivan. The taller figure in the back, however, the one whose face was hidden in the shadows, wasn't completely clear.

At least…not at first.

Panic swelled in her chest and she immediately stiffened in Killian's arms when she realized who the other man was. Sensing the sudden change in her demeanor, Killian stopped nuzzling her breast and lifted his head, giving her a quizzical look. Trapped somewhere between horrified and mortified, Sadie swallowed the urge to shrink into a corner and vanish. She jutted her chin toward the door as she dropped her legs from around Killian's waist and tugged her hands from beneath his shirt.

Breathless and looking entirely disheveled by lust, Killian snapped his head toward the door, a growl rumbling in his chest. Standing to his full height, he released Sadie and turned around to face the intruders. Sadie smoothed her hair and straightened out her shirt while Killian remained in a protective stance in front of her.

Letting out a beleaguered sigh, Killian slipped his hands in his pockets and said, "Hello, Father."

Chapter 12

"I TOLD YOU HE'D LOST HIS MIND," CHRISTINA HISSED. She started toward them, tossing her long, blond hair over one shoulder, but Ivan grabbed her around the waist, preventing her from coming any closer. "How dare you humiliate me like this, Killian?"

"*You're* humiliated?" Sadie asked with more than a little sarcasm. Peering out from behind Killian, Sadie became the focus of Christina's furious, burning gaze. "How exactly is any of this about you?"

"Watching him run around this disgusting city chasing after you is a complete insult." Christina shoved herself out of Ivan's embrace and adjusted her expensive suit jacket and skirt. "Everyone knows that Killian is going to mate with me, and yet here he is, wasting his time whoring around with you. A filthy vampire slut."

"Oh no, she didn't," Sadie seethed. "She did *not* just call me a slut."

She wanted to fly across the room and rip Christina's pretty blond hair out of her head, but she didn't. Losing her cool would be the worst possible move at the moment. Flicking her attention to Killian, she sensed tension in his body but also picked up on his restraint. She desperately tried to emulate it.

"That's enough." The king's clear, strong, and decisive voice cut through the club.

Stepping out of the shadows of the doorway, he

moved past Ivan and Christina with all of the regal grace
one would expect of a king. The two of them bowed
their heads and took a step backward, giving way for
their leader. Wearing a pristine charcoal-gray pin-
striped suit with a pressed white shirt and a cobalt blue
tie, he looked like the usual wealthy tycoon so easily
found here in the city. The only difference was the air of
absolute power the man exuded.

Power and confidence—just like Killian.

She'd met King Heinrich once before, about a year
ago, and he still looked exactly the same. He was a bit
grayer at the temples and possessed a few more lines on
his face, but all in all, he looked very much like his son.
Werewolves might not be immortal, but they aged far
slower than humans.

"What are you doing here?" Killian asked in a surprisingly calm tone. "I wasn't expecting you and Mother
to visit until the club opened next month."

"Your mother did not accompany me on this trip."
The king flicked a dark, intense gaze at Sadie and his
eyes narrowed. "If she had, I'm quite sure she wouldn't
have appreciated walking in on you and...*your friend*.
The poor woman may well have passed out."

Friend? Sadie touched Killian's mind sharply. *Right.
He doesn't want me to be your "friend."*

Let me handle it. Killian shot back.

"You didn't answer my question, Father." Killian
tucked his shirt in while he spoke. "Why are you here?"

"I received a phone call after your outing at that
vampire club last night. Apparently, you and this young
lady disappeared together for quite some time. They
were concerned that you'd lost your focus, the reason

you're here. Given how important you are to the future of our race, they thought it would be best if I paid a visit."

"They?" Killian asked with a growl edging his voice.

"Yes." King Heinrich clasped his hands in front of him and leveled that powerful stare at Sadie. "Ivan and Christina. Christina expressed her fears to Ivan and apparently he concurred. I was willing to allow you some freedom to live and work here so you could sow the last of your wild oats. I also hoped it would help strengthen our relationship with the vampires." His brows lifted. "This is not quite the tactic I had in mind."

"Father—"

"I'm not finished." King Heinrich didn't raise his voice, but his meaning was clear. "I had hoped that this added responsibility would serve as a good training ground before you assume the throne on your thirty-fifth birthday."

"I see," Killian said evenly.

"Based on what I've just witnessed, I'd say they were correct in their assumptions about your interest in this woman." King Heinrich moved closer while keeping his sights on Sadie. "I know I told you to learn more about the vampires, but I don't see how dalliances like this will help us. Tell me, Killian…why would spending time with this woman be of importance?"

"I told you, Your Highness," Christina simpered. A smug, satisfied look covered her heavily made-up face. "It's just like I said. Killian has completely lost his focus. I mean look at this place," she sputtered. "There's no way it will open in a month. He's wasting his time and our money."

"You are dismissed." King Heinrich, who seemed visibly annoyed by Christina's interruption, waved them off without looking back. "Ivan, take Christina back to her hotel. She and her ladies will be coming back to Alaska with me tomorrow."

Christina started to protest, but Ivan leaned down and whispered something in her ear. Whatever it was, it made the woman go silent, that smug, shit-eating grin reappearing on her face. Fury crawled up Sadie's back while she simultaneously fought the urge to flash that bitch her fangs.

"While you're at it, Ivan, you can go ahead and pack your shit too." Killian's hands curled into fists at his side. "I'll expect your room to be empty before I return to the penthouse. You're fired."

"As you wish," Ivan said tightly. He bowed his head, grabbed Christina by the hand, and disappeared out the door.

"You are the future king of the Werewolf Society. Do you really think it's wise to fire half of your security team?" King Heinrich turned abruptly to Sadie, and in spite of her bravado, she went absolutely still. "You look familiar." A sad smile played at the king's lips and he took a deep breath, as though carefully choosing his words. "If I'm not mistaken, I met you last year during my meeting with the czars. What is your name?"

A combination of fear and uncertainty whirled through Sadie's gut like that Tasmanian Devil from those old cartoons. How much should she admit to? What was she supposed to say to this guy? Saying too much could single-handedly cock up the treaty with the wolves in about thirty seconds. She shot a glance at Killian, trying to get a bead on where he was with all this. So far, he wasn't giving her much to work with. She still wasn't entirely sure what was happening between her and Killian, or where it was going, so how could she possibly explain it to the king?

"This isn't about *her*," Killian interjected in a cold, flat tone. He didn't even spare Sadie a glance, keeping his eyes on his father. If she had a heartbeat…it would have stopped. He seemed so totally dismissive of her, acting like she wasn't even in the room. "You're here to see me, so leave her out of it."

Her? Was this a fucking joke?

Sadie tried to touch his mind with hers but was met with an impenetrable wall—the son of a bitch had shut her out. She knew the sensation all too well from past fights with her sisters. What the hell was Killian doing? Why would he close his mind to her now? Why act so callous and cold? If he really wanted to be with her, wouldn't he gather her in his arms and stand by her side? Why was he—?

Tears pricked the back of her eyes as one answer filled her head—because being with her wasn't really about her. Not at all. Her wide eyes drifted between Killian and his father as the pieces came together. Killian didn't want to participate in the life of a royal— she knew that from his blood memories—and he didn't want to be king. And what better way to get out of it than to tell his old man he was going to mate with a vampire?

That deep ache in her chest, the one that made her feel empty and hollow, the one she felt when her family died, throbbed as the cold, hard truth settled inside her like ice.

Had Killian been using her?

Sadie almost laughed out loud at her foolishness. For a moment, for just a moment, she'd actually allowed herself to feel and to entertain the notion that maybe she could have something more with Killian.

What. A. Fool.

"My name is Sadie Pemberton." Sadie hopped off the table and stood next to Killian, forcing herself not to cry. She might have been embarrassed, but she'd be damned if she was going to hide behind him—or anyone else. These wolves were about to see what two centuries of survival could do to a girl. "I'm the new owner of The Coven, and, yes, you and I met at the Presidium offices here in the city."

"I see." King Heinrich looked her up and down with an expression that she couldn't quite decipher. His narrowed gaze lingered on the rips in her jeans before locking his eyes with hers once again. "I'm sure you can understand Christina and Ivan's discomfort regarding your dalliance with my son."

"Father, there is something I need to tell you."

"Silence." King Heinrich held up one hand and didn't look away from Sadie. "I'll deal with you in a moment. What is the nature of your interest in my son?"

The nature of her interest? Love? Lust? Friendship? Fun? Bloodmate? Partner? All of those words, among others, rolled through her head, and every one held far more meaning than the word she finally chose to utter.

"Sex," Sadie said with a casual shrug. "That's it. I'm a vampire, King Heinrich. I've been around for over two centuries, and sex isn't a big deal. Killian and I are both adults. It's just about sex."

"Is that so?" He arched one eyebrow and smiled.

"Yes." Sadie let out a short laugh. "I know how what you saw here looked… Well, let's be honest. It looked pretty bad. You caught your boy, the heir to the throne, in a compromising position with a vampire. Namely me." She jutted a thumb at her chest before sticking her hands in the back pockets of her jeans. "But you have nothing to worry about. It didn't mean anything."

"Sadie…" Killian said her name with an almost warning tone.

"Relax," she said abruptly. She looked Killian up and down. "I get it." She turned her calm gaze to the king. "I know that you're only here because you love your son, and you want what's best for him and for your people. You don't have to be concerned."

"Why not?" Heinrich folded his arms over his chest and seemed genuinely interested in her answer. "Why shouldn't I be concerned?"

Sadie swallowed the lump in her throat and forced herself not to look at Killian. She could feel his eyes on her. Even though she wanted to scream the truth, Sadie looked the king dead in the face and lied her ever-loving ass off.

"We had a fling, but it's done." Sadie curled her fingers around the specimen bags in her back pocket and fought the flood of tears that threatened to bubble up. Keeping her voice steady, she squared her shoulders. "I know Killian's future includes being king of the Werewolf Society, even if he's doing his best to sabotage that. I won't be a distraction for him anymore."

"So you don't wish to be queen?" the king asked quietly.

"Queen?" Sadie practically choked on the word and let out an incredulous laugh. "Yeah, right. A vampire queen for the Werewolf Society. I'm a vampire, Your Highness." Unable to bring herself to look at Killian, she dropped her voice to just above a whisper. "I cannot change who or what I am. Neither can Killian. I am a vampire and I always will be."

"Well, this has been quite enlightening," the king said with a wide smile to both of them. The smile faltered as he clasped his hands tightly in front of him and peered intently at Sadie. His brown eyes crinkled at the corners and his voice hovered somewhere around wistful. "What on earth would happen if the future king of the werewolves were to mate with a *vampire*?"

"I'm sorry you had to make a trip all the way out here." Sadie started for the door and spoke as though the sun was coming up and she was about to get fried. "Now, if you'll excuse me, I have to get back to the Presidium's offices."

"Sadie, wait!"

"There's nothing left to say, Killian." Sadie stopped by the door and curled her fingers around the knob. Glancing over her shoulder, she said, "We had our fun, Your Highness. I'd say it's time we get back to reality and down to business. Let's be honest. This thing between us never had a future. Not really."

Without waiting for a response, Sadie ran out the front door of the club. She turned the corner of the building and stumbled into the dark safety of the alley. Pressing her body against the rough, cool stone of the wall, she squeezed her eyes shut in an attempt to stem the flow of tears. It was no use. A loud sob escaped her lips before she shot up into the night sky like a bullet. With the sounds of the city surrounding her, she whisked through the darkness and let the tears fall. Like the silly young girl she once was, Sadie had allowed herself to believe in fairy tales. Tonight, reality had come crashing back in.

Bloodmate legend or not, Killian would never and could never be hers.

"You bastard." Never in his life had Killian spoken back to his father with such outright fury. He knew he was crossing a line but he didn't care. The wounded look on Sadie's face was more than he could take. He wanted to tell his father exactly who Sadie was and how much she meant to him, but he'd promised her he wouldn't discuss it with his father yet. Respecting her wishes hurt a hell of a lot more than he thought it would. "How could you speak to her that way?"

His father moved closer, standing eye to eye with his son. A deep, guttural growl rumbled in his barrel chest, his eyes glowing a burning shade of orange. For a moment, Killian thought his father was going to strike him. Instead, his father studied him closely and invaded his son's personal space with ease. The king was pushing him, daring him to back up, but Killian held his ground. It was the first time in his life he didn't back down from the king.

"The better question, Son," Heinrich said with a sad smile, stepping away from his son, "is why did you let me?"

"What?" Killian blinked as though his father had struck him.

"You heard me." King Heinrich let out a sigh and unbuttoned his jacket, the formality he'd been displaying swiftly dissipating. "Why did you let me speak to her in such a way if she is so important to you?"

"I—I don't understand." Killian shook his head and stared at his father in total disbelief.

"Do you really think I've been king for seventy-five years just because of my good looks?" Heinrich smirked at his son before slipping his hands in his pockets. "Your sister, Naomi, was with me when I received the call from Ivan. She overheard the entire conversation because apparently the dear girl thinks nothing of eavesdropping. At any rate, she told me that you had found the woman who bears the mark of the moon, the one you've dreamed about for so long."

"I thought you didn't believe in that 'hogwash.'" Killian leaned on the edge of the table, totally stunned by his father's revelation.

"Your mother does," the king said, smiling. "As you know, I have a very difficult time disagreeing with your mother. She informed me that if I didn't allow you the chance to explore your relationship with this woman, I was not going to see the inside of our bedchamber for many moons."

"Got it." Killian held up one hand, begging his father not to go any further with that line of thought. His father was an alpha in every sense of the word, but even alphas had weaknesses. "If you knew who Sadie was, then why didn't you say something? Why did you go on like that?"

"I didn't know what Sadie knew or didn't know. I had no idea if you'd spoken to her about the mark or your dreams." The king walked the perimeter of the room, looking up at the balcony. "She, however, was quite forthcoming. In spite of her denials, she obviously cares for you. I suspect she said what she did to protect you."

"Protect me?" Killian scoffed. "From what?"

"Political turmoil?" He waved his hand dismissively. "She's the progeny of one of the czars. I'm sure she doesn't want to rock the boat between our races."

"That's ridiculous." Killian squared his shoulders. "Olivia already knows about our involvement."

"I see." King Heinrich stilled. "Then what other reason could she have for saying what she said?" Killian stared at his father and irritation crawled up his back when a slow smile cracked the king's face. "You still have quite a bit to learn about women, my boy."

"What are you talking about, Father?"

"That young woman essentially threw herself on her sword and absolved you of any further entanglements with her." He folded his hands in front of him. "She believes that you don't care for her and that you were only using her to try and sabotage your place in line for the throne."

"Holy shit," Killian seethed. Running both hands over his face, he let out a growl of frustration. "I'm such an idiot."

"No, my son." His father laughed. "The heart, among other parts of the anatomy, has a funny way of making us say and do idiotic things. Why didn't you speak up and defend her?"

"I was trying to respect her wishes." Killian let out a beleaguered sigh and ran both hands through his hair, knowing he'd fucked it up. "Shit. It's complicated, Father. Far more than you would suspect."

"Of that I have no doubt. I tried to telepath to you but your mind has been closed to me for some time. Not that I can blame you." He stopped by the front door and an awkward silence hung in the air, filling the seemingly widening space between them. "I know you are reluctant to be king."

Killian opened his mouth to explain why he hadn't been able to speak with him telepathically, but his father held up one hand and shook his head.

"It's ironic. Your late brother, Horace, was poisoned and twisted by his hunger for power, and you, the one who can have it, are running from it like you're being chased by a silver bullet." He strode across the room slowly, closing the distance between them. "Listen to me, Killian. I will allow you to run your club and explore your feelings for Ms. Pemberton without any further interference from me or anyone else in the society. In fact, I will even reach out to the czar and let her know that I'm aware of your *interactions* with Sadie. In return, you must promise me that no matter what happens, you will remain open to the possibility of taking the throne. A great deal can change over five years."

"That's it?" Killian looked at his father warily. "You're just going to give me your blessing to mate with Sadie."

"That's not what I said." King Heinrich's voice remained steady and strong. "You still have five years until you are to assume the throne, and for now…I will not interfere with your personal life. We will revisit things in five years."

"Nothing will change, Father." Killian remained resolute. "If you want me to take the throne, then you'll have to take Sadie too."

"Things can change, my son."

"Sadie won't. She will not change what she is." Killian spoke slowly and clearly, wanting his father to hear every word. "In five years, she will still be a vampire."

"Like I said…a great deal can happen in five years."

"I love her, you know."

"Perhaps you should tell her that last part and not me." The king slapped his son on the arm and pulled him in for a rare hug. In that moment, Killian once again felt like the young boy who'd idolized his larger-than-life father. Pulling back, Heinrich smiled at his son. He gave him a playful smack on the cheek before walking to the door. "See you soon, my son."

"That's it?" Killian asked. "You're leaving?"

"Yes." His father buttoned his jacket and that weary look came over his face again. "The jet is at JFK waiting to take us back to Anchorage, and I think we'll leave tonight. Your mother will be pleasantly surprised," he said with a wink.

"One last thing." Killian ran his hand through his hair. "I want to buy out the general."

"You can't."

Killian opened his mouth to argue but his father cut him off.

"He's already sold his shares to me."

"Thank God," Killian said with a heavy breath. "Does Christina know that?"

"No." Killian's father cast his son a sly grin.

"Thank you, Your Highness," Killian said, bowing in deference to the king.

"You are most welcome." Giving Killian a wide grin, Heinrich opened the door and cast one serious look at his son. "Five years, Killian."

"Will I see you at the opening of the club?"

"Yes! Your mother and sister and I will be back for the grand opening." Letting out a low whistle, the king gave one last look around and muttered, "Better work fast."

As the door shut behind his father, Killian couldn't have agreed more. Only, he wasn't thinking about the club. He immediately tried telepathing with Sadie, but as he suspected, her mind was closed to him. Damn it. He'd shut his mind earlier to her because he didn't want to risk his father overhearing, even though it seemed he had nothing to worry about.

Unsure where she would have gone and not willing to waste any time, he yanked his phone out of his pocket. He called the one person who was sure to know where she was. He just hoped he wouldn't wake up the baby.

Chapter 13

Sadie had barely stopped crying since flying out of the Loup Garou like some scared little girl. Just when she'd get the tears under control, she'd recall the stone-cold look on Killian's face and the floodgates would open. She managed to hold it together at Xavier's lab when she dropped off the specimens, and even though her friend wanted to talk about the data he'd gotten from that watch monitor, Sadie couldn't deal with it. She had to get away and go to the one place where she could find some modicum of silence in the bustling, lively city.

In the dead of night, Central Park was one of the most serene places in Manhattan. In this city full of fluttering heartbeats, this was one spot where even a vampire could find some peace. Sadie landed silently on the grand turret of Belvedere Castle and swiped at her tearstained cheeks with the back of her hands. Looking out over the Great Lawn and the smooth waters of Turtle Pond, she closed her eyes and reveled in the warm spring breeze. The whisper of it drifted over her like a caress from Mother Nature. Her long, dark hair lifted off her shoulders and fluttered in the wind, while the sounds of the creatures in the park filled her head.

Her eyes flicked open and a wistful smile grew as she stared out at the surrounding view. From this vantage point at the top of the gray stone castle, she could see for miles. The twinkling lights of the buildings winked at her, as though telling her it would all be okay. Sure, she thought, with a roll of her eyes. Just great.

Sadie flew down to the wall of rocks along the bottom of the castle and landed on her favorite place to sit. Vista Rock, which overlooked Turtle Pond, was an oasis in the midst of the dark, gritty, and overly crowded city. Clusters of cattails grew high around the little pond, and the Great Lawn stretched out in seemingly endless waves of green. The light of the almost full moon glittered on the pond in silvery flashes, reminding Sadie of the river by that house in Arizona so many years ago.

The sound of pebbles skittering on stone captured her attention and brought Sadie to her feet in one fluid motion. She remained stone-still, ready for anything, sending her heightened senses in search of who or what was encroaching on her personal space. Another breeze whisked over Sadie, and her fangs erupted as the crisp, smoky scent of a werewolf surrounded her.

But it wasn't just any wolf.

Killian.

Sadie swore under her breath, retracted her fangs, and carefully walked down the rocks toward the edge of the water. So much for having her privacy. Sitting down, she drew her feet up and rested her arms on her knees, refusing to even look in Killian's direction. Based on the sounds of his steps, she could tell he was walking on two legs and not four.

"What do you want?" Sadie reached over to her left and picked a couple of cattails before running the brown velvety tips through her fingers. "I thought I made myself clear earlier. We had our fun, but the party's over. You got what you wanted. You pissed your old man off. Congratulations."

Ripples of heat washed over Sadie's arm as Killian moved closer, but to her surprise, he didn't respond. She plucked off the head of a cattail and flung it into the water, watching it drift on the surface. The ripples it made stretched wide across the pond and glinted in the light of the moon, giving her something to look at other than Killian.

"Are you just going to stand there staring at me?" Sadie brushed at her bare arm, wishing she'd worn a jacket. Maybe then she wouldn't feel his body heat, which seemed to heighten her intense attraction to him. *Ugh.* How annoying to feel this turned on even though she was hurt and angry. Pressing her lips together, she laced her fingers over her knees and stared out over the water. "Fine. Don't say anything. Why not, right? You were pretty fucking quiet earlier. So why should you speak up now?"

Sadie tossed the green stem of the cattail into the water and let out a scoffing sound. "You and I don't belong together, Killian. I'm not queen material. Even if I wasn't a vampire, I wouldn't be fit for a throne. I'm too rough around the edges, and I'm not one for pomp and circumstance. I prefer ripped jeans to haute couture. We just don't fit, so let's just call it a draw, okay?"

He still said nothing. What the hell?

"How did you know where to find me?" Sadie asked quietly.

Her impatience got the better of her and she finally turned to her right, planning to give him a piece of her mind. What she saw rendered her speechless. Standing in the pale light of the moon, with Belvedere Castle looming largely behind him, was Killian Bane in all his princely glory. A gentle breeze lifted the sweep of hair from his forehead, and those caramel-colored eyes glinted with flecks of gold as they peered down at her apologetically. In his hands he carried a single red rose, which he promptly extended to Sadie. The guy, quite literally, looked like Prince Charming from the fairy tales. All he needed was a horse.

"I'm sorry," he said quietly. "I called Olivia and she told me where to look for you. I know you came here to be alone and you have every right to be upset with me." Still holding the flower out to her, he bent at the knees, bringing himself almost to eye level with her. "Will you hear me out?"

Sadie tore her gaze from his and looked down at his gift, then curled her fingers around the thorn-free stem of the flower. When she brought the silky, soft bloom to her nose, her eyelids fluttered closed, and she reveled in the sweet perfume of the unexpected peace offering.

Sadie's heart ached with wanting.

She so badly wanted to accept his apology, to crawl into his arms and pick up where they left off, and yet she couldn't bring herself to do it. If it hurt this badly after only being with him once or twice, how much more hurt would she experience if she allowed herself to fall any further? Her lids flicked open and she found herself staring into a pair of familiar, warm brown eyes. The ache in her chest deepened and the familiar pain of rejection crept back in, but she shoved it aside. She nodded. "I'm listening."

"Based on what you said and the way you left, it's

clear now that you misunderstood what I was trying to do. I'm sorry I upset you, Sadie, but I was doing my best to respect your wishes." Killian held up one hand, immediately stopping any arguments. "Hang on. Right before we got out of the limo, you told me you wanted to keep this thing with us under wraps for a while. Didn't you? Weren't you the one who said you didn't want me to discuss it with my father yet?"

"Well…yes." Sadie's brow furrowed because he was absolutely right. She had said that. "But…since your father walked in on us fooling around…I thought…"

"Actually, I should be upset with you." Rising to his feet, Killian settled his hands on his narrow hips and looked out over the water. "Yup. You should be giving me flowers."

"What?" Sadie hopped to her feet and pulled Killian around so he would face her. "How am I the one who's in the wrong?"

"You left without letting me explain, and even worse than that, you called off our relationship without even discussing it with me." Killian inched closer, his tall, strong frame towering over her and filling the space around her with his powerful presence. "And… you lied."

"What?" Clenching the flower in her hand, she faced his accusation head on. "What did I lie about exactly?"

"You do care for me, Sadie." Killian brushed her long hair off her shoulder and trailed his thumb along her jawline. "You told my father that you don't love me, and we both know that's a lie. You may not love me yet, but I know you're feeling something for me. Because I feel it too. I want you physically, but it's more than that,

Sadie—and you know it. You're the first person I think about in the morning, and your face is the last one on my mind before I fall asleep."

"Killian," Sadie whispered, her lips quivering. "This is just too complicated. If Christina and Ivan caused this much trouble for us, what on earth would happen if all of your people found out? Or mine? It just can't work."

"You sure seem to say that a lot." Letting out a slow breath, he shook his head and tapped the tip of her nose with his finger. "I know I said I was sick of being surrounded by people who say 'yes' to me all the time…but you're taking this 'no' thing to the extreme."

"Because it's the truth, Killian." Sadie grasped the stem of the flower tighter and ran the velvety bloom along the tips of her fingers. Staring at the bloodred petals, she found her courage and forced herself to look him in the eyes again. "Being hot for each other is one thing. Getting involved—I mean, really getting involved with one another—is a whole other level of crazy. We would be out of our minds even to attempt it."

"Why?" Hooking his thumbs in his pockets, he stared at her and waited patiently for an answer.

"It will end badly." Sadie tapped his broad chest with the rose. "You'll hurt me or I'll hurt you, or our people will hurt each other. *Ugh.* Why on earth would you want to venture into a relationship with those kinds of risks?"

Staring at her intently, he looked like he was seriously considering what she said. A moment later, he extended his hand and cast her his charming smile, revealing that one dimple. "Walk with me?"

"Where?"

"Anywhere." Killian winked and leaned closer,

dropping his voice to a whisper. "There are two turtles staring at us from that log over there, and I want to talk to you in private."

"Well, this *is* Turtle Pond."

"Whatever. They're being nosy." Killian wiggled his fingers. "Come on."

"Oh fine." Sadie smiled in spite of herself and accepted his hand. As Killian's fingers wrapped around hers, a familiar heat spread over her skin. Smelling the rose, she peered at him over the petals. "But this better be good."

Hand in hand, they walked along the edge of the pond and continued across the Great Lawn. It felt natural to have his hand around hers, and in that moment, Sadie felt surprisingly normal. He wasn't a werewolf and she wasn't a vampire. They were simply two people walking through Central Park holding hands. It was one of the sweetest and most intimate moments of her life.

If only everything between them could be this simple all the time.

While they strolled along the moonlit expanse of grass, Killian told her about the conversation with his father that took place after she left. To say she was surprised would be a colossal understatement. Stopping along the edge of a grassy hill, Sadie reveled in the feel of her hand in his, and when she captured his serious gaze, that ache in her chest eased.

"So you're telling me that we have your father's blessing to pursue a relationship?" Sadie asked, still not believing it was true.

"He didn't give us his blessing to formally mate, no, but I'm confident that will come with time."

"And he's taking the two troublemakers back to Alaska with him and you're free to live your life here in Manhattan? Vampire girlfriend and all?"

"Well, I never said you were my *girlfriend*," Killian said dramatically. For a split second she thought he was serious, but the teasing glint in his eye quickly betrayed his intention.

"Hey." Sadie poked him in the belly and laughed as Killian put up both hands in surrender. An evil smile curved her lips when he squirmed while she poked him along the waist a few more times. "You're ticklish?"

"You should stop that," Killian said through a laugh, playfully attempting to avoid her attack. "I'm warning you."

"Why? What are you gonna do?" She laughed and stuck the stem of the rose between her teeth so she could torture him with both hands. "Where's the big, bad alpha now?" she said, the rose clenched in her mouth.

Laughing while trying to avoid the onslaught, Killian grabbed her by the wrists and dragged her body up against his. Sadie gasped, the rose tumbling from her lips as her breasts crushed against the hard planes of his chest. The beat of his heart pounded through his body and throbbed through her seductively as his eyes flickered to a deep shade of orange.

Allowing her body to melt against his, Sadie floated in the rich rush of lust that flared between them. Tangling her fingers in his, she reveled in the magnificent feel of him. This time, when her fangs begged for freedom, Sadie parted her lips and succumbed to the surge of bloodlust, allowing them to break free.

A growl rumbled around her, and she couldn't stop

staring at the devilish smile that played at Killian's lips. Loosening his hold on her wrists, he slid his hands along her arms. The whisper of flesh along flesh made Sadie moan. As she linked her arms around his neck, her lips parted. She flashed her fangs before flicking her tongue over his lower lip.

"This is going to be complicated," Sadie murmured as Killian tugged her T-shirt from the edge of her jeans. She let out a contented sigh when his heated palms rushed beneath the thin cotton fabric before cupping her breasts. Letting her head fall back, she closed her eyes and focused on the seductive feel of his talented fingers as they danced over her eager, sensitive nipples. "And it could get messy," she rasped. "I mean down and dirty, no holds barred. Messy."

"Look at me, Sadie." Killian tangled one hand in her long hair and lifted her head, forcing her to meet his hungry stare while his other hand paid thorough attention to her breast. Flicking the lacy fabric aside, he rolled her nipple between his fingers and brought her face just inches from his. The heat of his hardening cock seeped through the fabric of their clothing, an erotic, teasing reminder of what was still to come.

"I don't want you to hold anything back. Do you understand me? I want you to give me everything you have and take whatever you want, whatever you need. All that I am is yours. My body, my heart…my blood. Everything," he rasped, "belongs to you."

Stilling in his arms with the thick pulse of desire throbbing around them in the warm evening air, Sadie felt her chest tighten. Staring into his burning gaze, that odd, fluttery feeling swirled in her belly as the true weight of his words sank in. No one, not one person in all her two hundred years, had ever surrendered to Sadie the way Killian had. He was willing to give up anything and everything...for her. The man was offering himself to her in every way a person could, and he did it with an honest, open heart.

Tears pricked the back of her eyes because up until this moment her entire existence had been about surviving. Until connecting with Killian, she hadn't really thought much about living. Somehow, even without a heartbeat in her chest or breath in her lungs, he made her feel alive for the first time in centuries.

"Body and soul," Sadie whispered in a quivering voice filled with restraint. Reaching between them, she curled her fingers around the fabric of his shirt. She slipped the top two buttons open and ran her fingertips over the exposed patch of skin and its thin layer of dark hair. Her gaze skittered over the vein in his neck that throbbed with each beat of his heart, and before she could stop herself, she popped up on her toes and ran her tongue along that swath of skin. Killian shuddered and gripped her tighter, both hands slipping over her ass as Sadie murmured, "And blood."

"Take it." His heated stare clapped onto hers as the growl in his throat rumbled and his strong fingers dug into the flesh of her ass. "It's yours."

A strangled moan escaped Sadie's lips at the same instant Killian's mouth slanted over hers in a demanding, powerful kiss. Tongues tangling, Sadie tugged open his shirt eagerly and sent buttons flying. The sound of tearing fabric only served to heighten the frenzy of need between them. She had to touch him, to run her hands over that gorgeous chest and feel his flesh against hers. The fiery heat of his skin called to her like a siren song luring her in. Killian adjusted his stance and slid one leg between her thighs. He held her to him with one arm and tore her shirt off over her head with the other.

With a growl, he captured her mouth again with his, as though being apart was too much to bear. Carnal lust tinged with desperation permeated the kiss while his talented hands undid her bra and rid her of the flimsy fabric that remained between them. She sighed into his mouth as her breasts pressed against the hot expanse of his chest, allowing herself to feel him in every way possible.

In a frenzy of activity, they divested one another of the rest of their clothing until they stood completely nude, tangled up in each other's arms beneath the light of the moon.

Kissing her deeply, Killian swept Sadie up in his arms and carried her over to the grassy hill before laying her down on the soft bed of green. He stood over her and Sadie, mourning the loss of the warmth of his body, moaned and reached for him. The massive moon glowed brightly in the sky, and she had the silly thought that he'd hung it there just for her. The luminous disk loomed behind Killian, giving him an unearthly glow that only served to highlight his well-sculpted form.

"Do you know how beautiful you are?" Killian asked in an almost reverent tone.

Dropping to his knees, he nudged her legs apart before settling his long, strong body over hers. Placing both hands on either side of her head, he hovered above her, every taut inch of his body humming against hers with unfulfilled desire. His heated gaze skimmed over her face, and the hunger in his eyes deepened when they trailed over her. "So perfect," he murmured before dipping his head low and brushing featherlight kisses over her flesh.

Sadie writhed beneath him and let out a whimper of pleasure when he flicked her nipple with his tongue. Delicious waves of warmth rippled through her blood, and she knew that with each touch, with each caress, Killian was doing far more than marking her body as his. Before tonight, he'd made it clear that he was claiming her body. Now, Sadie knew, he was demanding far more. He was asserting his right to her soul, burrowing into her heart and taking what she knew was only his to take.

"I've pictured you like this for months." Settling onto his elbows, Killian rocked his hips against her slowly and deliberately. Sadie wove her fingers through his hair and opened her legs, urging him to put them both out of their misery and to take what she offered. He refrained. The hot length of his cock seared along the outside of her sex, and with each rock of his hips, it slid slowly over her clit. "Naked and spread out beneath me with that lustful look in those dark chocolate eyes."

"I want you inside me, Killian." The needy desperate voice that escaped Sadie's lips was barely recognizable. Arching her back and wiggling her hips, Sadie grabbed him by the hair and lifted his head from her breast, forcing him to look her in the eye. A slow smile lit up her face when she saw the hungry, lustful expression carved into his features. Baring her fangs, she hooked her legs over his and sighed as his sizable erection slipped over the wet flesh of her sex. Sadie brought his face closer and ran her tongue over his lower lip, her mind touching his. *Don't make me wait any longer.*

The instant their minds joined, the growl in Killian's chest rumbled and his mouth crashed over hers. Sadie opened her legs wide as he lifted his hips, and with one long, slow stroke, he slipped himself inside her to the hilt. Breaking the kiss, their bodies joined, Killian stared into Sadie's eyes and started to move. With each slow, deep, languid pump of his hips, she clung to him and reveled in the wicked licks of pleasure that fired through her body. *I want this to last, and I want to see the look on your face when you come apart for me.*

He thrust into her and filled her time and again as the bloodlust clawed at her, driving her impatience. She lifted her hips, wrapping her legs around him and rising to meet him with every pass. That was all the encouragement he needed. Killian swore as he pumped harder and faster, the friction and heat of his body rushing over her clit with exactly the right amount of pressure. The orgasm coiled deep in Sadie's belly. Killian's tempo increased, and she sensed he was close to the edge. That knowledge made her own pleasure surge.

He thrust into her, the hot, steely length of him filling and stretching her to almost impossible limits, and Sadie knew she only needed one more thing. With the thunderous beat of his heart calling to her and with his sweat-slicked skin sliding over hers, Sadie gritted her teeth, fighting the bloodlust. The pull was far beyond any she'd felt before, and as the orgasm built, her resistance crumbled. Killian's strong masculine body covered her while the sweet, torturous orgasm began to crest and her basest desires erupted.

I need to taste you, Killian. Licking the flesh along his neck while he pumped into her at a frenzied pace, she touched his mind and clung to him. *Just one more time...let me in.*

"Yes." Killian's voice hovered somewhere between human and wolf, and the guttural, animalistic sound of it pushed her beyond the limits. "Take all of me inside."

Surrounded by his touch, voice, and scent, Sadie's orgasm exploded as she sank her fangs into his throat and fed. The instant the warm liquid hit her tongue, Sadie came again, the powerful spasms of her orgasm racking her body with brutal force. Killian shouted her name and pounded into her with one final pass as his own pleasure flared and his body shuddered around hers.

Sadie absorbed Killian in every way possible and shivered when his blood memories filled her mind with a newfound familiarity. In a flash of light, however, a new image rose above and drowned out the rest.

Killian in his jet-black wolf pelt, his eyes glowing amber. He was standing in the middle of the Great Lawn, but he wasn't alone because next to him stood a smaller black wolf with eyes that burned red...blood red. The mournful howl of a wolf tore through her mind, and heat fired through her body as the clear, distinct beat of her own heart pounded in her chest.

With the ripples of their shared orgasm fading and the long-absent heartbeat throbbing strongly inside her once again, Sadie licked the wound on his neck closed. Killian collapsed breathlessly on top of her. Breathing heavily and with Killian's face buried in the crook of her neck, Sadie took a moment to enjoy the feel of his body on top of hers. Their hearts beat in unison, and she closed her eyes so she could shut out everything else except him.

Her skin hummed with energy and her body throbbed with life. Sadie sucked in a deep shuddering breath. Cool, clean air slowly filled her lungs as she breathed at a slow, deliberate pace. For the first time in centuries, Sadie didn't just feel alive...she *was* alive.

"Holy shit," she whispered. She tapped Killian on the arm and pushed at his chest with both hands, lifting him off her and making him look her in the face. A sleepy, satisfied expression swiftly changed to concern when he saw her distress. Fear, confusion, and excitement swamped her as she tried to decipher the latest development. "I'm alive, Killian. I mean, really alive."

"I feel the same way," he said with a cheeky wink. He gently disengaged from her body and stretched out next to her on the grass.

"Killian, I mean I'm actually alive." She sat up and grabbed his hand before quickly bringing it to her chest. The cocky, satisfied expression on his handsome face shifted to one of awe. "I'm breathing. I'm actually fucking breathing. Can you feel that?"

"How is that possible?" Killian's voice was quiet and almost reverent. He sat up and scooted closer to her, keeping his hand pressed to her chest. His warm brown eyes searched hers, and a smile played at his lips. "Before, when we were in the storage room, you got a heartbeat, but it wasn't this strong. And you didn't breathe like this." His brow furrowed and concern carved into his features. "Do you think it's my blood that's doing this?"

"I don't know," Sadie said quietly. "I—I think so. It must be part of the bloodmate connection, but honestly? I don't care what the reason is…it's incredible." She rested her hand over his on her chest, tears filling her eyes as they sat in silence and listened to the beat of Sadie's heart. A smile lit up her face as the cool, crisp air filled her lungs with refreshingly familiar ease. "It's like riding a bike, I guess. You never really forget how to do it."

To her surprise, Killian burst out laughing before grabbing her face with both hands and pulling her in for a long, deep kiss. It didn't have the hot, passionate, desperate touches of his earlier kisses, but was languid and sweet, reminding Sadie of long, hot summer nights that went on forever. Wrapping his arms around her without breaking the kiss, Killian lay down and pulled her with him. Feeling his cock stirring to life again, she smiled against his lips and straddled him.

She suckled his lower lip and rose up on her knees while trailing her fingertips over his hard, flat stomach. The tip of his cock bounced against the edge of her sex, and a tortured groan escaped his lips as he gripped her hips. A naughty grin played at her lips, and just when she was about to give them what they both wanted—the distinct sound of an intruder put an end to their stolen time together.

Her fangs erupted at the hint of danger and the pace of her breathing picked up, making her feel slightly off balance. Fangs and breathing didn't really go together. Killian obviously sensed the same thing because he wrapped her in his arms and brought her down to the ground with him, rolling her beneath him protectively.

Someone's here. Sadie touched Killian's mind gently. She felt a little silly about allowing him to protect her, but her senses were so screwed up, she didn't fight it. *In the trees behind us.*

I know. Killian nodded curtly and a growl began to rumble. *It's a vampire.* Both of their survival instincts were on high alert, but at the moment, Killian's senses seemed to be sharper. *Shane or Dakota?* he asked, refer-ring to the two sentries.

I can't tell. Frustration laced her voice. *All this breathing and beating-heart crap has my wires crossed.*

"Identify yourself!" Killian shouted in that voice that hung between animal and human. Eyes glowing, he tightened his hold on her. "Or are you a coward?"

What happened next seemed to happen in the blink of an eye.

Someone flew down in a rush of icy wind, slammed into them like a Mack truck, and ripped Killian away from her. Through the fog of sensations, she knew it was Dakota, the newest sentry in NYC. He was strong and fast, and from what Sadie had heard, the guy was a ruthless fighter. Struggling to find her voice, Sadie wanted to scream his name, to tell him not to attack, but no sound would come.

In that instant, Sadie knew what pure unadulterated fear combined with white-hot fury felt like as it fired through her with bone-clattering force. Somewhere in the distance she heard Killian growling and snarling and knew he had shifted, but she couldn't see anything. Her body, the one thing she could always count on for its predictable strengths and weaknesses, was betraying her brutally.

Sweat poured down her face, stinging her eyes, and even though she wanted to run after him, to fly and go to Killian's aid, she couldn't. She thought she heard Killian calling her name but he sounded so far away. Her entire body shook like she was being electrocuted, and the next instant her world exploded in a tsunami of heat and a blinding flash of light.

Fighting her way through the confusion, Sadie caught a glimpse of Killian and scrambled to her feet. He had shifted back into his human form and was standing next to Dakota, and both men had expressions on their face that were nothing short of stunned.

Feeling completely off her game and still horribly dizzy, Sadie shook her head in an effort to clear it, but all that did was make her more off balance. She went to steady herself with her hands, but she didn't have hands.

She had paws. Four furry paws.

The cold hand of fear grabbed her by the throat, and she shifted nervously on four legs instead of two. She looked up at Killian, who was moving cautiously toward her. She let out a low whine while she tried to wrap her brain around what had just happened. As Killian approached, and the wind whispered over her fur-covered body, Sadie tossed her head back and howled at the moon.

Chapter 14

Sadie's howl tore through Killian and made his heart ache. Her pain and confusion were evident in the mournful wail, and he fought the urge to shift so he could comfort her in his wolf form. Moving closer, he touched her mind with his as he dragged his jeans over his hips. *It's going to be okay, Sadie.*

What's happening? She whined and backed away from him, her eyes glowing bright red in the darkness of the park. Other than the color of her eyes, she seemed like any other pack member, and the jet-black fur of her coat shimmered in the moonlight. She was absolutely beautiful. *Killian?*

He was about to answer her when her body shook with what looked like a seizure. Her eyes rolled back in her head, and in a flash of iridescent light, she shifted back before collapsing naked on the grass. Killian went to her and quickly used his discarded shirt to cover her beautiful nude body from Dakota's curious gaze. He knew nudity wasn't a big deal, and it was irrational to cover her that way, but he didn't care. He never wanted another man to see her exposed and vulnerable the way she had been for him.

Gathering her in his arms, after ensuring she was sufficiently covered, he turned around and leveled his burning stare at the sentry who looked appropriately shocked.

"Holy crap," Dakota said none too delicately. He looked from Killian to Sadie and took a lollipop out of his coat pocket. Unwrapping it, he popped it in his mouth. "This coven gets weirder by the day."

"You're a vampire sucking on a lollipop, so I'd say you fit right in. Besides, your observations aren't helping," Killian said to the young, overeager sentry. Dakota had tackled him, but once he realized that Sadie was there, he'd backed off before any blood was spilled. "Call Olivia and tell her what's going on."

"How can I do that when I have no idea what *this* is?" Dakota rolled his eyes and snagged a phone out of his pocket. "This city is fuckin' weird, y'all. I shoulda stayed in Texas."

"You saw what happened," Killian bit out. Sadie stirred in his arms and moaned, but stilled when he pressed a kiss to her forehead. "It might happen again. I don't know. There's one thing for sure—she can't possibly open her club later today. And, to be honest, that's the least of our problems. Get the rest of Sadie's things. Then call Olivia and let her know that I have Sadie with me at my apartment. She should come there as soon as she can." With Sadie nestled against his chest, Killian strode toward the deserted street along the outskirts of the park where he'd left the car. Shouting over his shoulder, he said, "And tell her to bring Xavier with her."

"Sure thing, *Yer Highness*." Dakota's sarcastic tone wasn't lost on Killian. "Jeez Louise, you are a fuckin' bossy wolf man."

Killian knew he was being curt and risking a confrontation with the vampire sentry, but he didn't care. All that mattered was getting Sadie back to the safety of his apartment. Her body had cooled significantly and her new heartbeat no longer throbbed, but that almost musical hum of her energy still whirled in the air around him. Walking through the moonlit park, there was no longer any sign of the wolf within her. She was a vampire once again.

Pressing his lips to the cool, damp skin of her forehead, he murmured, "It will be alright, my love."

Had he said that for her benefit or for his?

Sadie had been asleep for hours, but Killian didn't leave her side for a second. With the room-darkening shades drawn in the bedroom of his penthouse, Killian sat motionless in the armchair next to the king-sized bed with his gaze pinned to Sadie's unmoving form.

It was the first time that Sadie actually looked like a vampire. Gone were the fleeting heartbeat and shuddering breath. She lay totally still as though frozen beneath the covers…frozen in time.

Killian rested his elbows on his knees and pressed his mouth to his clasped hands, recalling the frightened look on Sadie's face when she'd shifted. He'd been as stunned as she was, but had tried to remain calm for her sake. She may have only been in her wolf pelt for a few minutes, a blink in the span of her long life, but Killian knew the ripple effects would have far-reaching ramifications—for everyone.

"Killian." Olivia's gentle but insistent voice cut through the haze, pulling him from his thoughts. With a mug of hot coffee in hand, she strode into the room and held it out for him. "I thought you might need this."

"Thank you." He glanced at the mug briefly before taking it and giving the czar a nod of gratitude. Turning his attention back to Sadie, he sipped the coffee without really tasting it. "She looks…"

"Dead?" Olivia leaned against the wall and gave him a what-did-you-expect look. "She's a vampire, Killian. This is how we look when we sleep."

"She's a lot more than that now." He drained the coffee and placed the mug on the nightstand. "I still don't understand how *that* could have happened. How the hell did she shift into a werewolf? She wasn't bitten."

Even as the words escaped his lips, he realized how wrong he was.

"Yes, Killian, she was." Sadness laced Olivia's voice and she turned those earnest green eyes to him. "I'm sure it has something to do with the bite she suffered her last night as a human. I'm no scientist, but if you ask me, something in your blood triggered the change. She did feed on you, didn't she?"

Killian said nothing but kept his serious stare locked with the czar. He knew it was against the law for Sadie to taste his blood. He and Sadie both knew it, and yet neither of them had cared. With his body and mind fogged by lust and desire, all he could see, feel, or think about was Sadie. He *had* to be closer to her. It wasn't mere desire. It was a carnal, visceral, primal need to join with her in every way possible. While various excuses and denials ran through his mind, a smile spread across the czar's face and she waved one hand in the air dismissively.

"Do me a favor, Your Highness. Don't insult me and try to deny it, okay?" She arched one red eyebrow and gave him a pointed look. "I've been through the blood-mate bond, and there isn't a bloodlust or craving in the world that can hold a candle to it. Besides, Dakota gave me a full report on what he found in the park. The scent of blood and sex was thick in the air."

"Understood." Killian gave her a curt nod and looked back at Sadie, unwilling to discuss their personal escapades any further. "Will Xavier have some answers for us soon? I know you brought him another blood sample from Sadie, and I want to know if there have been any changes."

"You aren't the only one," she said worriedly. "Dakota will escort him over here after sundown, and if anyone can give us answers, it will be Xavier," she said with her usual calm, even-keeled manner. "Although poor Dakota may never be the same again. He thought two wolves were attacking a vampire in the park. Apparently Sadie's scent was completely unrecognizable, and given what happened, I'm not at all surprised at the mix-up. He feels like a jerk for attacking you the way he did, but to be honest, it's more than that." She rolled her eyes. "Like all sentries, the guy hates making mistakes."

Panic gripped Killian as he realized that word of Sadie's unusual transformation could get out before they even knew what was going on. What if Dakota shared what he'd witnessed? He was about to protest when Olivia held up one hand, preventing his response.

"Dakota is not going to say a word to anyone," Olivia said. "Trust me."

"How can you be sure?" Killian asked quietly. "If anyone else—"

"He's a sentry." Olivia's voice was edged with a

serious tone she rarely exhibited. "Aside from being skilled fighters, more than a little arrogant, and incredible trackers, they are the most loyal vampires you will ever encounter. They live and die for the Presidium. I know this is true because I used to be one." Moving toward the foot of the bed with her sights glued on Sadie, she murmured, "In fact, the rest of my coven doesn't even know what happened. Only you, me, Dakota, and Xavier." Her sharp green eyes flicked to Killian. "And Sadie, of course. I trust you'll be keeping this to yourself? You don't have any plans to put it in the Werewolf Society monthly newsletter or anything?"

"Of course not. I've kept Maya's secret and I'll keep Sadie's as well," Killian said firmly. "Ivan's been fired, and he should be on a plane with my father headed for Alaska as we speak."

"Should be?" Olivia tilted her head and inspected him curiously. "Haven't you telepathed with your father?"

"I can't anymore." Killian's mouth was set in a tight line.

"Of course." Olivia nodded her head in understanding. "The bloodmate bond eliminates telepathy with anyone except your mate."

"Yes. It didn't happen as abruptly for me as for Sadie, but it sure as hell happened."

"Okay, what about the other guy? David?"

"I told him I needed the apartment to myself. I put him up at the Plaza and gave him the week off. No one else can know about this yet. Hell, we don't even know if it will happen again." Killian quickly added, "There might not be anything to tell."

Silence hung between them and Killian shifted

uncomfortably in his chair. He knew that was bullshit. And based on the look on Olivia's face, so did she.

"Sure. We keep it under wraps for as long as we can." Olivia ran both hands through her red curls before folding her arms over her chest and leveling a concerned look at Sadie. "No one else finds out until we know what the hell is happening to her."

Movement in the bed captured their attention. Killian let out a sigh of relief as Sadie sat up, looking as bewildered as he felt.

"I'd love to know the answer to that too," Sadie said in a groggy, raspy voice, holding the sheet up to cover her naked breasts. "Did I actually turn into a wolf, or am I imagining things?"

In a blur of speed, Killian went to the bed and settled in next to Sadie. He gathered her in his arms. Sitting up against the massive leather-upholstered headboard, he held her against him and rained kisses over her, uncaring that the czar was standing only a few feet away.

"Thank God," he whispered. Stroking her long hair, he pressed his lips to her forehead and held her face in his hands. "I was starting to worry that you'd never wake up."

"It's still daylight?" Sadie nestled beneath the crook of his arm and glanced at the drawn shades, cracks of sunlight peeking around the edges. "Shit. I've been waking up a lot during the day lately."

"Yeah, that's true." Olivia sat on the edge of the bed. "But you don't usually shift into a wolf either, so it looks like you have all kinds of fun new things happening."

"Good point," Sadie said through a weak laugh. The smile quickly faded and a look of panic covered her face. Grabbing Killian's wrist from where it sat draped over her shoulder, she looked at his watch. "The club! Oh crap. What time is it?"

"Hold your horses." Olivia rose calmly from the edge of the bed. "We've got it covered. Damien is running the club tonight, and Suzie offered to help out too."

"Really?" Sadie said with genuine surprise. "But I thought she hated being around that many humans. It makes her super-uncomfortable."

"You know our Suzie." Olivia lifted one shoulder. "She may not *know* what happened to you, but...*she knows*. Anyway, I didn't even have to ask her to step in. Damien texted me a little while ago and said the girl showed up in her old uniform ready to rock 'n' roll." She pointed at Killian. "Your boy David is there too. Justine suggested that David work the door as bouncer tonight, since Damien will be on the floor running the show."

"I should have known," Killian said with a smile. He cradled Sadie's hand in his lap and brushed his thumb over her knuckles, needing to touch her and reassure himself that she was okay. "David is the go-to guy, you know? Steady and trustworthy, no matter what." His brow furrowed. "Too bad I can't say the same for Ivan."

"That's good. Really, it is," Sadie said with a hint of disappointment. Settling back into Killian's embrace, she smoothed the sheet over her body in a soothing gesture. "I guess you guys have it all figured out."

"Well, sure," Olivia said with a snort of derision. "Getting a nightclub open is a piece of cake compared to figuring out why my oldest and dearest vampire progeny is shifting into a werewolf. Now *that* is not so simple."

Killian held Sadie tighter and kissed her hair lovingly. *You scared the shit out of me, woman.*

I scared the shit out of myself. Sadie's voice touched his with a playful lilt. She peered up at him from beneath a fan of dark lashes.

Olivia cleared her throat, interrupting their intimate conversation, and the two of them looked at her with mild embarrassment. They'd forgotten she was even in the room.

"Anyway," Olivia said with a smirk. "We'll get this all figured out, but it will probably take some time. So, in the meanwhile, Sadie, I want you to lie low. Stay here in the penthouse with Killian." She nodded toward a bag on the overstuffed chair in the corner. "I packed you plenty of clothes and stuff. I'll tell the girls that the two of you needed some time alone together to get a handle on the whole bloodmate deal."

"What?" Sadie sat up and held the covers over her breasts, looking from Olivia to Killian. "Why do I have to go into hiding?"

"Are you serious?" Olivia tossed her hands in the air and looked like she was struggling to maintain her normally cool exterior. "From what Dakota and Killian tell me, you were experiencing some pretty intense emotions when you shifted, and you obviously weren't in control of what happened. Unless, of course, you've been shifting into a wolf for years and not telling me about it."

"I haven't." Sadie began to argue but thought better of it. She looked from Olivia to Killian before letting out a sound of frustration and sitting back. "Oh, fine."

"She's right, Sadie." Killian played with a long strand

of her hair and kept his voice low. "I don't know how or why it happened, but it was definitely triggered by your emotions. And that's not uncommon with newly turned werewolves."

"But I'm not a werewolf," Sadie whispered shakily. Her large dark eyes filled with tears as she stared up at him, her fingers curling against his chest. She lifted her lip and her fangs broke free. "I'm a vampire."

Lifting her hand to his mouth, he brushed a gentle kiss over her knuckles and murmured, "Did it occur to you that you could be both?"

"Let's not get ahead of ourselves," Olivia said calmly. "The point is that we can't risk you getting all wolfy in front of the humans, other vamps, or even worse, some of Killian's people. You have to stay inside and on lock-down until we have a clearer idea of what's happening. Xavier is running tests on your blood. He's comparing the sample I took from you this morning to what *he* took from you before all this happened, and he's comparing both of those against the one from the Presidium data-base. Xavier also said there was some interesting data from that watch monitor you wore, but the guy didn't want to say anything until he had more information." A sweet smile curved her lips. "You know how he is."

"Yeah," Sadie said softly. "I know. He needs all of the facts."

"So we're all on the same page?" Olivia leveled a deadly serious gaze at Killian and Sadie. "You do not, under any circumstances, leave this apartment until I give you the all clear. Right?"

"Right." Sadie made a saluting gesture. "Yes, sir."

"Bet your ass," Olivia said through a laugh. Her

expression grew serious again as she met Killian's gaze. "I'm counting on you, Killian."

"You don't even have to ask." Killian nuzzled Sadie tighter and held the czar's challenging stare. "I'll have David check on the club and get me progress updates. Sadie and I will be here... I'm sure we can find plenty of things to do to keep ourselves occupied."

"I'm sure you can." Olivia rolled her eyes and tried to suppress a knowing grin. The phone in her pocket buzzed and all humor faded when she read the message on the screen. "It's Xavier. He's hung up at the lab and won't be here for a few more hours. Something about retesting the samples."

"That doesn't sound good," Sadie muttered.

"Don't worry in advance," Olivia said while texting something to Xavier. "Listen, I'll be back here with him at some point after sundown. In the meantime, you two sit tight. Just to be safe, I'm going to have Dakota stick close to this part of the city, and I'll ask Shane to take the outer boroughs."

"Oh, he'll love that," Sadie said sarcastically.

"He'll be fine. Especially since he knows you two are going through the bloodmate bond." Slipping her phone back in the pocket of her Armani suit, Olivia headed for the open door of the bedroom. "That boy didn't know his ass from his elbow when he and Maya bonded. I actually felt sorry for the old stiff."

"Olivia?" Sadie's voice stopped her maker in her tracks. "Thank you."

"I got your back, girl." Olivia winked, and as she pulled the bedroom door closed, she said, "But it looks like I'm not the only one who does."

The door clicked shut, leaving Sadie and Killian alone in the dimly lit bedroom. Silence hung between them and he pulled her closer before gently kissing the top of her head. Gathering her hand in his, he could feel her shivering and a sudden feeling of helplessness swamped him. She was frightened, and he was fairly sure she'd started to cry but was trying to hold it together. Whether or not the woman would admit it, she was terrified of what was happening to her and there wasn't a damn thing he could do about it.

"Are you alright?" he asked quietly. Sadie didn't respond but snuggled deeper into his embrace and curled her arms around his waist. He played with her long hair and wrapped a silky strand around his finger before stroking her back gently. His fingertips glided over her satin-smooth skin, marveling at how wonderful it felt just to touch her. "I know that is the dumbest question in the history of questions but..."

"It's not a dumb question," Sadie said in a barely audible voice. Her cheek pressed against his chest, and as she spoke, he felt her tears seep through his shirt. Torture, he thought, this is pure fucking torture. "It's actually a really great question and I wish I had a great answer. I don't know what I am, Killian, and I haven't felt this way in a long time. I loved—I mean, I love—being a vampire. I always have."

"You weren't frightened after Olivia turned you?" he asked, wanting to know everything there was to know about the woman who'd stolen his heart.

"At first, sure, but not as much as you'd expect. Honestly, I was more in awe than frightened." She sniffled and curled her fingers around the fabric of his shirt. "Being a vampire is a dependable existence."

"Go on." Killian adjusted the sheet over her before tangling her fingers with his once again. "I'm listening."

"When I was human and living in the wilderness with my family, everything was uncertain. There were times when we weren't sure where our next meal was coming from, or if we'd survive the next winter. It was a terrifying way to live, not knowing what was around the corner of the next sunrise. But as a vampire, I've always known what to expect. The rules were clear. The boundaries have been solid and impenetrable. There were no surprises, and it made me feel safe."

"Until now," he said softly.

Sadie nodded but didn't respond as her tears continued to fall silently. Damn it all to hell. He wanted to fix it. That's what men do. Wolf. Human. Whatever. They fix shit. But this wasn't something he could fix, and it was making him feel totally useless. Selfishly, he wanted to kiss the fear out of her, out of both of them. Killian wanted to make love to her so that they could both fall into the sweet abyss of abandon...but he didn't. She was exhausted, both physically and emotionally, and what Sadie needed now, more than ever, was some rest.

"Just rest, Sadie." Holding her shivering form against his, he pulled the comforter over both of them and pressed a tender kiss to her forehead. "You're safe with me...I promise."

Chapter 15

WAKING UP FROM THE MOST SATISFYING SLEEP OF HER life, Sadie stretched languidly in the nest of soft bedding. Her body felt strong, rested, and even more powerful than usual, which was odd considering she hadn't fed in a while. A sleepy smile played at her lips when she recalled falling asleep in Killian's arms and hearing him assure her that she'd be safe. He was right, because she did feel safe with him.

Safe and loved.

Sure, she might turn into a wolf at an inopportune moment, but knowing that Killian had her back made it oddly…okay. The man was solid, steady, and totally dependable. Her stable and predictable existence as a vampire may be unsteady now, but having Killian in her life seemed to offset that somehow. Being wrapped in his strong, warm embrace made her feel like she'd come home.

She was safe and she was home.

Most men would probably have tried to get lucky with a naked and vulnerable woman wrapped in their arms. To her surprise, Killian didn't even make a suggestion about getting it on. He could have, and if he had, she would have gladly accepted. But he didn't. In that moment, he wasn't concerned with his own pleasure. All he had on his mind was *her* well-being…and his thoughtfulness was the biggest turn-on of all.

With the weight and warmth of his body absent from the bed, Sadie had no desire to linger there. Peeling her eyes open, she fully expected to see the shades still drawn over the floor-to-ceiling windows. To her surprise, however, they were wide open and provided a brilliant view of New York City at night. She pushed herself up onto her elbows, a smile playing at her lips as she looked around the spacious moonlit bedroom. Killian must have opened the shades for her. She shook her head as she pushed the covers aside and swung her feet over the edge. How funny that such a small, seemingly unimportant gesture like opening the shades could endear him to her even more.

Rising to her feet, she stretched her arms over her head but stilled when the sound of splashing water captured her attention. Her grin broadened. That meant only one thing. Killian was in the pool. Not bothering to put on any clothing, and knowing they were alone in the penthouse, Sadie padded quietly through the bedroom door and down the dark hallway toward the sound. Moving swiftly and silently, she crept over to the open sliding glass door and watched with rapt fascination as her lover swam through the aqua waters with strong, sure strokes. His nude, muscular body cut through the pool with all the power and precision one would expect from a werewolf prince like Killian Bane.

He was beautiful. Masculine. Strong. Enticing. Sweet Lord. The man was desire come to life. Killian Bane embodied everything a man should be, and not just in his physical form. His thoughtfulness, intelligence, and tenacity had drawn Sadie in and had her completely entranced. She smirked and stepped out onto the cool stones of the terrace. His wiseass sense of humor didn't hurt either, and when he looked at her with that wicked twinkle in his eyes, it just about did her in every single time. Hell, the guy had it all. He was, quite literally, Prince Charming, werewolf or not. Sadie knew it was time to stop fighting the attraction.

She loved him.

She might not know what the future held, but one fact would remain. Despite her best efforts to prevent it, Sadie had fallen in love with Killian.

Is there room in there for me? Sadie asked as she strolled over to the edge of the pool. She stifled a laugh when Killian popped up out of the water like a cork and swam directly to the water's edge. His heated gaze slid over her nude body from head to toe, and the hungry look in his eye made her wet. Naked and fully aware of her effect on him, she held her hands behind her back and gave him a coquettish look. "Or did you want to be alone?"

"Alone with you? Absolutely. Olivia and Xavier will be here soon enough. How'd you sleep?" Killian propped his arms on the edge of the pool and reached out, curling his hand around her ankle. He brushed his thumb over the top of her foot as his glowing amber stare drifted over her body before he finally looked her in the eye. "Did you get enough rest?"

"Plenty," Sadie said with a sigh. "And right now, I'd say that sleeping is the last thing on my mind."

Without waiting for him to respond, she playfully slipped her foot from his grasp and dove over his head into the pool behind him.

Before she could even emerge from the water,

Killian wrapped one arm around her and pulled her to the surface. Sadie linked her arms around his neck and clung to him, reveling in the swirl of sensations. The delicious heat of his flesh pressed against hers as the cool waters of the pool surrounded them, creating an exotic combination.

Killian's hands slid down and cupped her bare bottom as she wrapped her legs around his waist in one fluid gesture. His fierce, glowing gaze held hers and the thick length of his cock pressed between their bodies, its ridge sliding along her clit. Letting out a sigh of pleasure, Sadie wiggled her hips, tangling her fingers in his hair. Using the weightlessness of the water, she clung to him while slowly lifting and lowering her body, putting exactly the right amount of pressure in just the right spot.

She brought his lips to hers and brushed her mouth lightly over his while continuing to rock her hips against him. With every pass, the pleasure built. Tiny licks of fire sizzled through her blood as the orgasm coiled hard and fast. Killian held her bottom with one hand and grabbed her head with the other, taking control of the kiss. His tongue demanded entrance, and Sadie was more than happy to allow it. Kissing her deeply, and with Sadie sliding her sex along his cock, he walked over to the steps. Breaking the kiss, he hooked his hands under Sadie's arms and placed her on the top step in one swift movement.

A whimper of protest escaped her lips as her fangs broke free and she reached for Killian, already mourning the loss of his body melding against hers. Cool water sloshed over her sensitized skin and barely covered the swollen flesh of her sex. The sensation was surprisingly erotic and made her moan with wanting, but she needed more. She needed him. With that wicked grin, he shook his head and grabbed her wrists, preventing her from touching him.

"Put your arms over your head," he said in a firm, commanding tone. He knelt on the steps in front of her, sliding his hands along the slick flesh of her arms. "That's it." While he spoke, he kept his voice low and trailed his fingertips over her breasts and along her quivering belly. "Now, I want you to open your legs for me…wide."

Holding her arms high above her head, Sadie arched her back as she complied with his request. She whimpered as the water fluttered over her clit in wicked little passes, sending zings of pleasure to her core. Killian held her gaze as his strong hands curled beneath the crook of her legs and tugged them wider still. The sudden, abrupt motion sent another shot of gratification through her, making her practically beg him to fuck her. She wanted him put her out of her misery, to take her over the cliff that she clung to and make her scream his name.

"Perfect," Killian whispered. His glowing stare drifted over her as a gentle breeze wafted past, making her nipples harden into sharp points. Delicious shivers of anticipation flickered up her spine and she arched toward him, eager for his touch. "I don't think I'll ever get tired of seeing you like this, Sadie. Naked, vulnerable, and bared just for me to see."

"Please, Killian." Lips parted and fangs bared, Sadie tossed her head back and clasped her hands together. "Taste me," she rasped shamelessly.

His hands curled around the crook of her knee, and he pulled her wider before leaning in and blowing gently over her exposed sex. Sadie let out a sound of pure ecstasy as Killian finally caved in and gave her what she so desperately wanted. His hot mouth covered her, his tongue sweeping over her clit in one strong stroke. Pleasure ripped through her as he continued his merciless assault, licking and suckling her to the brink of orgasm. With the sweet, torturous coil of lust tightening in her belly, Sadie looked down and the erotic sight of Killian's head between her legs, combined with the feel of his mouth on her pussy, sent her right over the edge.

The powerful orgasm ripped through Sadie and she shouted his name as her body convulsed with wave after wave of pleasure. Needing more, wanting to give him the same carnal release, Sadie grabbed Killian's head with both hands and urged him to kiss her. In a blur of flesh, he rose to meet her and covered her mouth with his in a deep, searing kiss. With the strength of a vampire, Sadie turned Killian's body as she kissed him, putting him firmly on the steps beneath her. In one swift movement, she straddled him and impaled herself on his thick shaft.

Killian shouted her name as she rode him, his fingers digging into her hips with every pass. She tangled her fingers in his hair and he captured her nipples between his eager lips. Clinging to him and taking him deeper each time, Sadie tilted his head and scraped her fangs along the side of his neck. She knew she shouldn't. She'd taken enough of his blood already, but the voice of reason was no match for the bellowing cry of lust.

With her lover pumping into her at a more furious

pace, Sadie did the one thing that came most naturally to all vampires…especially with their bloodmates. As her fangs sank into his flesh and she took his powerful blood inside her, Sadie touched his mind with a shuddering whisper. *I love you, Killian.*

The now-familiar beat of her own heart began to throb as she merged with him on both the physical and mental plane. Warmth fired through her blood, and as the hypnotic pulse filled her, Sadie surrendered to it.

She surrendered to *him*. Her body, her heart, her life. All of it.

In one final thrust, and with minds and bodies merged, Sadie and Killian clung to each other as they plummeted over the edge toward an unknown future.

Killian stood at the stove, whipping up a midnight snack. Somehow pancakes always tasted better in the middle of the night. A smile curved his lips. Then again, after being with Sadie, pretty much anything would taste good. Hell, even the idea of being king sounded more palatable if he could have Sadie by his side. His smile faded as the thought drifted through his mind. His people were unlikely to ever accept a vampire for their queen.

Like his father said, a lot can change in five years.

Shoving thoughts of the future aside, Killian scooped the pancakes onto the plate before dumping the pans in the sink and going to the refrigerator for syrup. He was digging through the various containers of leftovers when a beautiful, sexy voice drifted over his shoulder.

"That's a hell of a view." Sadie's arms linked around his waist and she pressed a kiss to his shoulder. Her heart still beat in her chest and a steady breathing pattern still flowed through her lungs, but Killian refrained from commenting. They both knew the side effects of his blood were lasting longer each time and yet neither of them said a word. It was the proverbial elephant in the room. "Even with a pair of boxers covering it up, you have one fine-lookin' backside."

"Thanks. Yours isn't so bad either." Killian straightened and spun around to face her. Shutting the door behind him, he held up the syrup and kissed her lips firmly while linking one arm around her. He waggled his eyebrows at her and smacked her butt. "Then again, your front is pretty nice too. Even if you are obstructing my view with one of my shirts." He placed the syrup on the counter so he could wrap both arms around her. He settled his hands along the top of her round bottom and sighed. "Actually, my shirt looks much better on you than it does on me. But do you know where it would look even better?"

"Where?" Sadie giggled and looked up at him with those smiling dark eyes.

"Balled up in the corner of the room," he said with a wicked grin before leaning in and nibbling her neck, which elicited a louder giggle from Sadie. Killian stilled and lifted his head, peering at her intently as she tried to wiggle out of his embrace. "So it looks like I'm not the only one who's ticklish."

Without any warning, Killian leaned in and nuzzled her neck with his scruffy cheek. Sadie shrieked in protest as he blew raspberries along her throat, which had her shaking in his arms with laughter.

"Okay, okay, I give," she said through a shuddering

breath. An uncomfortable expression flickered across her face as she stilled in his arms and caught her breath. "Sorry…the breathing thing is still making me feel weird."

"Right." Killian nodded and kissed her forehead. "It's lasting longer this time," he said quietly.

"I guess." Sadie lifted one shoulder and slipped out of his arms. Her lovely bare legs peeked out beneath the hem of his shirt, which drifted along the middle of her thighs. She looked positively tiny and fragile as she walked to the end of the kitchen island. Keeping her back to him, she strolled around the open first floor of the penthouse before finally stopping at the enormous windows. "It will stop soon. It always does."

Killian stared at her with that same feeling of helplessness. As much as he wanted to help her, there was little he could do.

"Are you hungry?" he asked, knowing that food was about the only thing he could offer. "Olivia brought a supply of blood for you. I could heat some up."

"No." Sadie shook her head and continued staring out at the New York City night. "I'm not hungry." She let out a nervous laugh and glanced over her shoulder. "Actually, your pancakes and bacon smell really good."

"Do you want to try some?" he asked slowly.

"No," she said abruptly. She looked back out the window and shrugged. "I'm not hungry. I guess your blood was enough."

"Sadie—" Killian was cut off when the shrill chirp of his phone echoed through the apartment. He'd left the damn thing to charge because he'd let it go completely dead for the past several hours. Based on the series of alerts coming through, he had more than a few messages.

Taking care of Sadie took priority over his stupid phone, so whoever it was could wait. Before that thought had even finished, the damn thing started ringing with yet another call. "I have to answer it. It might be Olivia or Xavier with news."

He snagged it from the charger, and the number glaring up at him from the screen was not the one he expected. It wasn't Olivia or Xavier; it was David. Not only that, but he had about twenty missed calls and voice mails from his mother, his sister, and General Wolcott. Killian's brow furrowed and a knot of dread formed in his gut. It had begun. Damn it all to hell. His father had probably told the others about what was going on with Sadie, and if he hadn't, it was a surefire bet that Christina had. Damn that woman.

Killian punched the button and reluctantly answered the call.

"What's up, David?" Killian asked while turning his gaze to Sadie who still stood by the window. "I'm kind of in the middle of something, but it looks like I have a hundred missed calls from back home."

"We have a problem." David's voice was edged with anger.

"Aren't you bouncing at the club?" Killian glanced at the clock on the stove. It was after three in the morning and they were probably still cleaning up. "What the hell is going on?"

"It's your father." David was keeping his voice low, and based on the background noise, he was probably standing outside the club. "I just got a call from your mother. The king and the others never came home. The pilot isn't answering his phone either. I called JFK and the king's jet is in the charter hangar, but the damn pilot is nowhere to be found."

"What about Christina?" Killian asked as Sadie turned to face him with a concerned expression. "Did she check out of the hotel?"

"Yes." David's voice was edged with fury. "They checked out yesterday, not long after your father was at the Loup Garou. They should have been long gone and home by now. The general is ready to bring all-out war to the city. He's convinced that the vamps have done something to them."

"No one has been able to telepath with them?" Killian's jaw clenched and tension fired through him. "None of them?"

"Nope." David sounded as freaked out as Killian felt. "Total radio silence. General Wolcott is ready to declare fucking war. The only reason he hasn't hauled his ass here is because the king placed him in charge of the territory before he left. But I don't know how long the son of a bitch is going to follow protocol. If he doesn't hear from Christina soon…Killian…he's ready to send his soldiers here to confront the czars."

"That's ridiculous," Killian barked. "The czars would never—"

Sadie closed the distance between them in a blur. *What about the czars, Killian?*

My father, Christina, the girls, and Ivan are missing. His mouth set in a tight line and Sadie immediately wrapped her arms around his waist to comfort him. He rubbed her back and felt some of his tension ease but that nagging knot of dread lingered. *So is the pilot of my father's private jet.*

"No, *I know* the czars wouldn't do anything," David interrupted. "But what about the vamps who were threatening you for opening the club? Those cowardly fuckers who left all the anonymous notes? Come on, Killian. I realize you and Sadie have your *thing* going, but you can't put blinders on. You and I both know that plenty of vampires are pissed off as all hell that we're setting up shop in this city."

"Understood." Killian kept his voice even and controlled as he stared into Sadie's concerned face. "Tell Olivia and Doug what's happened. I know they're not involved, but they might have a good idea who is."

Me too. Sadie nodded and touched his mind with hers. *I'd put my money on Darius. He's got to be involved in it.*

"Get in touch with the general and my mother, and let them know we're working with the Presidium to find my father and the others. Tell them we'll have the full cooperation of the czars and the sentries. Sadie and I will meet you at the Presidium offices."

"Uh—are you sure that's a good idea? I mean do we know we'll have their cooperation?" David asked hesitantly.

"Absolutely."

"Fine, but you aren't going anywhere without me." David's voice took on a familiar stubborn tone. "I don't know what's going on with you, Killian, but I couldn't telepath to you tonight. It's like you were gone."

"I'm not gone." He let out a slow breath as he made the decision to acknowledge what he and Sadie already knew. "Sadie and I are mates. It's a long story and I'll explain more later." Sadie's eyes widened when he admitted to a member of his pack that not only was he fooling around with a vampire—but he'd chosen to mate with one. "We have more pressing matters to deal with."

"Shit," David said in a rush of air. "If the bloodsuckers that have your father find out about *that*, they'll fucking kill him. This gets worse by the second. We're going to have an all-out war on our hands if anything happens to the king. To say nothing of the general's only daughter."

"Other than Sadie's coven, you're the only one who knows about our *unique* pairing." Killian clung a bit tighter to his lover and said, "At least, for now. Let's deal with what's in front of us. Finding my father and the others is first and foremost. Sadie and I will meet you all at the Presidium in a half hour."

The line went dead. Killian swore under his breath as he wrapped both arms around Sadie. He stroked her long, silky hair and breathed her in, needing the comfort and serenity her touch always brought him. That unsettled part of him, the one that constantly fought to be free of duty and restraints, completely calmed within her embrace.

"You think vampires abducted your father and the others, don't you?" Sadie asked quietly. She tilted her head back and met his serious stare with her own. "Whoever wrote those notes did this, didn't they?"

"Probably." Killian cradled her face with both hands and brushed his thumb over the curve of her cheek. "Our best bet is to try and find my father and the others as quickly as possible. David's right. General Wolcott won't wait long for answers."

Sadie nodded and gave him a quick kiss before heading for the stairs.

"Where are you going?"

"To get dressed." A hard, dangerous glint flickered in her dark, almost ebony eyes. "Then I'm going to call Olivia and have everyone meet us at Xavier's lab. Time is of the essence and we're going to need weapons. I may be a breathing vampire with a heartbeat, but you can bet your ass I still know how to fire a gun."

"Sadie, I don't know if adding firepower to this is a good idea," Killian said hesitantly.

"See?" Sadie shook her head as she backed toward the steps. "Now I *know* that you're not a city boy. Trust me, baby, it's better to be safe than sorry. Listen, I know that in the Werewolf Society, you guys settle your differences with battles in your wolf pelts, but here in New York, things work a little differently. Don't worry. I've got your back."

Without another word, she whisked up the stairs in a blur and disappeared around the corner to the bedroom. Killian scrolled through the series of missed calls on his phone and cringed when he saw the multiple calls from the general and his mother. Among the voice mails, an unfamiliar number captured his attention.

It was a Manhattan area code.

He punched the screen and put the phone to his ear. A voice he didn't recognize, one that sounded like it was being distorted, came through in a static-laden message. As it played out, rage surged through Killian and his eyes shifted harshly to the eyes of his wolf.

Come to your club. Just you and Sadie. If you bring anyone else, your father and the others will die. You have until sunrise, and if you're not here by then...King Heinrich is a dead man.

Chapter 16

SADIE TIGHTENED THE WEAPON HARNESS AND ADJUSTED the throwing knives, making sure they were secure. Xavier's lab, normally quiet and sterile, had become a hotbed of activity with everyone getting fitted for weaponry while they hashed out a plan. When Killian told her about the message, Sadie was prepared to do what the kidnappers said and go right to the Loup Garou to retrieve his father, but Killian wouldn't hear of it. Her nerves were on edge, along with everyone else's, but at least the heartbeat and breathing had gone away and she was back to her regular vampy self. She couldn't imagine going into this situation feeling off her game.

"You're taking one hell of a chance, Killian." Olivia's voice, laced with concern, bounced around Xavier's cavernous laboratory. Her curly red hair was tied back in a tight braid, and she had dressed in the leather uniform of a sentry. The czar looked a lot less like a politician and more like a lethal weapon. She slapped an ammunition clip into her gun before slipping it into a holster with the ease of familiarity. "I know you didn't have to come here first. To be honest, if I had been in your position, I don't know if I would have."

"Like I said before, I want you to trust me and it's even more important now." Killian checked the ammo clip in the gun he was given and secured it before leveling a deadly serious gaze at Olivia and Doug. "But that's not the only reason I asked you to be involved in retrieving my father and the others."

"Okay," Doug said tightly. "We're listening."

David, Sadie, Xavier, Trixie, and Dakota went completely still. Even Bella stopped fluttering around and settled in behind Xavier like a ghostly guardian. All eyes were on Killian. Sadie moved in next to Killian and linked her hand with his. *I've got your back.* He smiled as her mind touched his and gave her fingers a reassuring squeeze before turning his attention back to the group.

"If my father were here, he would insist on your involvement. Olivia, he admires you and believes you have a bright and unique vision of the future." Killian's commanding voice, strong and steady, filled the space with ease. "We've had peace between our races, but we all know that it's been a strained peace at best. My father has always had a vision of bridging the gap between our people, and that's one of the reasons he gave me his blessing to move here. I won't allow a small group of fanatics to destroy what my father is trying so hard to build. If he were here, he would be enlisting your help, exactly as I am."

"Y'know this could cost your old man his life," Dakota said in his typically blunt manner. "If they get wind that we're with y'all, the king is as good as dead."

"I know, but it's a chance we have to take." Killian nodded slowly and Sadie's heart ached at the pained expression that flickered over her lover's face. "My father would tell you this isn't just about him. It's about what's best for our people."

"The prince is right." David, who'd been standing

by the doors and doing his best to stay out of the way, finally chimed in. "If the Presidium works with us to bring King Heinrich and the others to safety, that will help squash the idea that this attack was sanctioned by your government. We have to do this together."

"Together," Doug said with a deadly grin. "And quietly." He grabbed Olivia around the waist and gave her a quick kiss on the cheek. "Let's do this. We have a little girl who's going to want her Cheerios when the sun comes up."

"Emily's with Maya and Shane?" Sadie asked, her heart breaking to even think of that little girl losing her parents. "I don't know about this. Maybe you guys should stay here."

"Things like this are part of the gig," Olivia said with a wink. "And I don't plan on getting dusted any time soon. Besides, I think it's best that Maya steers clear of anything that involves the wolves. There's no safer place in the world for Emily than with Maya, because *Shane* is right there with her. Damien's with Suzie and Justine at the Presidium offices, so I think we have all of our bases covered."

"Let's go over this one more time," Doug said firmly. "Trixie and I will enter from the roof and listen from our vantage point in the stairwell. Olivia, David, and Dakota will enter through the emergency exit in the alley. It's too bad we don't have that underground entrance to use."

"I'm sorry," Killian said with a sidelong glance at Sadie. "I should've told you guys about that."

"Live and learn, brother. Olivia and I can telepath to each other, which will allow us to keep the two teams connected. Killian and Sadie will go in through the front door of the club, and we'll all keep our distance until we hear the code word from either of you—*Armageddon*. When the king is out of harm's way or you see an opening, then you say it and we bring it."

"Remember, we don't know how many vamps may be involved." Olivia's stance was rigid and the woman looked ready to explode into action at any moment. "Darius is nowhere to be found, and neither are his two partners in crime. Chances are it's just the three of them behind this fucking mess, but the truth is, we just don't know."

"Whoever did this had to subdue not only my father, but Ivan." Killian's body tensed when he mentioned his former bodyguard. "I'm betting on more than three."

"Like I said, we keep our senses alert and take it slow. Everyone watch your ass and each other's. You all have solid silver bullets. No liquid silver ammo, because we can't risk the king getting hit with it. There's no cure for that shit." Olivia nodded and shot a look at Doug. "Let's go."

"Thank you," Killian said quietly, bringing the activity in the room to a standstill. He leveled a serious look at each of them. "I know that you're all putting yourself in harm's way and—"

"You would do the same for us," Sadie interrupted. Leaning into his embrace, she gave him a reassuring squeeze. "Besides, you're my bloodmate and that makes you part of the family."

"This is one weird fuckin' family, y'all," Dakota drawled before popping a lollipop in his mouth.

"You're one to talk." Trixie cracked her knuckles and gave Dakota's lollipop a doubtful look. "Dude. You've got balls."

"Darlin'?" He removed the lollipop and pointed it at her as a sly grin covered his face. "Your hair looks like an Easter egg."

"Suck it, cowboy." Trixie flipped him the bird, which elicited a wide grin from Dakota.

"Like I said, y'all." He sighed. "Weird fuckin' family."

"Enough chitchat," Olivia said with a pointed look at Trixie and Dakota. "Or whatever that is." She made a circular motion with one hand toward the odd couple on the other side of the room. "Save all that energy because we're gonna need it. We've got under an hour until sunrise. Time to move."

The massive stainless-steel doors opened and the heavily armed group began to file out. Killian took Sadie's hand in his, but before they could leave, Xavier flew over to them and blocked their exit. A concerned expression covered his face and he glanced over his shoulder, ensuring no one else was within earshot.

"I didn't want to say anything in front of the others, but there's something you should know before you leave." Hovering in midair, he wrung his pudgy hands together before pushing his glasses on top of his head. "I ran the tests three times, hoping that the results were wrong, but I don't believe they were."

"It's okay, Xavier," Sadie said, steeling her resolve. "Just spit it out."

"Your DNA…it's…well…it's changed."

"What do you mean?" Dread curled in Sadie's belly

as Killian tightened his grip on her hand. "I—I'm still me. I mean, I'm still a vampire, Xavier."

"Yes," he said reluctantly. "But you're not only a vampire. I tested your most recent blood sample against Killian's blood *and* your original blood sample from when you were registered in the Presidium's data banks. They don't match."

"I don't understand." Sadie's brow furrowed and she heard Olivia call for them from the hallway. "Doesn't match what?"

"Any of it." Xavier's expression shifted to one of awe. "Your DNA is neither vampire nor werewolf, Sadie. My point is…it seems that you are both."

"Has this ever happened before?" Killian asked in an almost reverent tone.

"No." Xavier shook his head adamantly. "I didn't think—I mean—no one thought this was even possible. Sadie, your DNA was altered when you were bitten by that wolf, and when Olivia turned you, it must have left your werewolf traits in a dormant state. I think that feeding on Killian triggered something inside you that precipitated the change." He let out a sigh and held up both hands. "At least, that's my theory. Your body chemistry has completely changed. You, Sadie girl, are a hybrid."

"Holy shit," Sadie said in a rush. "So—so I could shift again."

"Yes." Xavier's mouth pressed in a tight line as he looked from Sadie to Killian. "It's not a matter of if you will, but when."

"Let's go," Olivia said from the doorway. Her brow furrowed when she saw the look on Sadie's face. "Sunrise is less than an hour away. We have to move."

"Okay," Sadie said absently. She nodded and slipped her hand from Killian's as she brushed past Xavier. Her entire body felt numb, and she was pretty sure she'd slipped into some weird stage of denial. "We'll talk more about it when I get back."

"Sadie, wait." Killian grabbed her by both shoulders and spun her to face him. "You can't go. When someone is first turned, they have little to no control over the shift, and usually it's triggered by intense emotion. There's no way I'm letting you do this. It's too dangerous."

"I'm not one of your subjects, Killian, and commanding me to do or not do something is never going to be okay." Sadie squared her shoulders and stepped out of his grasp, meeting his angry gaze with her own. "I may be turning into some kind of freak hybrid, but I refuse to allow it to control me."

"This isn't about controlling you." Anger edged his words and his eyes burned. "You're being unreasonable."

"I make my own choices, Killian," Sadie said quietly. "I always have."

"What's the holdup?" Doug shouted. "Let's go."

Turning on her heels and without waiting for Killian to respond, Sadie marched out to meet the others. Hearing what Xavier had to say was nothing compared to seeing Killian's furious, glowing eyes as she walked away.

"We're coming." Sadie glanced over her shoulder at Killian, who looked no less furious. "Both of us."

Killian was unaccustomed to being afraid, and he decided that he didn't like how it felt. Nope, not one damn bit. The stubborn woman refused to listen to reason and insisted on heading into what was sure to be a volatile situation with absolutely no idea how to control her wolf.

Shit.

He and Sadie got out of the car and strode down the block to the Loup Garou. The sidewalks were quiet and void of most humans, and the streets were empty except for a few delivery trucks and a taxicab or two. The city was relatively silent, and yet no silence was heavier than the one lingering between him and Sadie. He couldn't stand it one more second, and even though he risked pissing her off further, he stopped her before they reached the entrance of the club.

"Sadie, wait." Killian curled his arm around her bicep and pulled her around to face him. Her dark eyes glittered up at him with familiar determination, and in spite of their situation, a smile bloomed on his face. "I have one more thing to say before we go in there."

"I'm not going to change my mind."

"I know that." He released her arm and settled his hands on his hips as he cast a quick glance to the unlit entrance of the club. "If you do shift, you'll still be fiercely strong, and instead of two fangs, you'll have a mouthful of teeth."

"Got it." Sadie studied him carefully, her defensive posture softening, and she nodded. "Thanks."

"If you want to shift back, just picture yourself as you always are." Killian ran a finger along her jawline and her stony expression wavered. "Imagine this beautiful face. It's really as simple as that, but most new wolves panic and can't see the forest through the trees."

"Okay." Sadie nodded. She removed the gun from her holster, clearly not wanting to linger on the topic, and as much as he hated to admit it, she was right. "Got it. Power of the mind and all that jazz." She flicked her gaze to the sky. "Your father and the others don't have much time."

Killian looked around, ensuring there were no humans in sight, and took out the gun they'd given him. He knew how to handle a weapon and was actually a good shot, but it still wasn't the way he preferred to fight. In all likelihood he wouldn't even use it. If it came to a battle, he'd shift to his wolf and rip these motherfuckers in half. That would be far more satisfying.

With Sadie right behind him, Killian slowly opened the door of the Loup Garou and the two of them slipped inside. Back to back and with guns drawn, they slowly spun around. It didn't take long before they found the first victims.

"Holy shit," Killian said under his breath.

To the right of the club, dangling from the balcony level, were Christina's two friends. Linda's and Diana's naked bodies were hanging by their ankles from silver chains. Their flesh looked singed in some spots; their long hair hung in messy tendrils and drifted against their lifeless, blood-covered arms. The two women had been totally drained, and their open eyes stared vacantly out at the world, making them look like macabre dolls.

Oh my God, Killian. Sadie's quivering voice touched his mind. *Vamps definitely killed those women, but I smell...* Killian was about to go over to them when Sadie grabbed his arm and whispered into his mind. *Wolves.*

"Drop your weapons." A deep, familiar voice

resonated through the club from the upper left corner, an order immediately followed by the unmistakable sound of a gun cocking. "Put them on the floor now. Unless you want your old man to get a bullet to the brain."

Pure unadulterated fury fired through Killian as he realized who had betrayed him. Turning slowly, the prince lifted his burning gaze to the opposite side of the room. Killian's father was bound with silver ropes, making him weak. Killian could sense his father was breathing and his heart still beat, but he was completely unconscious—probably drugged. His bound body was draped over the side of the balcony at the waist and his captor held a gun to the back of the king's head.

"Ivan." A growl rumbled deep in Killian's chest and his eyes burned orange. "I should have fucking known."

"Weapons on the ground." Ivan jutted his chin toward them while he held the gun to the king's temple. "Now. Knives too. Lay them down on the floor, then step back."

While they did as he asked, Killian touched Sadie's mind with his. *The son of a bitch is up there so I can't fight him in my wolf pelt. We have to get him down here. I can't risk calling in the others while he's got a gun to my father's head.*

"What's your endgame with this? You're looking to start the war again?" Sadie asked while removing her weapons harness and the two knives. Hopefully, he wouldn't notice the one sheathed in the back pocket of her jeans. She tossed the harness on the floor and positioned herself next to Killian. "Where's that bitch? I don't see her strung up next to the others, and it's unlikely you pulled this off by yourself."

"If you're referring to Christina," Ivan said with a widening grin, "she's...around."

Shit. Sadie's voice shot into his mind on a hiss. *She's either dead or in on it.*

"Okay, Ivan." Killian opened his arms wide and stepped in front of Sadie, knowing that if a shot was fired, he could block it and keep her safe. "We're here. You've got my father and killed Christina's ladies-in-waiting. I imagine the pilot is dead too. Now what?"

"Nope. You're only part right." Ivan shook his head and inched closer to the railing, pressing the gun harder against the king's head. "I didn't kill those annoying twits. That vamp Darius and those two Dracula rejects took care of that for me. I had them pegged. I guess the lure of werewolf blood is just too strong for some blood-suckers to resist." He sighed. "Those three prejudiced assholes are like the preachers who talk about fidelity and then bang hookers behind closed doors. Anyway, Darius and his boys got so fuckin' hopped up, they couldn't stop."

"They combusted, didn't they?" Sadie's voice was flat and hard, matching the expression on her face.

"Yup," Ivan said through a laugh. "They were fucking and sucking and then...well...let's just say they went out with a bang. The girls were already dead by the time the fangers went all *Firestarter*."

"You sick fuck," Sadie growled. "You let them drain those girls."

"They were annoying anyway. As for the pilot, he's drugged like your old man. I drugged their asses. Poor bastards won't remember a thing. Except, of course, that I came to their rescue. Then the pilot can fly us all home.

Well, not all." An evil grin curved his lips. "Not you and your vampire slut. No. You'll be dead. The slut and her coven of bloodsuckers will be blamed for your death and the king's abduction. We may not get an all-out war, but you can bet your fucking ass we won't have a vampire whore on the throne."

"Really? That's all ya got?" Sadie arched one eyebrow. "Calling me a slut? Dude. That's so lame."

"I have to agree," Killian scoffed, while slowly moving toward that side of the room. "And using a gun to kill me is about the most chickenshit way to do it."

"Sure looks that way to me, Ivan," Sadie taunted. "It looks like you're afraid to fight his vampire-loving ass."

"No. This is just far more efficient," Ivan said in a deadly tone. He raised the gun and smirked. "Bye-bye, Killian."

Chapter 17

"I ALWAYS KNEW YOU WERE A COWARD." KILLIAN'S quiet, taunting voice echoed through the club. "I guess you're not wolf enough to take me on. Are you, Ivan? If you've gone to all of these lengths in the name of keeping our race secure, then I would think you would at least fight me the way nature intended. You know the rules of the society. If you challenge an alpha, it's a fight to the death."

Killian. Sadie knew Killian could handle Ivan one on one, but he couldn't outrun a bullet. *Be careful.*

"You know what?" Ivan lowered the gun and pointed it back at the king's head. "You're right. If I'm going to take you down, then I should do it the right way." A sick smile covered his face as he shouted, "Christina, get your pretty little ass out here!"

I fucking knew it. Sadie touched his mind just as Christina emerged from the shadows of the doorway by Killian's office. *That bitch was involved all along.* Sadie stilled when Christina's bruised and battered face came into view. Her right eye was swollen shut and the flesh had turned an ugly shade of purple. She had a fat lip and looked like she'd been crying. In that instant, Sadie's entire opinion of the woman changed. She might have been a snotty bitch, but nobody deserved a beating like that. She held a gun in her shaking hand that was pointed right at Sadie. *Or not. Jesus, look at what he'd done to her.*

"Hey, baby. Just stay right there. I know Killian will behave himself because he doesn't want his little vamp to get a belly full of silver." Ivan grabbed the king as though he weighed nothing at all and tossed him over his shoulder. He leaped over the balcony and landed squarely on both feet. The sound echoed through the space, sending tremors through Sadie right to her bones. Based on Ivan's strength, Sadie knew this would not be an easy fight for Killian. A moment later, Ivan dropped the king on the ground like a sack of potatoes, keeping his weapon pointed at Sadie the entire time. "Get over here, Christina."

Christina didn't move but kept her frightened stare, to say nothing of the gun, directed at Sadie. She looked totally terrified.

What the hell? Sadie whispered into Killian's mind. *I've heard of Stockholm syndrome, but she hasn't been with him that long. Why wouldn't she use the gun on him?*

"Now," Ivan barked. Christina flinched and quickly scurried over to Ivan. "Good girl." He grabbed her by the arm and pushed her to her knees. "You keep that gun on the king. If either of them come near you, you blow his head off. Remember what I told you. There's no going back now, and if everyone finds out that you were the one leaving those notes, you're fucked. No refunds or returns, baby. You're in this for the long haul. If I go down, you're coming with me."

"I know," Christina whimpered. Kneeling behind King Heinrich, she held the gun to his head as her shoulders shook. "I'm sorry…I'm so sorry."

"Shut up!" Ivan shouted. "You are such a whiny bitch."

"Let her go," Killian said evenly.

"What? You suddenly give a shit about her?" Ivan scoffed. "Please. All you've been thinking about ever since we go to this shithole city is *her*." He glowered at Sadie and kicked the king with his booted foot. King Heinrich groaned but didn't wake up, and Sadie could feel the rage oozing from Killian. "Your old man is so fucking weak, he was willing to look the other way while you wasted your time with a damn vampire."

Sadie flicked her gaze to Killian. That was probably why she didn't see Ivan turn the gun her way. Sadie heard the shot a second too late. The silencer made it sound like a whistle. When the silver bullet punctured her shoulder and emerged through her back, it felt like her blood turned to liquid fire. Killian's outraged scream filled her head.

She dropped to the floor in a heap and a blinding flash of light erupted as Killian and Ivan shifted into their wolves. Hackles raised and with teeth gnashing, the two massive wolves tangled with each other in a flurry of fur and claws at the center of the room. They were about the same size in their wolf pelts, but Ivan was a bit bulkier than Killian, giving him a slight advantage. Snarls ripped through the room as they rose on their hind legs and tore at each other ferociously with snapping jaws.

Writhing in pain, liquid fire coursing through her body from the effects of the silver, Sadie fought through the dizziness and pushed herself to a sitting position. She'd been hit by silver before, and luckily this time the bullet had passed right through. Her vision blurred and she felt like she was in the middle of a nightmare.

Everything spun as she tried to focus. Christina had dropped the gun and lay on the floor next to King Heinrich. The woman was curled up in a fetal position like a terrified child, shaking and whimpering and no threat to anyone.

Sadie didn't have to say the safe word to bring her friends to their aid. Having heard the gunfire and Christina's screams, they were already there. Blinking, trying to clear her vision as she rose to her feet, Sadie saw Olivia's red hair fly by in a blur as she went directly to the king. The heavily armed group swiftly entered the room and surrounded the battling wolves, who were seemingly unaware of the latest arrivals.

Muzzles bloodied and circling one another, both Killian and Ivan were wounded and breathing heavily. Sadie could tell that neither would give an inch for fear the other would take the advantage. The sound of Dakota's gun cocking echoed through the room and was immediately followed by loud rumbling growls from Killian and Ivan. Ivan snapped his jaws and the hackles on his brown-and-beige fur-covered body rose higher.

"No!" David shouted and put one hand on Dakota's weapon, stopping him from going any further. "Killian has to finish this himself. If you interfere, it will do him more harm than good. If he's ever going to be king, he has to finish this on his own."

Dakota looked at the czars, currently in the process of trying to revive King Heinrich. Olivia sat on the ground with the king's head in her lap. She exchanged a knowing look with Doug and nodded her agreement. Dakota reluctantly lowered his weapon with a sound of disappointment. A split second later, Ivan lunged toward Killian and the sight of his sharp mouthful of teeth lunging toward her lover was almost too much for Sadie to bear.

Ivan knocked Killian to the ground and his jaws sank into Killian's shoulder while fear swirled inside Sadie like a tornado. Amid that rush of energy and intense emotion, her heart began to beat again.

A cool wave of air filled her lungs as her heart pounded in her chest. Sweat dripped into her eyes while she watched Killian fight for his life. The fire in her blood seeped out to her skin, and it felt like flames flickered over her sweaty flesh, making the effects of the silver seem like child's play. Squeezing her eyes shut, she fought the change that she knew was coming, but it was too late. In a brilliant explosion of light and a painful rush of heat, Sadie's body erupted into the sleek, furred body of her wolf.

A growl rolled in her chest and her hackles rose as she got her feet under her, stalking closer to the center of the room. The look on Ivan's furry face when he saw her shift into her wolf pelt was nothing short of pure shock, and that was exactly the distraction that Killian needed. He was pinned beneath Ivan's larger frame, and now with a rumbling snarl, Killian latched his jaws around the traitor's neck.

In one fluid motion, Killian leveraged his body weight and swiftly flipped Ivan onto his back before biting down and crushing his neck. Snarling, Killian bit down further and shook his opponent brutally. Ivan's body went limp. In an instant, the traitor shifted back to his human form and lay motionless on the floor. Killian— breathless, weakened, and bloody from battle—released

Ivan's neck and stumbled away from his naked, life-less form.

Without waiting for Killian to shift back, Sadie ran to the center of the room and nuzzled the warm, damp fur along his neck in the closest thing she could muster to a hug. Killian whined and immediately returned her affection as he touched her mind with his. *Now, you did that just to prove me wrong, didn't you?*

Yup. Sadie sat on her haunches next to him and licked his nose playfully. *I told you I could handle myself.*

"Well, that's new," Trixie murmured. She was squat-ting on the ground next to Christina, who looked equally shocked. "Shit. This bloodmate legend sure has some freaky side effects. You can count me out for that one, and the pregnant thing too. No thanks."

"Like I said, y'all." Dakota put his gun in his holster and shook his head. "This is one weird fuckin' family." He hooked his thumbs in the waist of his leather pants and shot a glance at David. "Is it crazy like this back in Alaska?"

"Well, it wasn't," David said with a small laugh. "But something tells me things are about to change."

––––⁓––––

It had only been a few days since the nightmare with Ivan and yet somehow it seemed far longer. Once King Heinrich regained consciousness and heard what had happened, everyone went into serious damage-control mode. Ruffled feathers had to be smoothed and bruised trusts were in need of repair.

Sitting in the waiting room of the Presidium offices, Sadie had never been more nervous in her entire life.

Her entire future was riding on whatever happened in that meeting—the one she wasn't allowed to attend. All of the bigwigs were in there deciding her fate. Emperor Zhao had even flown in from Hong Kong. King Heinrich, General Wolcott, Olivia, Doug, and the emperor were all in that conference room listening to Xavier as he told them everything he knew about Sadie's...*situation*.

At least she wasn't in *Christina's* situation. Hell, she actually felt sorry for the girl. Her father and mother had arrived in the city within hours of hearing their daughter was safe. Naturally, the general wanted all the vamps in Manhattan strapped with silver and staked out for sunrise. The czars and King Heinrich thought there would be a hell of a fight getting him to believe what happened, but to everyone's surprise, Christina confessed to it all. She'd sent the notes, and when Ivan found out, he'd used that information to blackmail her and help his cause.

The woman was back in Alaska in a padded room, but the general kept referring to it as a vacation. Right. Sadie rolled her eyes.

Wearing a simple black suit and the ruffled white shirt she loved so much, Sadie was terrified. Once again that feeling of uncertainty had crept back inside, threatening her sanity. Killian sat next to her, his hand secured safely around hers, and when she shot a glance at him, she didn't miss the smirk on his handsome face.

"What are you grinnin' at?" Sadie elbowed him but didn't miss the shy smile from Suzie, who was watching them less than discreetly from behind her computer. "Why aren't you nervous? What if—"

"What?" Killian released her hand and draped his

arm over her shoulders before placing a warm kiss on her temple. "What are they going to do? Banish us? This meeting is just about sharing information and making sure we're all on the same page. I bet Xavier has them eating out of the palm of his hand."

"You're right. I know you are, but…what about you?" she asked quietly. "I mean…I kind of screwed you."

"Yes." Killian wiggled his eyebrows. "You did. Several times."

"Killian," Sadie said through a giggle that she was unable to stop. "I'm being serious."

"So am I," he said innocently.

Sadie opened her mouth to argue with him and tell him he was being ridiculous, that he wasn't taking their situation seriously, but he kissed it right out of her. His strong hand cradled the back of her head as he shifted her body and melded his lips with hers. Sadie sighed and opened to him, reveling in the spicy taste that had become so wonderfully familiar. His body pressed against hers, making her sink deeper into the buttery-soft leather couch. He softened the kiss and suckled her bottom lip before resting his forehead against hers.

"Everything will work itself out," he murmured.

Sadie was about to answer him when a familiar, deep voice interrupted them.

"Your mother says that to me all the time."

King Heinrich appeared and once again had Sadie scrambling to get out from under Killian. She tucked a loose lock of hair behind her ear and quickly rose to her feet to find Olivia standing behind the king, rolling her eyes. Sadie felt like a teenager getting caught by her parents making out in a closet or something.

"Father, your timing continues to be impeccable."
Killian stood next to Sadie and linked his arm around
her waist. "I take it the meeting is over."

"Not quite." King Heinrich glanced quickly at Sadie
before looking back at his son. "We'd like to speak with
the two of you before our decision is announced to the
various communities."

Decision? Sadie touched Killian's mind and grabbed
his hand as they headed to the room. *What the hell?*
They're going to announce that I'm a freak and that you
won't be king. Wonderful.

Killian and Sadie followed the king into the conference room and closed the door tightly behind them.
Xavier stood on a stool by the large screen on the left
side of the room. A colorful graph glared brightly from
the projector, one that Sadie could only assume had to
do with her condition. Xavier winked as she made her
way toward the table, Killian's hand linked tightly in
hers. She gave him a strained smile.

Emperor Zhao was seated at the head of the long
table, with King Heinrich and General Wolcott on the
right. Olivia and Doug were on his left, and the emperor
gestured for Sadie and Killian to take the empty seats.
Sadie made eye contact with the powerful ancient
vampire only briefly before sitting down. She'd only
met him once, the last time they had trouble in the
city, and he'd unnerved her just as much back then. He
was thousands of years old and possessed more power
than any other creature she'd ever encountered. His
energy was thick and pulsed through the room in pal-
pable waves.

"Hello, Sadie." Emperor Zhao's deep baritone

resonated through the room and Sadie's entire body stilled. Even with that quiet, almost imperceptible tone, he was commanding. "Xavier was enlightening us about your…evolution. According to his tests, this is a permanent condition. Isn't that correct, Xavier?"

"Yes." Xavier pushed his glasses back onto his nose and pointed at the chart on the screen. "As I mentioned earlier, her DNA has been completely altered and, well, Sadie girl is basically a new race all by herself. Not vampire. Not werewolf." Pushing his glasses onto his forehead, he looked back at the table. "She's both. An entirely new breed—a hybrid. In addition to the shifting, she is also a daywalker in both forms."

"Do you understand what this means?" Emperor Zhao asked. "Not just for you, Sadie, but for our people?"

"Yes, sir," Sadie said in a surprisingly confident voice. "My DNA was permanently altered the night Olivia found me, but it was dormant until—"

"Until we found each other," Killian said firmly.

"I know what it means." She forced herself to look each of them in the eye before saying what she knew they were all thinking. "I'm a threat—an abomination."

"Yes." Zhao flicked his serious ebony eyes to Sadie and her heart sank.

She could feel Killian's anger and touched his mind with hers. *Please, don't do anything. Let them say whatever they want and then we'll get the hell out of here.*

Zhao folded his hands on the table in front of him. He raised one dark eyebrow when a growl rumbled in Killian's chest. His enormous muscular frame was dressed in a five-thousand-dollar suit, but it couldn't hide his size or strength. Killian wasn't stupid; he wasn't going to attack the Emperor of the Presidium, but he also wasn't going to hide his outrage.

"In years past, that is probably what we all would have thought. Between your new genetic makeup and the unique mating between you and the prince, well, none of it would even be *considered* an acceptable event—not by either race." Killian opened his mouth to respond, but the emperor gave him a small smile and held up one hand. "Allow me to finish, Your Highness."

"Apologies." Killian tilted his head in deference. He glanced at his father, who seemed visibly annoyed with his son's impatience. "Please continue, Emperor Zhao."

"As I was saying, even a year ago, this mating would be seen by all of us as undesirable. However, given recent developments, we all feel that it comes at a most opportune moment in history. King Heinrich has always been eager to improve the relations between our people, and what better way to bridge the gap than with a royal pairing?"

"Royal pairing?" Killian looked at his father with confusion. "You mean you still want me to assume the throne in five years?"

"No." General Wolcott straightened the front of his jacket, which was laden with various medals on the lapels. Sadie felt Killian stiffen next to her, but to his credit, he held his tongue. "Not just you. Both of you." An uncomfortable look flickered across the general's face as he said, "My daughter's actions were inexcusable, and we cannot allow dissent like that to spread within the society."

"The two races must stand together if we are to not only survive but thrive in an increasingly changing world." Emperor Zhao gestured toward King Heinrich and the general. "If everything goes as we hope, you and Killian will help educate both races."

"We still have five years until you are to assume the throne," King Heinrich interjected. "She may be a vampire, but as Xavier has pointed out, she is one of us as well. In preparation for your impending positions on the throne, however, both of you will also serve as senators for the Presidium. Our hope is that by the time of your coronation, both of our races will have had time to adjust to the…changes. It will make for a smoother transition for you and build the relations between our people. And if they need more time to accept your pairing, then we'll take it. I am, after all, the king. Perhaps I'll linger on the throne a bit longer than is traditional."

Sadie and Killian looked at each other with total surprise and then back at the table full of power players.

"Is this for real?" Sadie asked, with a pointed look at her maker. "You want us to be politicians?"

"Think of it as goodwill ambassadors or liaisons between our races." Olivia smiled as though she had just thought of something great. "Just like Pete. Right? He's a vampire sentry but he's mated to an Amoveo shifter, so he's our liaison with them. See? No big deal."

"This is so you can keep an eye on me, isn't it?" Sadie leveled a serious look at the general and King Heinrich, and then at the emperor. "And on Killian."

"In part, yes," Emperor Zhao said, lifting one shoulder. "As we've seen with the other two bloodmate couples, this bond is unshakable. Therefore, we must use it to our advantage." He looked around the room and tilted his head in deference to King Heinrich. "All of us."

"You will live here in New York but make frequent visits to Alaska in an effort to familiarize Sadie with our people." King Heinrich turned his serious eyes to Sadie. "Then, when the time comes, both of you will come back to Alaska permanently. By that time, Sadie, you should have full control over your wolf." A sly smile curved his lips. "I wouldn't be surprised to find out that you already do."

"I have been practicing." Sadie nodded and looked away, holding Killian's hand tighter. The king was irritatingly perceptive. In the past couple of days, she'd been able to stop and start the shift with ease. In fact, instead of panicking at the idea of shifting, she'd found it an exhilarating challenge. "It's kind of like riding a bike…or breathing." She couldn't suppress the grin that emerged. "Once you get the hang of it, it becomes second nature."

"There is only one restriction for Ms. Pemberton," General Wolcott said in a deadly serious tone. "It is nonnegotiable."

"Okay," Sadie said slowly.

"You will not be permitted to turn anyone." His eyes flickered briefly and glowed before returning to their human state. "Ever."

"Fine." Sadie nodded and gave them a thumbs-up. "No new hybrid race. Got it."

"What if we have children?" Killian asked in a remarkably casual tone. "It is possible, isn't it, Xavier? They would be hybrids or something along those lines."

All eyes turned to the scientist. He looked a bit nervous and wrung his hands together while he seemed to be contemplating how to answer the question. No one was more interested in that answer than Sadie. Xavier pushed his glasses onto his head and locked gazes with her. Based on the tender gleam in his eyes, she knew what the answer was before he even said it.

"Yes, I suspect that it's possible," he said quietly before looking at the others. "Although we'll just have to wait and see."

Sadie looked at Killian who was smiling at her with nothing less than love. The others at the table responded, but Sadie didn't even hear them because she couldn't stop staring at Killian. *You heard him, didn't you?* Killian's seductive voice touched her mind as the others continued talking about next steps. *We could have children. I, for one, would like to start trying as soon as possible.*

Dude, take a chill pill. Sadie's eyes widened. *We've been together for like five minutes and I don't even—*

Oh fine. Killian rolled his eyes and looked back at the group, pretending to listen to them while he touched her mind. *But we should at least start practicing making babies. That's the fun part.*

After a bit more conversation about what was expected of Sadie and Killian, and confirming that they would be staying in New York for now, the czars escorted Zhao, Heinrich, and Wolcott out before bidding them farewell. Xavier flew over and placed a quick kiss on Sadie's cheek, which was immediately followed by a fluttering noise from above.

"She's like a daughter to me," he shouted without looking up. Bella materialized behind him and drifted over to the door, waiting not-so-patiently. "You see, Sadie girl. I told you it would all be just fine."

"Thank you, my friend," Sadie whispered. Gathering him in her arms, she hugged him tightly and kissed his cheek. "You are a true gentleman and one of the most trustworthy men I've ever known. I can always count on you."

Bella's fluttering grew louder.

"Yes, dear." Xavier winked at Sadie before flying out the door with his ghostly gal pal. "I'm coming."

The door shut quietly behind them, leaving Sadie and Killian alone in the conference room. Nibbling on her lower lip, she faced the screen and stared at the color-coded chart that compared her DNA to that of vampires and werewolves. That nervousness, the swirling ball of uncertainty, was gone and had been replaced by confidence. She knew what she was, and in a few hours, so would the rest of the community. And it was all okay, because not only did she have her family behind her… she had Killian.

At the same instant that thought whisked through her mind, Killian's arms linked around her waist and he nuzzled her neck with butterfly kisses. Sadie let out a contented sigh and settled her hands over his. Their linked hands rested on her belly while he gently rocked her in his embrace.

"Tell me what you're thinking," Killian murmured in her ear. "We can refuse, you know. If you don't want to do this, then I can call them all back in here and put a stop to it right now. We can leave and go start a life someplace on our own. No Presidium. No Werewolf Society. Just us."

"What about you?" Sadie turned in his arms to face him and leveled a serious look at her lover. "You never really wanted to be king," she said quietly. "Why would *you* agree to all of this?"

"Because of you." His caramel eyes crinkled at the corners and he settled his hands on her hips, pulling her close. "Assuming the throne, taking on all of that responsibility, it never made sense to me until I found you. Being king and mating only out of obligation or duty felt like a death sentence. But now, with you as my mate, my future is wide open. I know that having you by my side as my partner will make me a better leader for the society."

"But not yet," Sadie said with a wicked grin. Popping up on her toes, she flicked his lower lip with her tongue. "We've got the next five years here in New York."

"Yes, we do." Killian's eyes glowed amber as he captured her lips, kissing her deeply. Suckling her lower lip, he broke the kiss and murmured, "And I realize we have paperwork to fill out, but do you think the czars would mind if we…"

"I'm way ahead of you." Sadie's grin widened. Slipping out of his embrace, she went to the door and flipped the lock. "I think our first duty as senators should be to test out the sturdiness of that table."

That wicked grin she so adored covered his face as she stalked toward him. In a blur, she leaped into his arms, curling her body around his like a baby chimpanzee. He grabbed her ass with both hands and carried her over to the table while capturing her mouth with his.

I love you, Sadie. Killian's mind whispered along the edges of hers as he settled her on the edge of the table. Breaking the kiss, he pulled back and cradled her face with one hand. "Always. I can't promise there won't be surprises or challenges. I know that your life as a vampire was stable and steady, and your life with me will be…uncertain."

"No." Sadie shook her head and pressed her finger to his lips. "You couldn't be more wrong. I was wrong about something too. The future isn't promised to anyone, Killian, and all these years I fooled myself into thinking that it was. But you know what? There is something I'm sure about."

"What's that?" He brushed a lock of hair off her forehead and she shivered at the feel of his flesh rushing over hers. His intelligent, loving gaze met hers and he murmured, "Tell me."

"You," she said in a quivering voice. Staring into his handsome face, her heart swelled with love, and as the emotion surged, her heart began to beat. She took his hand and placed it over the now familiar, if not sporadic beat of her heart. "I love you, Killian, and my heart literally beats only for you."

IF YOU ENJOY SARA HUMPHREYS'S
DEAD IN THE CITY SERIES, BE SURE TO CHECK OUT
THE AMOVEO LEGEND SERIES FOR PARANORMAL
ROMANCE OF A *DIFFERENT* BREED.
READ ON FOR AN EXCERPT FROM *UNCLAIMED*.

"OKAY, PAL," TATIANA SAID EVENLY AS SHE STROKED the puppy's coat and carried him to the exam room. "I know you're not going to like this, but you need some stitches."

Bumping the door open with her backside, she placed the puppy on the table. He lay quietly and timidly, watching her with those soulful brown eyes as she gathered the supplies she needed.

Tatiana found the poor thing on the side of the road, but she'd felt his energy signature—red with pain and anguish—before she ever saw him. The only good thing about being half Amoveo was her ability to connect with animals on a psychic level. It made her an extremely effective veterinarian and had her patients' owners calling her an animal whisperer.

It wasn't that she actually spoke to them or that she could hear them speak with words—it was more like the ability to feel what the animals were feeling. Tatiana was able to sense their emotions and in turn could send the animal soothing energy waves. It allowed her to connect with them on a deeper level, which made the animals more willing to let her treat them.

Tatiana made quick work of cleaning up the little beagle as he responded to her calming energy, lying perfectly still while she sutured and dressed his wound. He licked her hand as she finished, and though she sensed gratitude in his energy waves, she also saw it in those gorgeous eyes.

She could connect with all animals but had an affinity for dogs, which was probably from being part of the Timber Wolf Clan. Sometimes she wondered if the animals knew she could shapeshift into a wolf.

"You're just a big flirt, aren't you?" she asked as she scooped him up and placed a kiss on his head. "Made me fall in love with you with one look from that sweet face. So you know what? I'm going to keep you."

Tatiana leaned back to get a better look at him and smiled.

"Yup," Tatiana said through a smile. "You're a heartbreaker, alright. So what do you think about the name Casanova?"

The puppy answered with a face full of warm licks and a nibble on her ear.

"Alright." Tatiana giggled. "Casanova it is, but I think we'll go with Cass for short."

Satisfied with his new moniker, he snuggled against her chest and lay still as her sister's voice floated into Tatiana's head. *Hey, sis.* Layla's familiar sound filled her mind. *Are you alone, or is Matt with you? I need to see you right away.*

I'm alone, Layla.

Tatiana grinned. Matt was her assistant and only friend outside of her siblings. Like her, he never knew his parents, but instead of being raised on a farm by a loving aunt like she had been, he grew up in foster homes and had no family to speak of.

Tatiana and her twin brother, Raife, may not have known their parents, but at least they had each other and their aunt Rosie. They were adopted and moved in when they were twelve, but they couldn't have been closer to Rosie than if they were actual blood relatives.

Matt always said he and Tatiana were like two peas in a pod. Tatiana felt a bit sorry for him because he really didn't have anyone other than her. He showed up looking for a job about a year ago, and they'd been thick as thieves ever since. However, as close as they were, he was still unaware of her unique heritage.

I'm in the exam room, but meet me in the waiting room, okay?

Tatiana held Cass a bit tighter as she made her way to the front office. Within seconds, the air-conditioned space filled with static electricity, and the air shimmered. Layla materialized in the center of the room. Her unruly red curls flowed wildly around her, and her brilliant green eyes sparkled brightly as she made quick work of kissing her sister on the cheek.

"I'll never get used to that," Tatiana said quietly as she hugged Cass for some much-needed reassurance, and to her surprise, the puppy snuggled closer and licked her neck. "Can all of them do that?"

"You mean all of *us*?" Layla said playfully as she let the puppy sniff her hand. "Yeah. The pure-blood Amoveo can do it, and the hybrids like us can do it." She lifted one shoulder and scratched Cass behind the ears. "At least, the few that I've met so far. Once you find your mate, you'll be able to do it too."

"No thanks, sis. I'll stick to regular forms of human travel *and* human dating, for that matter. So what's up?" Tatiana asked, changing the subject. She sat on the edge of the reception desk and watched her sister carefully. "You don't usually *pop in* like this."

"Hardee har har," Layla said with a roll of her eyes.

"Sorry," Tatiana said. "I couldn't help myself."

The smile faded from Layla's eyes, and Tatiana sensed the tension in her energy waves as they swirled faster through the room. It was something akin to a breeze that only another Amoveo could feel.

"We need your help."

"We?" Dread crawled up Tatiana's back.

"Richard, the Prince of the Amoveo, asked me to come here to see if you'd be willing to help him. He has about a dozen Arabian horses that have all come down with something. And before you ask, *no*. Richard doesn't want to use the vet he usually hires because he's concerned the animals might have been poisoned, and if that were the case, then the vet would want to get the police involved. He suspects it was either a Purist, or possibly, part of the recent Caedo activity. Either way, we obviously can't involve the human community."

"No way."

"Hear me out." Layla put her hand up to stop the inevitable protest, and Tatiana snapped her mouth closed.

Tatiana made no secret about her feelings regarding the Amoveo. Purist Amoveo killed her father for mating with her human mother. After their mother died, none of *them* came looking for her or her twin brother, Raife. The two felt as though they'd been completely abandoned. Therefore, she had no love for the Amoveo or their world.

Tatiana's mouth set in a tight line as she waited for her sister to continue.

"Thank you." Layla let out a slow breath. "Now, listen. I know you aren't jazzed about getting involved with the Amoveo. Believe me. I get it. You know that until I met William, I was on the same train as you. I thought they *all* hated hybrids—hated *us*—but it's simply not true. Yes. There are *some* Amoveo—the Purists—who would sooner see us dead than sullying their bloodlines with human blood, but most Amoveo aren't like that." Her jaw tilted determinedly. "William isn't," she said, referring to her new husband. "He's a Loyalist, just like the prince."

"I know," Tatiana said in a gentler tone. "I met William only a couple of times, but it's obvious he's crazy about you. I mean, he hovers around you and is more protective of you than Raife has ever been of either of us. I'm happy that you found someone who makes you so happy." Tatiana's face twisted with confusion, and she paused for a minute. "Wait a minute. Back up. Who or what is a Caedo?"

"The Caedo are a human family who know about us and hate us," Layla said with a casual shrug as she sat on the sofa. "Apparently, they were the big bad enemy until the Purists got their panties in a bunch about us hybrids."

"That's a lovely little tidbit—hard to believe you've been keeping that to yourself," Tatiana said sarcastically. "So there are two different groups that want to kill us. Awesome."

"Richard and the others thought the Caedo were a

nonissue, but it seems they started acting up again. They got wind of the little civil war we had with the Purists and decided to exploit the rift. Anyway, you wouldn't have to worry about that. All you have to do is come to the ranch and check out the horses. When you're done, you can split."

"You're killing me, you know that? Today was supposed to be my first day of vacation in the three years since I opened this place."

"Perfect." Layla smiled brightly. "You can vacation in Montana at the ranch. It's gorgeous in the summer. Actually, it reminds me of the farm where we grew up."

Tatiana glanced down at the sleeping puppy in her arms.

"You can bring the dog."

"Thanks." Tatiana chuckled. "Actually, he seems to be an empathetic little soul. I have a hunch he'd be a great therapy dog." She locked eyes with her sister as an idea bloomed. "I'm bringing more than the dog. I'm bringing Matt too."

"Shit." Layla laid her head back on the sofa and tapped her jean-clad legs with her trimmed fingernails. "Bringing a human to the ranch is not going to go over well with anyone, especially not with the Guardians. Dominic in particular—he's a big one for rules and tradition."

"Sorry, sis," Tatiana said all too sweetly. "That is a deal-breaker. No Matt, no doc. Whoever this Dominic guy is, well, he'll just have to like it or lump it."

Tatiana meant it. She wanted to help her sister, but she needed a security blanket, a way to be sure she wasn't going to get schooled by the Amoveo twenty-four-seven—a bunch of shifters trying to talk her into this mate nonsense. If she brought a human with her, then the Amoveo would have to be on their best behavior. Otherwise, they would risk letting the proverbial cat out of the bag.

"Fine. I'll run it by Richard and Salinda. If that's the only way we can get you to help, then I'm sure they'll be okay with it." Layla stood up. "So you'll come to the ranch and help us find out what's making the horses sick. Right?"

"Yes." Tatiana rose from her spot on the desk and met her sister at the center of the room. "I'll book Matt and me a flight and be there in a couple of days."

"Right." Layla nodded. "I'll pick you up at the airport."

"No," Tatiana added quickly. "I'll rent a car and drive there myself. Really, it's fine."

Layla let out sigh of frustration as she hugged her sister vigorously, which elicited a whine from Cass.

"It's okay, little buddy." Layla rubbed his ears and looked fondly at Tatiana. "I'm sorry as hell that the horses are sick, but I can't say I'm disappointed to have you visit." Her smile brightened. "Hey, you never know, maybe you'll find your mate, or at least get a visit from him in the dream realm."

"No thanks." Tatiana laughed and shook her head vehemently. "When love finds me, it will be the old-fashioned way. No dreams. No weird shit. Just good, old-fashioned, true love and romance. We *are* half human, in case you've forgotten."

"I guess that means that you and Matt aren't…"

"Nah." She made a face. "I think he'd like more, but

we're better as friends. No sparks. Y'know? I want a guy who will knock me out and have my head spinning."

"Oh, I know exactly what you're talking about." Layla's face turned as red as her hair, and she stuffed her hands in her pockets. "Actually, until I met William, I didn't really know what sparks were, and *believe me*, when you find your mate, you'll know what *I'm* talking about."

"When I find the love of my life, there will be plenty of sparks." Tatiana winked. "See you in a couple of days."

Tatiana watched as Layla's image wavered as though she were underwater, and as static crackled in the air, she vanished in a blink. As quiet settled, guilt swamped her.

She lied to her sister.

Tatiana already found her mate, or more to the point, her mate found her. She watched him time and again from the shadows of the dream realm as he hunted and stalked her in his tiger form. She had no idea what his name was or what he looked like as a human, but she *did* know he was dangerous. A predator. Yet for all his searching, she managed to stay hidden, and if she had anything to say about it, she would keep it that way.

"I'd have killed him twice if I could've," Dominic growled, his voice bouncing through the sterile medical facility.

"Easy there, tiger," Steven teased as he inspected the injury on his face. "You may be a badass from the Tiger Clan, but you're still my patient, so sit still or you won't get a lollipop."

Steven's teasing did nothing to improve Dominic's mood. He was itching to get back outside and patrol the property, but the doctor was taking his sweet time. Steven, a member of the Coyote Clan and an excellent healer, was known for his use of humor to put his patients at ease, but right now, the last thing Dominic wanted to do was laugh. He was surprised Steven even had a sense of humor left given the suffering he had endured over the past year.

Dominic's sense of humor, on the other hand, was nowhere to be found. There was nothing funny about what had transpired in the past week. Two Caedo assassins, members of the one human family who knew of the Amoveo's existence, snuck onto the ranch and attempted to murder the prince. Dominic killed one, but another shot Eric, the other Guardian, and escaped into the surrounding mountains.

Dominic sat unmoving on the hospital bed as Steven inspected the almost-healed injury, which ran down the left side of his face. Hands balled into fists in his lap, he stared past the healer to the blank wall behind him and concentrated on keeping his fury in check. Getting pissed at Steven wouldn't help anything.

"The stitches have dissolved, and the wound is beginning to fade. You'll have a scar, but from what I hear, chicks dig scars." Steven removed the latex gloves and tossed them in the trash. "I have to be honest. I'm surprised you healed this quickly, especially considering you haven't found your mate yet. Most fully mated Amoveo take longer to heal from a laceration as severe as this one."

Steven picked up the tablet on his desk and entered information as he continued speaking.

"I guess you Tiger Clan boys are as tough as they say

you are. Some say the tigers are the fiercest of all ten clans, and after treating you, I'd have to agree. However, you can't avoid the inevitable outcome if you don't connect with your mate."

Frustration flared, and despite Dominic's best efforts, his sharp brown eyes flickered and shifted into the glowing amber eyes of his tiger. He breathed deeply as he struggled for self-control and willed them back to their human state.

"A mate is irrelevant," Dominic said evenly. "As Guardian, my loyalties and responsibilities lie with the prince and his family. Wounded or not, I will continue as Guardian and keep our prince, and everyone else on the ranch, safe."

"Right." Steven ran a hand through his shaggy blond hair and shook his head. "I get it, dude. You are not one to fuck with. You more than proved it when you killed that Caedo assassin and ripped his head off like he was made of tissue paper."

"I would've done the same with the other one if I'd found him, but Eric's wound looked severe and—"

"And you did what anyone would do. You stopped to help your friend and fellow Guardian. Eric healed as quickly as you did, by the way. It's too bad we can't figure out what's making the horses sick, but from what I hear, they've got someone in mind to help."

"Yes." Dominic's mouth set in a tight line. "One mare died this morning, and given the recent Caedo activity and the continued animosity with lingering Purists, Richard is reluctant to bring in the local veterinarian."

"You're pretty good at changing the subject, Dominic."

Dominic swore and hopped off the bed. He snatched his black T-shirt off the chair before quickly pulling it on. "Why do you feel the need to bring up the issue of a mate, or more to the point, my lack of one?"

Dominic knew he sounded like a defensive asshole, but he couldn't help it. Steven was right. He still hadn't found his mate, and if he didn't find her soon, his Amoveo abilities would vanish, leaving him to live the rest of his existence as a human.

That was the fate of any Amoveo who didn't bond with a life mate by the age of thirty, and it wasn't one he was interested in participating in. However, with his thirtieth birthday just a year away, he knew the reality of what awaited him.

No shapeshifting, minimal strength, no powers of visualization.

How would he effectively serve as Guardian if he was void of his Amoveo abilities? Dominic shoved the dark thoughts from his mind, refusing to believe that it was actually a possibility. His military training brought him to this place, and he would be damned if some bullshit legend of fated mates would take that away. Mate or no mate, he would stay the course and fulfill his duties.

Even if it meant dying in the process.

"Hey, man." Steven raised his hands in surrender. "I'm just stating a fact, and it's only out of concern for you as a healer and a friend."

Dominic nodded and tucked his dog tags beneath his shirt. Even though he hadn't been in the human military for four years, it was still a part of who he was, and he'd feel naked without that cool stainless steel pressing against his skin. It was where he learned his combat skills and intense focus, both of which were crucial to his position.

"Have you connected with her at all?" he asked. "Any sign of her in the dream realm?"

"Not exactly," Dominic bit out, unable to look Steven in the eye.

All Amoveo connected with their mates in the dream realm before the physical plane. It was a crucial part of the mating process and one he hadn't experienced yet.

"I don't see her, but sometimes I can feel her there in the shadows and mists. I can sense her energy signature, and just when I think I have it, it slips away. It's frustrating as hell, and if I didn't know better, I'd think she was intentionally avoiding me."

"I see." Steven went to his desk and connected the tablet to his computer.

"And vanilla." Dominic crossed his arms over his broad chest and breathed deeply as the memory of the scent filled his head. "Sometimes I catch the scent of vanilla and cherries."

"Interesting." Steven shucked his white lab coat and draped it over the back of the desk chair, revealing an Iron Maiden T-shirt and torn jeans. Without his lab coat he looked more like a roadie than a doctor. "I never saw Courtney in the dream realm either, not clearly at least, and if I hadn't stumbled on her at that blasted Purist compound, I may never have found her. Don't use us as an example though, our mating has been… unorthodox."

"How do you mean?"

"Never mind." Steven waved him off. "As far as your mate avoiding you, that is certainly a possibility, and if you're concerned, I would suggest having a chat with my boy, Willie."

"Layla avoided him?" Dominic's brow knit in confusion. "That doesn't make any sense. Why would our mates avoid us?"

"Dude, are you serious?" Steven smiled and punched a few buttons on his computer before looking back at Dominic. "If she's a hybrid and has been raised away from our people, God only knows what she *knows* or *doesn't know* about us. *If* she knows what she is, she may think all Amoveo are like the Purists and want her dead for being a hybrid. *Maybe* she thinks we're all a bunch of chauvinistic pigs looking to drag our women into servitude. Hell, she may be a human and not even *know* that the Amoveo exist."

Dominic was quiet as Steven's words settled over him, and he felt like a dope for not thinking of these things sooner. This whole mate business was far more complicated than anyone ever let on.

"Or—" Steven sighed. "She could think you're buttass ugly and be running in the other direction."

Dominic cracked a smile in spite of himself and ran a hand over his cropped black hair.

"My point is," Steven said solemnly, "avoiding your mate or ignoring it isn't doing you any good, my friend. Your mate is out there somewhere, and if you don't find her soon, then you'll have to face the music one way or another."

Dominic clenched his jaw and strapped the leather weapons belt securely around his waist. He pulled the massive hunting knife from its sheath and briefly inspected it. Seeing that shiny blade instantly put his anxious heart at ease, but the reality of what Steven said still weighed heavily.

"I appreciate your concern, but I can assure you that finding, or not finding my mate, will not impact my ability to protect the prince. I would give my life to protect our people from anyone who threatens our existence."

"Yeah, I'm getting that," Steven said through a laugh. "Listen, I don't want to sound like an ungrateful ass. Courtney and I live here too, so your quick actions with those Caedo assassins protected her and the baby. She's already been through so much and still isn't fully recovered emotionally. The pregnancy is making it so much worse."

Steven's face darkened at the memories. Dominic heard about what some of the women were put through as involuntary participants in the Purist breeding program. He couldn't imagine the helplessness and rage that Steven must have felt knowing his mate had suffered. Whatever it was, it must've been bad, because he never talked about it.

"It's good to know that you and Eric have our backs." Steven stuck his hand out, and Dominic promptly accepted. "Thank you."

Dominic shook his hand quickly and gave him a brief nod of understanding before opening the door.

"Hey," Steven called. "Catch."

Dominic turned around and caught a lollipop as it came flying in his direction. He gave Steven a friendly smile as he stuck the lollipop in the pocket of his camo pants and headed out the door.

It's not that he didn't appreciate Steven's gratitude,

but it made him uncomfortable to be thanked for doing his job. Hell. He hadn't even done it that well. One assassin got away, and as far as Dominic was concerned, that was a failure.

However, it was not one that would be repeated.

As Dominic headed up the steps from the medical facility to the main floor of the house, he couldn't stop thinking about what Steven had said. Perhaps he was right. What if his mate had been avoiding him all along out of fear or ignorance?

Dominic swung the door open at the top of the stairs and instantly sensed familiar energy signatures, the spiritual fingerprints made by all Amoveo. Then an unfamiliar ripple in the air sent his protective instincts on high alert. He detected fear and apprehension flickering through the enormous house, and it was coming from an unknown Amoveo… and a human.

Caedo? That was all he could think. Another Caedo assassin or a Purist had infiltrated the property.

Dominic cut through the grand entry hall and in a blur of speed, he went immediately to the lavish living room to the left of the main hall. The scent of vanilla swamped him as he came to a halt in the doorway, ready for battle with glowing eyes and his knife drawn. The room was empty, but movement to his left captured his attention.

Without thinking, moving only on gut instinct, he spun to the left and grabbed the intruder, throwing them to the ground. In a matter of seconds, he straddled the small body and pinned the stranger easily beneath him. His knees held struggling arms to the floor, one hand curled over a slim shoulder, as the other held his knife poised high in the air, ready to strike.

As the haze of rage receded and the imminent danger was stifled, Dominic found himself staring into a pair of beautiful, furious golden eyes. A stunning hybrid Amoveo woman who smelled of cherries and vanilla glared at him, and if looks could kill, he'd be toast.

Shoulder-length dark hair framed a heart-shaped face stamped with anger, but through it all he detected a hauntingly familiar energy signature. It was the same one that slipped in and out of the dream realm and eluded him night after night.

Layla's voice drifted over his shoulder.

"Do you think you could get off my sister?"

Sister? Dominic blinked in surprise and sheathed his knife as he stared at the woman still trapped beneath him. Her eyes burned brightly in their clan form as her intoxicating scent filled his head.

As he remembered those nights in the dream realm, his body tightened and responded to her on an instinctual level. She wiggled, attempting to get out from under him, but he kept her there as the pieces fell into place.

Mate. That one word ran through his head over and over like an ancient mantra. This woman, the one he just tackled, as if she were a Caedo or Purist assassin, was his mate. *Son of a bitch.*

Vampire Trouble

Dead in the City Series
by Sara Humphreys

—‹‹‹—

A fledgling vampire ignites a war

Maya Robertson remembers the last moments of her life as a human with haunting clarity, and every man she meets pays the price…until Shane. Finding herself in the middle of a bloody fight between vampires and werewolves, Maya has no choice but to let the devastatingly sexy vampire guard get close to her.

And that's not all that heats up

Shane Quesada, a four-century-old vampire sentry, is known for his cold, unemotional precision, but once Maya begins to invade his dreams, his world is changed forever. His job to protect her is swiftly replaced by the all-consuming need to claim her as his own.

—‹‹‹—

"Humphreys is undoubtedly a rising star in the genre… The sparks that fly between the leading couple are totally irresistible!" —*RT Book Reviews*, a July Top Pick for Paranormal Romance

"A powerful love story that proves that while our past is inescapable, it is the core of our strength." —*Washington Post*

For more Sara Humphreys, visit:

www.sourcebooks.com

Tall, Dark, and Vampire

Dead in the City Series
by Sara Humphreys

—◆—

She always knew Fate was cruel…

The last person Olivia expected to turn up at her club was her one true love. It would normally be great to see him, *except he's been dead for centuries*. Olivia really thought she had moved on with her immortal life, but as soon as she sees Doug Paxton, she knows she'd rather die than lose him again. And that's a real problem…

But this is beyond the pale…

Doug is a no-nonsense cop by day, but his nights are tormented by dreams of a gorgeous redhead who's so much a part of him, she seems to be in his blood. When he meets Olivia face-to-face, long-buried memories begin to surface. She might be the answer to his prayers…or she might be the death of him.

—◆—

"Shines with fascinating new characters… Readers will not want to wait for more from the very talented Humphreys!"
—*RT Book Reviews* Top Pick of the Month, 4.5 Stars

For more Sara Humphreys, visit:

www.sourcebooks.com

Unclaimed

The Amoveo Legend Series
by Sara Humphreys

She works hard to be normal...

Tatiana Winters loves the freedom of her life as a veterinarian in Oregon. It's only reluctantly that she agrees to help cure a mysterious illness among the horses on a Montana ranch—the ranch of the Amoveo Prince. Tatiana is no ordinary vet—she's a hybrid from the Timber Wolf Clan, but she wants nothing to do with the world of the Amoveo shifters.

But there's no escaping destiny

Dominic Trejada serves as a Guardian, one of the elite protectors of the Prince's Montana ranch. As a dedicated Amoveo warrior, he is desperate to find his mate, and time is running out. He knows Tatiana is the one—but if he can't convince her, he may not be able to protect her from the evil that's rapidly closing in...

"The world that she has created is so fascinating, and the characters so engaging, that each new book is like catching up with old friends." —*RT Book Reviews* Top Pick, 4.5 Stars

For more Sara Humphreys, visit:

www.sourcebooks.com

Undone

The Amoveo Legend Series
by Sara Humphreys

—⁓—

She's far from human...

With her secret race of shapeshifters embroiled in civil war, all Marianna Coltari wants is to stay far from controversy. Even so, when her overprotective brother insists on hiring his human friend Pete as her bodyguard, Marianna is furious.

Does she dare to love one?

Like most retired cops, Pete Castro resents his new job as a bodyguard. It's even worse because he'll be babysitting a party girl like Marianna. But that's before he meets her for the first time and discovers his instincts on red alert. Would he kill to protect her?

—⁓—

For more Sara Humphreys, visit:

www.sourcebooks.com

Untamed

The Amoveo Legend Series
by Sara Humphreys

Her worst nightmare is coming true...

Layla Nickelsen has spent years hiding from her Amoveo mate and guarding a devastating secret. But Layla's worst fear is realized when the man who haunts her dreams shows up in person...

He has finally found her...

William Fleury is as stoic as they come, until he finds Layla and his feelings overwhelm him. She won't let him get close, but then an unknown enemy erupts in violence and threatens everything Layla holds dear...

—⁓—

"Compelling... Deft world-building and sensuous love scenes make this paranormal romantic thriller an enjoyable journey." —*Publishers Weekly*

"Humphreys's spectacular talent is on full display... You will feel as if you are entirely immersed in her world... This series is getting better with each book." —*RT Books Reviews*, 4.5 Stars

For more Sara Humphreys, visit:

www.sourcebooks.com

Untouched

The Amoveo Legend Series
by Sara Humphreys

She may appear to have it all, but inside she harbors a crippling secret...

Kerry Smithson's modeling career ensures that she will be admired from afar—which is what she wants, for human touch sparks blinding pain and mind-numbing visions.

Dante is a dream-walking shapeshifter—an Amoveo, who must find his destined mate or lose his power forever. Now that he has found Kerry, nothing could have prepared him for the challenge of keeping her safe. And it may be altogether impossible for Dante to protect his own heart when Kerry touches his soul...

"Outstanding... Red-hot love scenes punctuate a well-plotted suspense story that will keep readers turning pages as fast as they can." —*Publishers Weekly* Starred Review

For more Sara Humphreys, visit:

www.sourcebooks.com

Unleashed

The Amoveo Legend Series
by Sara Humphreys

What if you suddenly discovered your own powers were beyond anything you'd ever imagined...

Samantha Logan's childhood home had always been a haven, but everything changed while she was away. She has a gorgeous new neighbor, Malcolm, who introduces her to the amazing world of the dream-walking, shapeshifting Amoveo clans... but what leaves her reeling with disbelief is when he tells her she's one of them...

And shock turns to terror as Samantha falls prey to the deadly enemy determined to destroy the Amoveo, and the only chance she has to come into her true powers is to trust in Malcolm to show her the way...

"The characters haunted my dreams and I thought about this book constantly." —*Long and Short Reviews*

"The love scenes are steamy... The plot is intriguing... The reader will be entertained." —*Fresh Fiction*

For more Sara Humphreys, visit:

www.sourcebooks.com

About the Author

Sara Humphreys is a graduate of Marist College with a B.A. degree in English literature and theater. Her initial career path after college was as a professional actress. Some of her television credits include A&E *Biography*, *Guiding Light*, *Another World*, *As the World Turns*, and *Rescue Me*. In 2013, Sara's novel *Untamed* won two PRISM awards: Dark Paranormal and Best of the Best. Sara has loved both paranormal and romance novels for years. Her sci-fi/fantasy/romance obsession began years ago with the TV series *Star Trek* and an enormous crush on Captain Kirk. That sci-fi obsession soon evolved into a love of all types of fantasy and paranormal—vampires, ghosts, werewolves, and of course shape-shifters. Sara is married to her college sweetheart, Will. They live in New York with their four boys. For a full list of Sara's books and reading order, please visit her website.